Tornado Express

Tornado Express

Levi Johnson Mountain Man Scout

Book Thirty-Two

Ash Lingam

Tornado Express
Paperback Edition

Wolfpack Publishing
1707 E. Diana Street
Tampa, Florida 33610

www.wolfpackpublishing.com

Ebook ISBN 979-8-89567-371-3
Paperback ISBN 979-8-89567-372-0

Tornado Express

Trading Posts

The outlaws heard the faint rumble of wagons creaking in the distance, signaling they weren't too far ahead. They were keeping up a good pace, but they knew the teams of draft horses that pulled the cargo wagons couldn't outrun fast horses.

They spotted the cargo train a half-hour later. Leather reins slapped the backs of the six-horse teams. Circles of dust trailed the ponderous creaking of wooden spokes and iron-rimmed wheels, rising into the air and forming a thick cloud that made it hard to see the target.

That morning, when they set out to run down the cargo wagons, the outlaws expected them to be traveling much more slowly. They lingered at their campsite, thinking they had all the time in the world. By the time they targeted the small cargo wagon train, it was much closer to Fort Hall than they liked. The outlaws pressed their horses to catch up before the train made it to the safety of the fort, which had just become the property of the United States government.

What the outlaws knew—and most people didn't—was that the fort no longer flew the British Union Jack above its walls. Given the departure of the Hudson's Bay Company, most British subjects had departed for Fort Vancouver and other postings. It left the fort understaffed and weak.

The United States Army had only recently taken control of the fort and had yet to replace the security forces provided by HBC. Like most branches of government, the Army moved slowly when it came to manning installations on the Western frontier.

Fifteen riders rode recklessly toward confrontation. Most clutched a revolver or rifle in one hand and the reins in another. They dug in the spurs and rode hell-bent-for-leather, gaining on the struggling cargo train. The lead horse cracked off a shot, striking a wooden barrel. A spout of corn liquor poured onto the wagon bed, its rich smell filling the air. Bullwhacker Billy Rooster didn't dare look back because keeping the team moving in a straight line and the wagon from tipping over as it rounded a bend in the trail required all of his skills.

The six cargo-laden wagons raced for the safety of the fort. If they could make it before being overtaken by the thieves, they would rest and continue to Fort Boise, their final destination. If they lost any wagons in the attack, it would cut into their profits and impact the soldiers who were assigned to protect the settlers moving west along the Oregon Trail.

Tommy Verde led the charge, with his closest men riding a few feet behind. Andy Irons, Red Hawkens, and Slim Parkins all had pistols in their hands, raised in the air and ready to fire. Behind them raced another eleven men who were just as determined. Each one hoped to benefit from the seized cargo of the armed wagons.

GARROTT SNEED and right-hand man Howey Dundurn had gleaned news of the cargo shipment while sitting at the table next to a corporal and a sergeant at Fort Boise. Several suppliers chipped in to make a massive shipment that would last for months. It was supposed to be top secret, but the two soldiers never suspected the men sitting behind them were highwaymen. As soon as they heard the news, they rode back to Fort Hall to get their old gang together.

Three hundred miles later, they sat in Pearl's Cantina, sipping rotgut whiskey and filling in the other six gang members on their plan.

"But where are we gonna sell that cargo once we steal it?" Red Hawkins asked, worry lines crossing his brow. "I don't doubt we can take it, but I'm not so sure how to turn it into money."

"We'll sell it back to the very people who ordered it in the first place," Sneed, the gang leader, said. "Do you really think they'll say no? We'll have them over a barrel, and they'll have no choice but to pay us any price we ask. If not, half the settlement is gonna dry up and blow away. Without supplies, Fort Boise will become a ghost town."

"GET YOUR ASSES MOVIN', you old hags!" Rooster yelled as he popped his whip over the heads of his six-team.

Red curly hair peeked out from under a black hat brim, and freckles sprinkled his sun-wrinkled face. "I can see the fort walls, Buster. I think we're gonna make it!"

BOOM! BOOM!

Buster Balls fired a double-barreled shotgun at the oncoming riders. He knew he was out of range, but the loud noise spooked the outlaws' horses. That meant that they were far too close. It was a toss of a coin if they would make it through the fort's gates before the outlaws shot them dead and made off with everything—cargo, wagons, and draft horses. Balls knew that was why the outlaws hadn't tried to shoot the draft horses first. They would need them to pull the heavy cargo wagons. Without the horsepower, they couldn't get away.

Verde calmly aimed and popped off another round with his long rifle. It initiated a reply from guards who rode in the back of the wagons. They had fair cover behind wooden boxes and barrels full of rice and grain. When bullets flew from all six wagons, their pursuers spread out, making themselves harder targets. The ropes holding down the cargo squeaked and groaned under the weight. Occasionally, Rooster's wagon would hit a bump, and his companions would fly a few feet into the air. Rooster had the wagons moving so fast, all the teamsters were on the verge of losing control.

Wagon wheels creaked and churned, and harnesses strained as the wagons burst toward safety in an explosion of wood, leather, and horseflesh. The bullwhackers pushed their animals within an inch of their lives as the outlaw gang came into range. Bullets began to close in on their targets.

A gunshot rang out from a heavy-caliber rifle. The

cargo wagon's horses bared their teeth. Their ears fattened against their skulls as they swung their heads from side to side in panic. Fear made the run harder, finding a new burst of speed. Whipcracks popped from each wagon, urging them on. Chunks of lead slammed into the wagons' wooden sideboards and whined off rocks and stones. Gunsmoke hovered over the trail, making visibility difficult amid the dust from the churning wheels.

Horses ran blindly, trying to flee the pandemonium with wide-spread eyes and hooves hammering the ground. The teamsters urged them on, knowing they would be killed if caught and their precious cargo would be lost. More importantly, they wouldn't get paid, and their families would go without. Only desperate men took such jobs, and they had no intention of giving up without a fight.

Rooster drove his wagon to the brink as though messengers from hell were chasing his wagon. He focused on the horizon, searching for the tall turret of Fort Hall. He knew it couldn't be much farther. As the outlaws closed in on the heavily laden wagons, everyone knew they were playing for keeps. They were engaged in a life-or-death race.

Amazingly, the cargo train had covered a thousand miles without mishap. Now, near the first stop on their journey, they might be killed before they reach the fort. Then, all the grief and wear and tear would have been for nothing. The money their families counted on wouldn't materialize if they failed.

All they had to do was reach Fort Hall. After a rest and maybe gathering a few more men, they would make the last and most dangerous stretch, the three hundred and thirty miles remaining to Fort Boise, located along the Snake River. It was right on the mail trail, so they were assured solid ground for the heavy wagons.

As the outlaws pushed their horses harder, they saw that each wagon had a heavily armed shotgun rider and a guard lying on top of the cargo, returning fire with revolvers and rifles. Some had shooters firing from the back of wagons. Their Colt Patterson revolving, five-shot pistols were still well out of the seventy-five-yard range to be effective. Once close enough to lay down a solid spray of bullets, they would be able to stop the flight of the wagons once and for all. They knew that a barrage of bullets from the fifteen outlaws would do the trick, but they had to make sure they didn't kill any of the draft horses.

It was fifteen against eight, so the odds were against the men from The Tornado Express Cargo Company. On horseback, the outlaws had the advantage of agility and speed, and most of the gang members were sharp-shooters.

The odds ran through Rooster's head as he continued to scream and crack his whip over the animals' heads. That was when he got the first glimpse of the tower rising from Fort Hall. They were almost there. He held his breath and prayed they could survive the last few hundred yards.

As THE CARGO wagons roared down the Oregon Trail, the creaking wood, jingling harnesses, and thundering wheels could be heard from a long distance. A shotgun guard with a pair of long rifles clung to the top of piles of barrels and wooden boxes as the prairie schooners roared down the rugged and rutted trail. The bull-whacker in the lead wagon wore a brace of pistols and had another shotgun leaning up against the spring-loaded, wooden seat. Lately, they have had more than hostile Indians to deal with, but no bandits had found out about the cargo shipment's schedules, and the prices of the necessities had soared.

Some of the items were nearly as valuable as silver. The Fort Hall merchants were waiting for part of the cargo to replenish their quickly depleting stocks. Most of the supplies were destined for Fort Boise, if they managed to make it that far. Right then, they were hoping to get to Fort Hall before the outlaws caught up, killed them, and took everything they had.

Even though the workhorses had stamina, they could only maintain short bursts at a top speed of thirty miles per hour. The most significant advantage of the mule teams was their ability to gallop at slower speeds for much longer periods of time and with less feed and rest. It made them perfect as working animals. At a casual gait, they would last much longer. A good thoroughbred could sprint to over forty miles per hour.

These horses were bred from American Percherons, at seventeen hands and one thousand two hundred pounds. Some teamsters preferred jack mules over fourteen hands and jennies at thirteen hands. They weighed some nine hundred pounds each. For this transport, they were too slow. They were deemed unsuitable for the job, given the threat of attacks from outlaws.

They did not discard being ambushed by hostile Indians, but believed their superior weapons would ward off the Bannock or Shoshone as long as they didn't run into a major war party, which was unusual. In a typical clash, the hostile Indians generally cut and ran after suffering a few losses. It was on a rare occasion, Indians seldom risked their lives on reckless attacks. The Indian Nations valued the lives of their warrior braves, unlike the renegade leaders.

Gunshots continued to ring out as the teamsters managed to stay out of range of the outlaws. Buster Balls clutched his Mississippi Rifle, a US Model 1841 muzzle-loading percussion rifle, while waiting for a good target. Hemp ropes creaked as the cargo shifted its weight when the wagon took a corner at full speed. He and the other guards waited as the outlaws wasted ammunition, firing well out of range. The occasional bullet pinged off the tailgate of the drag wagon.

Meanwhile, Rooster cracked his whip over the heads of the six-horse team. The bullwhacker glanced to the rear, realizing the trailing wagon soon would be within range of the outlaws, who had blood in their eyes and bared their teeth. Rooster hoped they all made it to safety.

CARGO for the forts along the Oregon Trail sometimes came via Vancouver and the main offices of the Hudson Bay Fur Trading Company. Occasionally, supplies were shipped from Oregon and Santa Fe. Most often, cargo trains from back East carried goods from places like Missouri and Iowa. The fur companies not only bought buffalo hides and, before that, beaver pelts, but they also provided most of the store goods purchased by the settlers crossing the country and heading west along the Oregon Trail.

Fort Boise and Fort Still were both situated in remote areas of the wilderness beyond the Great Plains. British flags flew over both forts until the United States gained control following the boundary settlement of 1846. Even some of the friendly local Bannock and Shoshone Indians frequented both forts to purchase items such as coffee and sugar. They weren't as friendly when they were out on the plains, looking for migrating settlers whom they believed were encroaching on their land. This strange paradox made coexistence possible. Each had something the other wanted.

The treaty establishing the boundary at the Forty-Ninth Parallel pushed British interests north, solidifying United States control over Fort Hall, Fort Boise, and the surrounding region. It left a gap in armed protection for the forts, which the British abandoned. The American Army had yet to arrive in full force. It was an opportunity for brave and reckless men to take what wasn't theirs and sell the stolen goods to the highest bidder, of which there were many in such remote places.

Soon, United States Army patrols would arrive to help protect the travelers on the Oregon Trail from hostile Indians and highwaymen. Post-treaty travel increased, and those making the journey west surged. With the growth of both forts' businesses and populations, the local economies and fur trade shifted to support emigration. For this part of the West, the British era had come to an end.

The economy and protection of both forts depended on these chains of supplies from private outfitters or teamsters. The journey was long, dangerous, and expensive, even when all the supplies reached their destination. The demand for fur dropped, but the need for supplies increased tenfold. Trading posts at the forts supplied the overlanders on their way west. Mountain men, buffalo hunters, and Native Americans were all clientele of the new regime.

The most reliable transport company of the time was Russell, Majors, & Waddell. The company's teamsters and bullwhackers were responsible for ensuring the forts were serviced frequently due to the never-ending, ever-growing demand. More and more pressure was put on them to deliver goods in larger quantities and faster. As the passage became more dangerous, smaller private companies subcontracted the work.

In general, many of the cargo trains were pulled by oxen or mules. Although stronger and more resistant when attacked, they had no chance of outrunning pursuers. The increased danger and higher wages often left goods overpriced by the time they reached the western territories. The cargo in question was loaded in Missouri and passed through Fort Laramie before reaching Fort Hall. From there, the last stop was Fort Boise, just over three hundred miles west.

Horse-driven, heavy cargo wagons often snaked along the trail just ahead of a hundred settlers' wagons. The ten men who raced across the prairies knew to ride before the giant cloud of dust kicked up by wagon wheels, horses, and people walking alongside all the possessions they had in the world.

Due to the location of the two forts, limited farming was possible because of hostile Indians. Even with what little they could grow in the greener areas, like Fort Boise, they still relied heavily on the supplies raced to them by The Tornado Express Cargo Company. It was far from the largest transport outfit, but it was known to take anything, anywhere, and anytime for a price. It was supposedly the fastest of the various companies that provided cargo service, and the most expensive due to the risks the teamsters and guards had to endure. The heft price also covered the wear and tear on resources that ran from first light to dusk, hardly stopping for food and rest.

When a shipment was lost, the prices of replacement goods would be even higher than before. The higher the demand, the more exuberant the prices, and still, the people waiting would be fighting over the goods regardless of how much they cost. Without the service, settlers would never reach their dream of milk and honey at the end of the Oregon Trail.

In the early years of the Oregon Trail, the main dangers were limited to Indian attacks by the Shoshone or Bannock Tribes. By driving several teams of wagons with heavily armed guards, they had discouraged the attackers enough to avoid losing shipments. Of course, the Indians didn't know what was in these scattered wagons that raced across the countryside. If it were White man's food, except for coffee and refined sugar, they would easily do without. They preferred their own diets.

Since they often traveled with wagon trains of settlers, the local Indians presented a lesser threat. The remains of a few cargo trains that had been successfully stopped and everyone murdered were visible along the trail. Skeletons of wagons and people alike glistened in the harsh landscape. Here, the businessmen died alongside the pioneers, never to see or touch the pots of gold government promoters promised.

Skillets, pans, utensils, along with barrels of spirits and miscellaneous supplies, were scattered across the landscape, where they were inspected and discarded. The war chiefs frowned on their braves drinking White men's spirits. So, they used tomahawks to bust the wooden barrels open and poured the contents onto the ground.

At times, there were secret shipments of weapons of all sorts and ammunition, enough to supply the local law, the soldiers, and the growing population. These were stored below barrels of whiskey and flour, and up until then, they hadn't been discovered.

This run was all food stocks and ammunition, but still very important to the settlement's survival. The wagons roared forward with six-team horses as the sound of hammering hooves echoed across the countryside. Still, they were on their toes. The gossip from back East was that bands of outlaws were crisscrossing the Oregon Trail in search of easy pickings. Some of the foreigners who crossed didn't own guns or know how to use them. They became easy targets for the desperate and greedy alike.

Generally, hostile Indians could be held off by the overlanders' wagon trains. The growing threat of thieves and highwaymen created an even greater danger. Ruthless men and gangs attacked with reckless abandon and no regard for civility.

As times changed, and more people began to cross the trail and frequent both Fort Boise and Fort Hall, many of these thieves passed themselves off as fellow travelers. Among these were everything from flim-flam men to out-and-out thugs. Most of these types stayed outside the fort walls, where they could better blend in with the crowd of strangers. Among these were even a few murderers.

In the middle of the western wilderness, there was little law other than that provided by a settlement's sheriff and a few small army patrols that came and went. They are supposed to be keeping the hostile Indians in check, but they were outnumbered. As weapons advanced, the tide slowly began to turn. Until then, bows and arrows could easily overwhelm early settlers. Innovations like the Colt Patterson pistol and the Sharps rifle, which were being manufactured in mass quantities, were stirring the tides of change.

Still, until a reliable repeater rifle was invented, the Indian tribes would hold the upper hand. Plus, their skills at guerrilla warfare, along with the knowledge of the land, kept them ahead of the struggle to expel White men from the land that the Indians had populated for thousands of years. As soon as the right weapons were developed, the Native Americans' demise would begin, and the Indian Wars would end.

Of course, wagons full of food, grains, sugar, coffee, canned goods, and hardware were valuable objects when crossing the wilderness. They provided the occasional delicacy. If the season was cool, cargo trains delivered chocolate bars to towns across more than a thousand miles. Fancy cigars from a place called Cuba, in the Caribbean Sea, were gaining in demand.

The fort staff included a self-appointed sheriff, traders, and support personnel, along with a mix of Native, British, and American residents. All these people kept their small enterprises going because of the constant flow of travelers. They ensured that wagons were repaired, supplies were provided, and a certain level of protection was offered while resting inside or around the forts. It was important for delays to be avoided because wagon trains lined the Oregon Trail. There were always fifty to a hundred wagons pulling into the fort, while another pulled out. When the occasional traffic jam ensued, all hell broke loose due to the excess of people.

The settlement on the Snake River was in dire need of new shipments of supplies as the number of overlanders traveling the trail to Fort Boise grew with each passing day. For them, the supplies usually came from Fort Hall, which was three hundred miles as the crow flies. But the goods still had to reach both forts. By then, the farthest fort west was nearly out of stock, and the population was in near panic. Travelers frequently rebelled against authority when supplies ran short during stops along their journey. Soon, the streets of Fort Boise were packed with angry settlers, who thought nothing of turning on the locals.

Smoke

"Whatcha lookin' at, Rusty?" Money Penny asked. "Are those smoke signals I see up there? I hope they don't have anything to do with us. Every time I see you readin' those puffs in the sky, it spells trouble for somebody. Hopefully, we'll get a break, and it's not for us."

"Maybe this time you might be right, young man. The thing is, I don't understand what this is all about. Up there's the Crow stronghold, so Potak must be responsible. That's where these signals are coming from, but I figure they were relayed from somewhere else, farther away. If Chief Wanata had a problem with us, he'd come down and tell us himself. He's never shy about such things, so it's gotta be something else."

Rusty Steel used the flat of his hand to shade his eyes from the sun as he stretched his neck and stared up at the sky, watching gray, intermittent puffs of smoke from a fire made of green wood. He mumbled as he read the message. For little Money, it seemed to go on and on. Even Rusty looked puzzled.

"Tornado? I think that's what that one means."

"But what does it say, Uncle Rusty? Levi said that I didn't need to know how to read smoke yet. He claims there were more important things to learn first. I reckon he knows best."

"Only Levi, his wife, Dahteste, and I are good at readin' smoke. Angus, too, but since he's gettin' on in years, he leaves it to us. Most tribes have their own codes, but some things are intended for everyone to understand across the board, like this message. It says it comes from one of the forts up on the Oregon Trail. That must be Fort Boise because Fort Hall is three hundred miles east along the Snake River. Then again, the Indians there use smoke signals, too."

Nine-year-old Money Penny called all the compound members uncle or aunt, except for Levi Beaver Johnson, who was his mentor. Marshal Joseph Walker and his Crow wife, Bar-chee, were his pa and ma. For him, it was like one big happy family, and everyone watched out for one another. Despite being with Rusty, the young boy still had a look beyond the brick-and-rail fence as paranoia nibbled at his guts. He glanced at the corral to confirm the horses were calm. He had recently learned that one could never be too careful while in the wilderness, even when you're near home.

"Do you have to go up and talk to the medicine man and the chief?" the youngster asked in a small voice.

Penny felt happy and safe in the compound, but he wasn't so sure about the Crow stronghold being so close to their cabins. Hundreds of teepees housed four or five times as many Indians. It was the largest Crow village in this vast area and dominated the mountain, at least, most of the time.

Ever since the young boy was kidnapped with the intent to be sold as a slave, he never left the compound unaccompanied. If it was with more than one adult, it was all the better. It wasn't that mister paranoia sat on his shoulder all the time, but he wasn't stupid either. He had learned his lesson well and never let his guard completely down. You just never knew what awaited you outside the safety of the compound fence. Sometimes, maybe even inside.

That didn't mean Money had a change of heart about dedicating himself to becoming the best mountain man he could, under the guidance of Levi, the most famous frontiersman in Yellowstone Valley and the surrounding mountains. His fame had even surpassed that of *his* mentor, Rusty Steel. The nine-year-old was like a sponge as he soaked up every word he heard and repeated each skill until he mastered it like Levi, despite he was less than half his size. He had lowered his time to reload a percussion rifle down to twenty seconds, but his target was fifteen seconds, like Levi. A quick reload was just as important as knowing how to shoot a gun.

Not many men in the Rocky Mountains were six feet seven and weighed north of two hundred pounds. Money was buckskin-clad like his mentor. Levi's long hair and beard were known across the mountains and out onto the Great Plains, where he and Captain Will Forrester fought in the Indian Wars before arriving in the Rockies.

"Nope. It says we're to stay put and that a messenger is on the way. The Crow stronghold is only a half day's ride up Bear Tooth Mountain. I wonder who Potak trusts enough to share important information. Pine Needle is already here for the warm weather, she would be the perfect person for the job because we can trust her. I reckon we'll have to wait and see who it is and what they have to say," Rusty said.

"How do you know it's important, Rusty?" Money asked as he looked up at the wise and aging frontiersman.

"They wouldn't send up smoke if it wasn't. From what I've read, there's somethin' goin' on between Fort Boise and Fort Hall. I reckon this is gonna be a call for help. What I can't figure out is what I read about a tornado. Oh, I know they occasionally exist around here, but if one's comin', no humans can do anything about it or predict when it'll hit. Maybe I've mistaken the word. I reckon we'll just have to wait and see if we hope to solve our mystery. It'll give us somethin' to think about the rest of the day. It takes about six hours to ride down here. So, the messenger will be here before dusk."

WHEN POTAK REALIZED where the smoke signals originated, he knew it was serious. Word came all the way from Fort Hall and Fort Boise, then south down to Yellowstone Valley and west to Bear Tooth Mountain. With smoke signals, what would take a messenger days or even weeks was accomplished in forty-eight hours. But what could be so important that such a long chain of messages was necessary? It could only mean trouble, but for whom?

"WHAT'S ALL the smoke about? Is it more trouble from those pesky White men and women I allow to live on my mountain and below our Crow's stronghold?" Chief Wanata gruffly asked. "I don't know why we haven't run them off years ago."

Despite Chief Wanata's gruff attitude, more than any of the others, he knew how powerful Potak was. He could only push things so far. If push came to shove, he felt tribe members would pick the medicine man over their chief, meaning he had to tread carefully. It still irritated him, and he struggled to maintain a respectful tone. Potak ignored him because he believed the chief was a stupid man. Were Wanata only ignorant, that could be remedied for anyone willing to learn. But Potak knew that you couldn't teach a simple person to do an intelligent man's tasks.

If Wanata pushed too hard against Rusty Steel and his clan, he knew that some of the older warriors and elders would revolt. Old Chief Hachta, now deceased, had been the White leader's blood brother. Although dead, it was believed Hachta watched over the White men from the spirit world.

Only occasionally did Potak have to put the chief in his place. Of course, there was nothing stupid about the tribe's medicine man. He was considered one of the wisest men west of Missouri by both Indians and many Whites alike. Only those inexperienced in the wilderness thought him to be a buffoon. Many considered the shaman the best medicine man in the mountains and knew he could be dangerous. Many tribes believed Potak could speak to the animals and walk the earth invisible to the human eye. What more dangerous an enemy could there be than one you couldn't see?

Potak never denied or confirmed any of the gossip. He recognized it for what it was and chose to ignore it. He let people believe what they wanted, which they would do regardless of what he said. He also knew the power of a mystery and kept his personal life shrouded in doubt and unbelievable stories. Such tales made him appear more powerful than he really was.

If the truth were known, he never claimed to do any form of magic or talk to the bats at night or other animals. Some of the gossip he heard made him laugh out loud. Still, he didn't deny anything. If it helped his people's faith in him grow, there was nothing wrong with that. Especially as Potak always had the best intentions while considering his followers. He even treated his enemies well, to a point.

"I must go and speak to Levi Johnson and the captain. I know Rusty and Beaver both can read smoke, but this message was tricky even for me. Plus, it comes from hundreds of miles away. To us, it is unimportant, but for my friends in the compound, it may well be valuable," Potak told the chief.

"It doesn't take much to get Captain Forrester excited and ready to ride into a fight," Wanata replied. "I doubt he could resist a battle, even though it is a many-day ride. What else does it say?"

"Nothing," Potak lied, shaking his head. "Not anything important for a chief like you, Wanata. Just something about the forts, but they're hundreds of miles away from us here on Bear Tooth Mountain. Nothing for us to worry about. Not when we have a chief like you." Potak looked at him out of the corner of his eye as the chief puffed out his chest—almost undetectable curls formed at the edges of the Tonkawa Indian's thin lips.

"Let me take care of this simple matter," Potak said, waving his hand as if it were nothing. "I would like to do it for my friend Angus, who feeds me so well when I visit the White men's compound. Have you ever tried his cooking? Of course, you haven't. If you are ever invited, make sure you don't miss the chance. You don't know what you're missing, Chief. His wild turkey is the best I've ever had. Hopefully, he will invite me to join him as payment for delivering this message to Levi and the captain. You could go and visit your sister anytime you want. I will leave at once. If I leave now, I'll be there before dark."

Wanata didn't even make an effort to reply. On one side, he loved his sister, Bar-chee, as any brother would. On the other hand, he despised her for marrying a White man, even if Marshal Walker did prove to be honest in the eyes of his village. Back then, the chief had tried to kill him but failed. Then, Walker married his sister, making it all but impossible to throw him off Crow land. He cursed the marshal under his breath.

Potak's stomach grumbled as though on cue as he unwrapped his legs, stood, and turned to go, tossing the end of his blanket over his shoulder. Fluttering feathers hung from long ear lobes, and his hair was braided in many trances and nearly hung to his waist. His prominent nose made him unmistakably recognizable, even from a distance. It stood out between his sunken eyes. If you locked eyes with his, you were instantly drawn into something profound, almost hypnotizing, just beyond his innocent look. It made a man feel that there was vast knowledge locked inside.

The chief looked down for a second, but when he looked back up, Potak had already vanished. It was as though he was never there. Only the strange smell of eucalyptus lingered in the air. The rumors said it was bark from a tree found in the forests along the Urubamba River in the Andes Mountains of Peru. How he always had a supply—no one knew how—but he claimed it was vital to his daily rituals.

On the other side of the world, in a place called Australia, it grew abundantly and was used in Aboriginal cleansing rituals. Potak wasn't the only one aware of the tree bark's value. Whenever you entered Potak's campsite, the end of a piece of eucalyptus bark glowed as the flameless cinder burned, and the camphoraceous, minty, woody, and slightly sweet undertones were found invigorating as they floated on puffs of air.

Mystery was one of many things that made the Tonkawa shaman special and separated him from all the other medicine men of the five Yellowstone Valley tribes. He was the only Indian allowed to cross boundaries and not be harassed, wounded, or killed. Some believed that Potak's dead spirit could be more potent than the simple man who currently walked the earth. In his presence, most men were humbled and respectful. Everyone but Wanata, the leader of his own tribe. Still, the chief knew his limits and what would happen if he were to harm Joseph and his sister. It surprised him, but he believed Bar-chee would protect her White man with her life, disregarding the fact that the chief was her brother.

Still, the shaman saw Wanata as a fool and knew

that one day soon his end would come. If he didn't grow up and act as a chief, he would be banished in shame. Meanwhile, he watched his follies as they unfolded. For the shaman, it was just more of the theater of life, played out in real time.

POTAK RAN down the mountain more like an antelope than an aging man. He was so surefooted and balanced that he seemed to dance down the rugged path gracefully and with no apparent effort. As he raced past forest animals, they didn't stir, keeping their eyes on their food as if the shaman weren't even there. In motion, he created a mild rustle in the leaves as he passed under trees and left nary a footprint.

Soon, he saw smoke snaking into the sky from the fireplace in Angus's kitchen. Potak smiled as he stopped and smelled the air. He heard horses nicker in the distance as they recognized his scent.

Peach Pie for supper. I hope I'm in time to be invited.

Potak smiled and picked up his pace.

As the sun began to disappear behind a mountain, a colony of bats raced across the sky, darkening the land with winged shadows. Not five minutes later, he heard the incessant ringing of a dinner bell, obsessed with its evening message. The shaman chuckled because he knew why the aging mountain man rang the bell with such tenacity. His friends didn't, not even Pine Needle, his wife. Being patient, observant, and aging gave you answers to questions others didn't believe possible.

"*Sho'daache Kahee*," Potak called out. "It's me, Potak the medicine man."

"*Sho'daache Kahee*," Little Money replied, making everybody laugh, including their unexpected guest.

"I figured you'd send somebody else to deliver the message," Rusty said. "I saw the smoke well enough, but I must have been mistaken about what it said. What's all this about a tornado, Potak? I've gotta admit, I'm a mite confused."

By then, all the members in the compound were making their way toward Rusty and Angus's cabin. As Potak walked toward them, he stopped briefly, closed his eyes, and inhaled deeply. A smile grew across his face. When he opened his eyes again, they were full of life and twinkled like tiny sparks of fire.

"An army captain named Crow had his Tonkawa scout send the message from Fort Boise. The people living there are quickly running out of supplies. Outlaws tried to stop the cargo train en route to Fort Hall. Outlaws ambushed them, hoping to steal the wagons and their contents. The people in Fort Boise are getting desperate because they're running out of many of their main food and hardware supplies. Now, they have wagon trains piling up around the fort with no supplies to sell to the overlanders, who are getting nervous."

"Yeah, Captain Harvey Crow is a stand-up fella," Levi replied. "I figure since so many settlers are traveling across the Oregon Trail, the prices of everything have skyrocketed due to the excessive demand. At first, the folks at McKay's hardware store were as happy as pigs in a wallow. But soon they had difficulty keeping enough stock to feed both the settlers and the settlement. I reckon the cargo's value has become a handsome prize for any outlaw gang, albeit a might difficult to sell. Then again, some might be so brash as to sell it back to the rightful owners, the folks at Fort Boise. It doesn't seem possible, but I reckon it's a mite better than starvin'."

"So, what does all this have to do with Levi and me?" Captain Forrester asked. "I don't see how we fit into the picture. What can we do that the Army can't?"

"The Army captain wants to hire you two to guide the embattled cargo from Fort Hall to Fort Boise. With the new boundaries act, lots of the British men who protected the fort have headed back to Vancouver. So, the fort is short of men. The smoke said the bad White men were experts and something about a tornado. I don't even understand exactly what that means, but the shape of the smoke was clear," Potak explained.

"But it's huntin' season, and I wanted to get a good stock of meat and fish for the winter," Levi said. "Joseph and I were gonna go fishin' tomorrow. The streams nearby are full of trout."

"There is one more detail that I have not mentioned," Potak added, staring like a mute monk pondering what he was about to say. "This Captain Crow said the businessmen are willing to pay you a thousand dollars if you get the goods to Fort Boise."

"How much?" Levi asked as he stuck his finger in his ear and wiggled it. "My ears must be clogged with wax."

"What was that you said, Potak?" Captain Forrester asked.

"You heard what I said. I don't make mistakes. Make of it what you will. I am just telling you two what I read in the smoke. Mind you now, if they are paying so much money, it must be a dangerous job."

"That sure is a lot of gold coins, boys." Marshal Walker grinned. "If you're gonna stick your necks out for all of us, I reckon I best go too. I never like to miss a good scrap. Especially at a thousand dollars a pop. How hard can it be, anyway? I'm sure we've dealt with worse situations and come out unscathed."

"Let's not claim victory until we've seen the battlefield," the captain said. "I've got to admit, it's too much money to turn down. We can live off those double eagles for a year or maybe even two. We can use the extra funds now that there are thirteen of us."

"Thirteen, who'd have ever thought?" Angus whispered. "Once upon a time, there were just three of us."

"And all one big happy family. With Potak, we'll be fourteen today. Virgil, could you bring a chair from y'all's cabin? I reckon we'll fit, now that Money has his new chair," Angus ordered and grinned like an opossum.

Angus had taken it on himself to make a special chair for Money, one with longer legs and a place to rest his feet when he ate at the table with the rest of the clan. Before, when he sat in the grownups' seats, all that showed was his head from his mouth up. Now he sat a half head taller than everyone else, and the young whippersnapper was tickled to death. The old cook even painted the chair red, which Money claimed was his favorite color.

Angus reached for the iron rod to ring his dinner bell again, but Rusty snatched it out of his hand before he could start.

"You've already rung that fool bell enough for one day. I don't wanna hear it again until tomorrow. You're gonna have to wait. Come on now. What's to eat, Angus?"

"Rocky Mountain Oysters, and have I got a passel of

'em. They're sliced, breaded, and fried crispy just like you like 'em," the ornery old cook replied.

Potak smiled and said, "I knew I'd be glad I brought the message myself." He held his plate up as Angus used a large, palm-sized spoon to scoop the fried bison testicles onto their plates.

"I got 'em from baby calves wandering around a valley full of carcasses from the hide hunters. At least we got something out of it. Try 'em, Potak. I bet you've never tasted prairie oysters like mine."

The shaman's face disappeared into the steamy aroma. His face turned into a mass of wrinkles as he smiled from ear to ear.

AFTER DINNER, they sat around the porch, sipping corn liquor and smoking hand-built cigarettes, pipes, or cheroots. Potak smoked a strange mixture of herbs and leaves that smelled sweet. Dense smoke circled his head.

When Levi took a drag, the end of his cigarette glowed orange and reflected in his eyes.

"So, whatcha think about this cargo wagon security job, Will?" Levi asked. "I reckon if they're payin' a thousand bucks, there's gotta be a catch. Most guard jobs don't get a tenth of that. It ain't no normal job, that's for sure. I wonder what it is that makes it so valuable."

"Are you saying that you don't want to take the job?" Will asked, raising his eyebrows. As he sat on the porch, a gust of wind made his empty sleeve flutter in the breeze. He brushed his mustache with his knuckles, then he rubbed his stubble of a beard and frowned.

"No, I ain't sayin' nothin', but don't expect somebody to give us a thousand dollars for doin' nothin'. All I wanna do is consider the risks first."

Potak raised his head from his empty plate As he licked his fingers, he said, "If it sounds too good to be true, it *is* too good to be true. Now all you must decide is if it's worth risking your lives for all that money. It's what White men value most, is it not? I value my life more. Shiny gold eagles sure are pretty, but you can't eat them —especially if you're dead." Potak stated. He smiled, and it reached his eyes. It was his attempt at humor. But, at the same time, it was a serious message.

"But a man *can* buy the things that make him happy," Joseph said. "With enough money, you can buy whatever you want."

"Do you really think that happiness is something you can purchase as you do a hat?" Potak asked, again smiling. There was nothing he liked more than a healthy conversation. "Happiness is a state of mind, not some object to trade for pretty things. Sure, you can pay others to do your work, but then you would be denying your soul self-respect. If you could put a price on them, how much would Money and Bar-chee be worth, Joseph? In gold coins, I mean."

Potak had always had his reservations about the marshal. Since the kidnapping of his son, he seemed to have changed, though. Not a lot, but there were little signs there. So, rather than ignoring him as unusual, Potak turned his attention to the old lawman. Since he had taken a Crow wife, he deserved respectful consideration.

"Why, how can you ask such a question?" Joseph replied, shocked. "You can't put a price on your family."

"Exactly, my friend," Potak said, showing a sign of acceptance of the old Indian fighter. "Those two humans are your happiness, and you could not have bought them for all the money in the world. You only got them because you were deserving. That is what happiness is. Not some shiny object you can't love or eat."

First Light

A wedge of yellow lamplight spilled onto the ground from the barn's wide, double doors. Horses nickered and whinnied in the stables as they nervously stomped their hooves. Steam disappeared before their nostrils from the morning chill. A pack mule was loaded with supplies to get them to Fort Hall if necessary. If there were no supplies available in Fort Boise, Levi, Will, and Joseph would have to fend for themselves for the last three hundred and thirty miles of the journey if that was what they were really supposed to do. At this point, it was all speculation. Until they spoke with the Army captain, they remained in the dark, though they believed they had the general idea of their mission.

In the past, Levi and the captain had been contacted by Captain Harvey Crow from other jobs over the years. He was a fair man and understanding for a military type. He and Will understood each other just fine. Under Crow were Sergeant Clay Carson and Corporal Shane Holmes. All three were men to be trusted. They could only hope that the Army hadn't sent replacements. It was much easier to work with someone you knew, especially when it involved the military. Out west, the rotation of soldiers was continuous. Some were killed or wounded, a handful could not tolerate the isolation and went mad, and a few simply ran off, never to be seen or heard from again.

If Captain Crow was still in charge, they knew they would have his full cooperation. Knowing the captain like they did, if the business owners were putting up a thousand dollars to get six cargo wagons to Fort Boise, there had to be information yet to be revealed. It was too much money for such an apparently easy job. Of course, there were always hostiles looking for easy targets along the Oregon Trail. The Indians had grown wiser, picking and choosing the easiest travelers to attack.

The local natives weren't as reckless as White men when confronting their enemies. They always calculated the risks and took the time to assess their target's defenses before making a full charge. Their usual method of taking on smaller numbers of wagons was by ambush, often using the cover of the six-foot-tall prairie grass. Wagons struggled to get through the thick growth, slowing their progress as the wiry strands of greenery tangled in wheels and axles. War parties used the thick cover to hide until they popped up and started shooting. By then, it was too late for the settlers. In minutes, they would all be dead. That was why the Indians were so effective, they were silent, calculating, and as deadly as a bolt of lightning on the open prairie.

As the full moon descended to the world's western edge, the first hint of light shimmered on the eastern horizon. Simultaneously, the thick carpet of stars rolled back and quickly disappeared, revealing a clear blue sky. When the sun blinked its orange eye over the horizon, multicolored rays of light rained across the sky. A bald eagle soared across the horizon, circling over a small body of water in search of breakfast. It tucked its wings and dropped into a dive, disappearing over a distant mountain only to reappear again moments later with a large fish in its talons.

Its seven-foot wings flapped, quickly propelling it into the sky, despite the heavy load. It climbed higher until it reached a flat ledge on the rock formation, where it ate. Its sharp talons effortlessly sliced the meat and fed it to its beak. When it finished, it would return home. Bald eagles only brought food to their nests if they had baby eaglets to feed.

One by one, the trio ducked under the barn door as they rode out into the corral and into the main yard. Little puffs of dust followed their hooves like dogs chasing cats. As the sun began to climb into the sky, long shadows grew on the ground like black paint. The other ten members of the compound, plus the medicine man, stood on the main cabin's porch.

The look on Rusty's face told the story. He knew a year prior that he would have been riding with them. Now, he used the excuse that his new wife, Silvia, was afraid to be alone, and the other women needed protection in case the compound was attacked. No one was sure if he had decided he was simply too old to challenge Mother Nature and a gang of wicked men. That was an assumption that would require testing.

"Don't look at me like that, Rusty," Levi said. "We both know damned well you're up to the chore, but someone sharp with all their wits about them has gotta stay here and protect what's ours. Our whole lives are here in this compound. We've got to protect our homes —and who better than you and Angus, all that remains of the original crew? My, how things have changed since Mountain Dennis died."

"And even more from when Dennis first arrived. He was the first one here, you know. A lot of our friends died since you boys came to become my apprentices," Rusty said half-heartedly. "All you've gotta do is look over in the corner of the compound where those white crosses are. But don't you worry. I won't let anything happen to the women, Angus, or Virgil while y'all are gone. Then again, most of us can take care of ourselves, women included."

"I'm leavin' my wife and boy with you, Rusty," Joseph said. "For me, that's no small thing. I'm beholden to you for caring for them while we're gone. Everything I have in the world that's important to me is here in your charge, pard. Who knows. We might get to Fort Boise and discover it's already sorted out. Or we find out it ain't right for us after all."

Marshal Walker paused for a moment before continuing. It was almost like he wasn't quite sure if he should go or not, but he had committed himself, and there was no turning back. He shrugged it off and continued, "Still, a thousand dollars for the compound kitty sounds pretty good to me. That's a lot of money. With the beaver pelts gone and the buffalo herds dwindling, we can't let such an opportunity pass. In the old days, I've hunted down dangerous career criminals for no more than my monthly wages, and some of 'em took me six months to catch or kill. Whatever this is, by nature, it surely won't take long. The way I see it, all we've gotta do is move some objects from point A to point B. It doesn't get much simpler than that."

"If it's the Army that's called us, it won't be an easy job, you can be sure," the captain said while securing a safety pin to the empty sleeve of his shirt to keep it from festooning. His limb had been removed by a hostile Indian just above the elbow, but it didn't seem to hinder Forrester at all. It was as though he ignored the missing appendage and expected his friends to do the same.

Rusty nodded but didn't speak for fear of choking up. It was true, it rubbed him the wrong way not to be going along. At the same time, he knew he would just slow Levi, Will, and Joseph down. Sure, he could still outshoot Joseph with his eyes closed, but there were other things that he didn't have the strength to do that he once had not so long ago. He understood that a weak link in the chain could jeopardize the whole job. It could cost them one thousand dollars and maybe their lives. He could never do that.

Bar-chee somehow managed not to cry this time. She held Money so tight in her arms that his face turned red. Two tears ran down the boy's cheeks. His eyes were red from crying while hiding under his covers the previous night. It seemed like they had just gotten back together, and now his father was running off again. He understood this was the life of a mountain man, but it made him feel a little insecure. Lucky for him, he had Rusty to watch over him and teach him while Levi and his father were gone.

Angus stepped down off the porch and gave Levi a cloth sack. "Inside, you'll find warm biscuits filled with berries. Eat 'em on the way so they don't get cold. I reckon you boys have had your last good meal for a spell. I don't know which of you three is the worst cook." Angus cackled like an old hen.

"We'll have a sit-down meal in McKay's Saloon at Fort Boise before we head for Fort Hall," Levi said. He always had his meals planned ahead of time. Once he got food on his mind, he seemed to forget everything else. "Rusty, do me a favor and take over with Money, my apprentice, for a spell. We don't want him getting behind in his mountain man learnin'. And who better to teach him than the man who taught me? Whatcha say, amigo? Is that all right with you, Money?"

"You think you've got it all figured out, do you?" Rusty spat. "You boys just remember. Nobody is gonna pay anybody that kind of money unless you've gotta risk your lives, so don't be kidding yourselves about this. Don't let the money go to your heads. Just make sure all three of you come back in one piece. Lately, I'm gettin' like Potak. I don't give a damn about the gold coins. We've never needed much before. We provide ourselves with most of what we need, except for coffee, tobacco, sugar, and bullets. Over the years, we've become nearly self-sufficient."

Money looked at Rusty, waiting for him to answer Levi's request, but he was disappointed when he didn't say anything one way or the other. He glanced at him for a second, realized the aging frontiersman was staring at him. They locked eyes. Levi's mentor winked and nodded, as if it were their personal secret. Rusty wanted Levi to think about what he said. He had already planned to continue guiding Money down the path to become a frontiersman. Rusty was curious to see how the young fellow's mind worked. From what he had seen, he seemed to catch on very quickly.

THE MEN TIPPED THEIR HATS, and without another word, they wheeled their horses toward the south entrance of the compound and the trail to Yellowstone Valley. They stood in their stirrups on the first steep stretch of the trail, being careful not to put excessive pressure on the horses' backs and joints. The trick was for the rider not to lean too far back. Then, man and horse had a safe and comfortable ride on the steepest grade.

When Marshal Walker initially offered to come along, Levi and the captain exchanged looks. They knew he was handy with his guns and never backed down from a fight, but they also were aware he couldn't travel as swiftly as they could. He was going to slow them down. They would have to keep a close eye on him for signs of cracks in his façade. He was more than twenty years older than Levi and Will. They would push him to his limit, but without breaking him.

Still, Joseph was as brave as they came and was used to dealing with ruthless outlaws, if that was what they would face. Levi and Will were better Indian fighters, but it sounded like this time it wasn't the case. In the end, the three provide a unique combination of fighting men. Still, at that point, everything remained to be seen. They wouldn't have the whole story until they talked to the captain. Now, they had to focus on reaching Fort Boise undetected so that they wouldn't take any longer than necessary. What was clear from the smoke signal message was that time was of the essence. It sounded like people might starve.

They traveled so smoothly and with so little effort that it appeared they were in no hurry. Even the marshal had managed to keep the pace and catch their rhythm. He didn't tire. They seemed to glide along like graceful animals rather than men riding horses. It was almost like they were at one with the environment. The days passed by like pages of a book, turning one by one in a soft breeze.

In no time, they were at the end of the trail and nearing Fort Boise. The three had hardly spoken the entire way, each man contemplating his own thoughts. At times, they wondered what they would do with so much money, other times, they focused on what mysterious dangers lay ahead. Each of them had more questions than answers.

WHEN THEY GOT near Fort Boise, they could smell the stench from the banks of the river far before they caught sight of the fort. The docks were just a short distance from the main fort's double gates. It looked like there were more than a hundred wagons and tents set up around the fort's perimeter. Too many people milled around outside. The foul odor of humanity was almost overwhelming to the men fresh from the clean air in the forests. Ferrys bobbed up and down, tied to the docks, waiting to take someone to the far banks of the Snake River.

Strangely enough, the Indians' teepees had vanished, leaving no sign of Native Americans around the military compound, inside or anywhere else. Normally, Indians erected a couple of dozen teepees so they could watch the settlers come and go, sometimes trading hides and skins for tools and coffee.

"I wonder why all the Indians disappeared and where they went," Will whispered, as though speaking up would break the serenity of the moment. The mountain men had hardly spoken for days.

The sight of so many strangers took them aback. They sensed things were not right. The migrants glared at the mountain men like rabid dogs ready to attack their pack animals. Some men become mean and dangerous when they ran out of coffee, tobacco, and whiskey. All were considered luxuries in the wilderness. Anywhere else in the country, such things were taken for granted.

Some of the wagons closest to the fort gates had missing wheels and axles propped up on wooden barrels. Foreigners argued near the fort gates in a language few understood. A shot was fired, and one fell dead as the other one instantly vanished in the chaotic crowd. Before they realized it, all the mountain men had their revolvers in their hands, ready to fire if threatened. They could feel the tension and wondered if it would be worse inside.

"Steady now, fellas. This is my kind of work. Keep sharp now. These innocent folks are like a herd of cattle ready to spook, and the slightest thing will set 'em off," the marshal warned.

"I wonder how Sheriff Tom Hand is dealing with all this. From here, things don't look so good. I suspect inside it'll be worse," Will added.

"Well, what are we waitin' for? I'm so hungry I could eat three whole chickens. First thing, we get something to eat. Then, we can see Sheriff Hand and the captain. The order of things has changed since the Brits were kicked out." Levi said, rubbing his belly and thinking about apple pie.

Levi pushed his way through the crowd to the batwing doors of McKay's Saloon. They swished shut behind them as the captain slipped by. As soon as they walked in, they saw who they were looking for at the bar. Sheriff Hand leaned over, talking to Captain Crow and Sergeant Carson. They were so engrossed in their conversation that they didn't even look up or notice the mountain men enter the saloon.

Will tipped his head toward a table by the door, and they sat down as they watched what was becoming a heated argument. They waited until things died down to step up and let them know they had arrived.

"Damn it, that won't do!" Crow roared as he hammered his fist on the bar top. Neither Levi nor Will had ever seen him lose his temper like that.

"We can't take the chance of waiting much longer. At any time, we're gonna have the settlers outside the gates rushing our warehouses and stores. They'll take anything that's not nailed down. Things are getting dire. I say we close the gates and let only the residents remain inside these walls. Otherwise, we risk them taking over the town. As the wagons pile up, there are gonna be more of them than us. It won't be much longer until we're outnumbered. We've gotta act immediately, or it'll be too late. So far, nobody has been killed, and we wanna keep it that way."

"I'm afraid that you're incorrect, there, Sheriff Hand. A man was just shot dead outside the gates, not fifteen minutes ago," Johnson called out from a nearby table.

"Is that you, Levi?" Captain Crow asked. "Why, ain't you a sight for sore eyes. I didn't think you'd get the message or wouldn't be able to make it. If it weren't for my Tonkawa scout, I'd never have had such an idea. Smoke signals, of all things. What will we have to do next?"

"It's Marshal Walker and Captain Forrester, too." Sheriff Hand said, nodding as he forced a smile. His eyes told another story. "I'm afraid that things have gotten out of hand here, boys."

"We got the message, but it was kind of garbled. Even for Potak, the medicine man who reads smoke better than anyone we know, was confused. What was this about a tornado?"

"The Tornado Express Cargo Company," the sheriff said. "They usually deliver the general stores and other business stock along with feed, ammo, and weapons for the armory. They were on their way here with six wagons full of supplies—enough for months—but an outlaw gang learned they were running a special delivery. They ambushed them before they could arrive. They usually travel with a wagon train, but this time they were running flat out on their own. It's risky business these days. Lucky for them, it was just before they hit Fort Hall. So, the cargo wasn't stolen, and the drivers and guards survived. But I heard it was a close call.

"Messengers on fast horses were sent out as soon as it happened, and we've been trying to sort it out ever since. The folks here are about to riot. You haven't been able to get a coffee in town for two weeks. Tobacco and whiskey are runnin' low, too."

"Hey, whatcha doin' out there?" Marshal Walker growled as he stormed for the door after spotting a man stick his hand into their aparejo mule pack full of supplies. The marshal pulled his Colt revolver and put the barrel to the thief's head. The thief's teeth clenched when he heard the hammer click into action. It rattled in his brain. Walker grabbed him by the ear, dragging him into the middle of the courtyard. He kicked him in the butt, sending him flying into the dust.

"Next time I'm gonna shoot ya, mister. Ya see this badge?" Joseph growled and forked his thumb at his chest. "That's gonna make it legal. Now, get out of here before I change my mind."

"Junior," Charlie Fox, the bartender, said, "take that mule and these boys' horse over to the stables and stick him in a stable. Unload their gear and get it over to the sheriff's office."

"We can lock it up in a jail cell, so your traveling supplies are safe until you need them," the sheriff said. "I'm afraid that's gonna be real soon."

"You're kiddin', right?" the captain asked.

"Not these days, I'm not. The folks outside these walls are as angry as a woodpecker with a broken beak. We don't have any supplies to sell them. Many of them don't have anything to eat and are too green to know how to hunt. The game is pretty much hunted out around here anyway. Those who do hunt charge too much for what they bring in. It's flat-out robbery. Did you see the line of people on the riverbank fishing? There ain't been a fish pulled out of there for a week. It's all fished out, too. I swear, the whole place is falling to pieces. There ain't a live game animal worth the price of a bullet within a twenty-mile radius. I've even seen dogs roasting on spits, and they weren't Indians eating 'em—they were White folks."

The Apprentice

"Rusty, how about you and I take young Money Penny on a hike through the forest for a couple of days?" Potak asked after supper. He was smoking a long-stemmed pipe and popping smoke rings so big he blew little balls of smoke through the holes in the center. "I bet that between us, he will learn some interesting things. Maybe some things that even Levi Johnson doesn't know."

The medicine man chuckled at the thought of a White man ever knowing what he had learned in his journey through life. The shaman didn't know of another medicine man with his wisdom or skills, at least not anywhere he had traveled.

"How about that, Money?" Rusty asked, raising an eyebrow. "Do you wanna do a little exploring in the forest? Just the three of us."

"Can we go fishin', too? That's just about my favorite thing to do." Money replied with a grin from ear to ear. "Yeah, that'd be dandy. Who's gonna take care of the women while we men are gone?"

The comment about him being a man wasn't lost on his two elders.

"Virgil's here. He talks all about peace and nonviolence, but I've seen him in a fight. He can handle himself with a gun. And you know Angus is a dead shot," Rusty assured him. "Remember, Levi's wife is a Crow war chief, too. Things seem pretty quiet up here right now. I don't think it'll do us much harm if we're only gone for two or three days."

"Now, be a good young fella and go inside and ask Angus if you can have that last piece of apple pie." Potak chuckled. "But don't tell him it's for me, or he might say no. I've been eating him out of house and home. And don't worry, I'll give you a little bit."

Potak's eyes twinkled with mirth. They were full of mischief and magic.

As soon as Money disappeared through the cabin door, Potak turned to Rusty and asked. "How about I take you and Money to a secret place that nobody but me has seen or knows of? Do you think the boy can keep a secret forever? Can you keep a secret forever, Rusty Steel?" The Tonkawa medicine man's eyes twinkled, but his expression told Rusty how serious he was.

"There ain't no place around here I ain't seen or scouted. I know this land like the back of my hand. How far away is this secret of yours? A hundred miles? It can't be less, or I'd know about it."

"No, it's less than ten miles from right here in your compound. You've never noticed it before, of that I am sure. Don't be surprised or offended, my friend. Nobody but me and shamans from hundreds of years ago have set eyes on it. I've found traces of their trinkets and saw paintings on the walls. I believe it was a spiritual place for ancient tribes. At the time, I think the Ute, Arapaho, Cheyenne, Shoshone, and Apache traveled through these mountains. Pretty much all the tribes came here for the excellent hunting and fishing. There is always plenty of food. It has been like this for a thousand years."

"Save the stories for the boy," Rusty replied and laughed. "He'll be more likely to believe you. So, go ahead. We'll let you show us this secret place you're talking about. I ain't sayin' it's a lie, but I have a hard time believing it's true. Not with me living here for nigh on fifteen years and Mountain Dennis before that. He never mentioned any secret place to me."

"Of course, he wouldn't. Then it wouldn't be a secret, would it? You wait and see for yourself. You're lucky. If it weren't for young Money, I doubt I'd ever share my secret. It came to me in a dream last night. You, me, and the boy were sitting on the water's edge talking to an ancient turtle. It was the turtle that said that I should take you two there. He seemed to know who the boy was."

"I must admit, Potak, you come up with the strangest things. I swear I've never heard the likes. And what is the name of this talkin' turtle?" Rusty asked, laughing voraciously. "Were you talkin' to the fish too?" he asked sarcastically.

"Whatcha talkin' about, Uncle Rusty? Were you and Potak talkin' about me?" Money interrupted.

"As a matter of fact, we were," Potak said happily. "You have good instincts. You will make a fine mountain man one day. Maybe even a white Indian. There can always be a first."

"So, when are we goin' on that walk through the

forest? How far are we gonna go? What are we gonna see? Does it take long to get there? Are we the only ones going? Is it dangerous or is it fun? I prefer fun, if that's all right with you, Uncle Rusty. I've seen enough danger to spot me for a spell. I ain't like the captain. Levi says mountain men don't look for trouble. What kind of fish will we catch?"

"You asked how far we are going?" Potak replied mysteriously. "As far as a man can go."

"You sure are full of questions, boy," Rusty snickered. "How about askin' one at a time. I can't remember them all. And, what do you mean by as far as a man can go? You just told me that this place isn't but ten miles away."

"Some things appear close when in fact they are very far away," the Tonkawa medicine man replied mysteriously. "I must admit, the boy is observant for his age. Maybe this young fellow *is* something special."

THE FOLLOWING MORNING, they were up an hour before dawn. Money was so excited that he'd hardly been able to sleep. Potak said they wouldn't need their horses because they would be going slowly, so they wouldn't miss anything or make a misstep on the rough terrain. The shaman claimed that most people rushed through life, never noticing the beauty right before their eyes. They think they're too busy or were in too much of a hurry to go somewhere unimportant.

Rusty grumbled, still not believing that there could exist a place within ten miles of the cabin that he didn't know about, discounting everything the medicine man said. He was somewhat doubtful of the Tonkawa on a good day. The story he was telling them now seemed to be too outrageous to be true. But he also knew that you just never know what surprises you might dig up in the Rocky Mountains. Things worked differently among the tall peaks than anywhere else he had been. That much he could admit. Especially when dealing with a renowned medicine man.

Angus rushed up as they were just about to climb over the back of the brick-and-rail fence, which led to a fire wall they cut to keep the hostile Indians and Mother Nature's fires at bay. It was a stretch of land full of tree stumps until you reached the tree line on the other side.

"Here's a bag of food for lunch, fellas. From then on, you'll be eatin' your own cooking. There's a can of peaches for each of ya, too. Now, don't linger too long. Get back home safe and sound, and you two take care of that little man."

FROM THE NEXT cabin's window, Bar-chee was watching her boy go out into the wilderness again. She wanted to refuse to let him go, but she knew that her husband would disapprove, and it wasn't the right thing to do. She was afraid Money would grow up to be a man before she had time to enjoy the best thing that ever happened to her. A son had been the furthest thing from her and Joseph's minds. Neither one ever expected that they would get married or have children. Joseph assumed that, at his age, it might be too late. Bar-chee never awoke from their marital bed with the morning sickness. What she hoped might happen never did. She forced a tight smile, not feeling much like laughing.

Now that she had Money, she felt everybody was stealing her precious time with her newly adopted boy. She had thought he would belong only to her, but it seemed that everyone wanted a piece of his time. She knew that jealousy was a distasteful trait, so she bit her tongue and did what she knew was best. She didn't even go outside to hug him before he left. Bar-chee knew it would only embarrass the young boy, who wanted so much to be a man, and she might crack and start to cry again. She refused to spoil the mood. From where she stood and worried, she could see his happy eyes.

The Crow woman had been crying a lot since Money had been kidnapped, and now paranoia sat permanently on her shoulder. He was growing up before her very eyes, and all far too fast. She felt like her time with her son was slipping through her fingers, and she had resisted coddling him. At the same time, she knew her responsibilities and held her tongue.

THE BUCKSKIN-CLAD males jumped the fence and headed for the forest. When Money looked, Rusty grinned and winked his approval.

As they walked the first part of the trek, Potak looked back at the boy, and an amused smile curled his lips. Money saw him and grinned appreciatively. He had the feeling that Potak would show them something very special. Unlike Uncle Rusty, Money believed anything was possible, like most young men. The youngster wondered if the medicine man could hear the bass drum hammering in his chest. He seemed able to perceive everything else.

Their eyes traced across the rolling hills and mountains that were peppered with lodgepole and ponderosa pine. Englemann spruce and subalpine fir were abundant in the forested areas, along with the cottonwoods and aspens. When they looked up, nine thousand feet to the Bear Tooth plateau, it was treeless. The vegetation at lower altitudes was replaced with sagebrush, alpine aster, alpine arnica, and moss campion wildflowers. Using their spyglasses, they saw high-elevation plants like dwarf willow and bog birch.

After a few hours, they saw a column of Indians winding down the trail, a mile below them. They could see how they slowly marched in dreary unison, never missing a beat.

"Don't worry, they can't see us from here. For now, we are invisible," Potak continued without even turning to look at his friends.

Rusty shot him a doubtful glance.

"And what the hell is that supposed to mean? I might be superstitious, but I ain't no fool," he said as he scratched his bushy beard and squinted his intelligent eyes.

They walked past a massive field of sunflowers, standing high over their heads as their yellow faces dished toward the sun. The shaman looked back and tossed the boy another wistful smile as he observed the beauty of the mountainscape.

Rusty suddenly stopped, mumbled something, and squatted, his hands dangling before him as he studied the tracks. "That's a big grizz all right. I hope he hasn't taken up residence in your secret paradise. Keep your eyes peeled for tracks, boys. We don't wanna run into this big fella and spoil our day."

Money bunched his lips in doubt, then shrugged. He looked at the medicine man to see his reaction, but there was none. Maybe the bears weren't dangerous where the medicine man was taking them. The White men followed the dark-skinned Indian as they resembled wise men following a falling star.

"Most men only see what they want to see. I look for things that others don't. Then again, I have an advantage. I am a shaman. It is normal for me to see things that you don't. You are brainwashed to look for what is normal. If you really want to see, you need to look for the abnormal. Maybe we can teach Money how to look at things clearly before he is brainwashed like most men. It not only happens to White men. Indians are blinded sometimes, too."

"I never knew you could wash somebody's brain. Did it hurt, Uncle Rusty?" Money asked, puzzled.

Potak and the old mentor both laughed.

"Attaboy!" Rusty yelled as he slapped his knee. "Let this witch doctor know that he's talkin' foolishness. I, for one, know that I ain't brainwashed. I have a mind of my own with my own thoughts on things."

"Is that what Uncle Virgil means when he says that some men have dirty minds?" Money asked, which brought another round of laughter. His face showed he didn't understand.

FIVE HOURS AFTER THEY LEFT, they reached a narrow cliff cut right out of the mountain with a three-hundred-foot drop below. It was right along the main trail and was no secret as far as Rusty knew, but the Tonkawa shaman stood on the very edge and peered into the depths below.

"There it is," Potak said as he stared into the abyss.

"Whatcha mean, there it is? All that I see is air," Rusty replied. "There's more than a hundred yards to the bottom—maybe two hundred."

Potak stepped to the side of the shelf and pulled a loop of rope from under some dry limbs and broken bushes. It was obviously stashed there for his convenience. The hemp blended in with the foliage, and it was hard to see, even when you knew it was there.

Rusty became suddenly curious as he watched the shaman attach the rope to a hidden hook in the cliff's wall, something else he had not noticed. However, he didn't spend much time near dangerous drop-offs. More than one horse and man had dropped from the cliff and fallen to their deaths.

"See? I tied knots in the rope so it would be easy to climb down. You can't see them from here, but there are also small steps to put your feet on. Some Indian tribes cut them decades, if not centuries, ago. I'll go down first, then Money can follow. You can help him over the ledge, Rusty. Then, you come. We'll be waiting for you at the entrance to the cave."

"What cave?" Steel asked as he peered over the ledge and down again. He stood so close that a small stone broke loose, and all three watched as it fell, taking forever to hit the bottom.

No sooner had Potak finished talking than he grabbed the rope and disappeared over the edge, falling out of sight. When Rusty looked down, the shaman had vanished. He knew he hadn't lost his footing or fallen because he would have yelled, and there would be a body at the bottom. To make sure, Rusty quickly glanced through his spyglasses, but he saw nothing, making him more curious and puzzled than ever.

Money disappeared just as quickly, vanishing out of sight in the blink of an eye. Rusty looked again but saw no sign of the boy. He knew it would take him at least four seconds to hit the bottom if he had slipped. Worried, Rusty launched himself off the edge of the cliff. Fifteen feet down, he saw Potak and Money sitting on a rock in the shade, but he still didn't see any signs of the shaman's secret spot. They and everything around them were shrouded in shadows and lush green vegetation.

"So where is this place you're talkin' about?" Rusty asked." "I don't see anything. Everybody knows about this cliff because so many horses have slipped and fallen to the bottom. You can see their bones from here."

"The entrance is right there." Potak pointed, chuckling. He pointed to a spot not four feet behind them.

The Tonkawa Indian spread his arms expansively as they walked through to the cave's entrance. The eyes of Rusty and Money grew wider as broad grins showed rows of white teeth.

Rusty did a double-take, seeing that the cave entrance was covered in layers of shadows, making it difficult to see, even though he stood right next to it. The outside was damp and covered in vines and plants, lush and green.

Without a word, Potak lit a lantern as soon as they stepped into the dark natural tunnel, leaving a yellow circle around their feet. After walking through the hidden cave for nearly half a mile, they saw a crack in the mountain at the end of the dark tunnel. Sunlight slanted on the cave's stone floor from the inside entrance. They felt bats' wings touch their heads as they spooked and scattered. They walked through the vertical break in a boulder and into something that resembled the Garden of Eden.

For the briefest of moments, everything froze like a painting on a wall. They held their breaths and took in every minute detail before taking another step. The allure was heart-stopping. Money stood as mute as a tailor's mannequin when he first set eyes on Potak's secret. He gobbled air. The stone walls were dotted with colorful lupine, alpine forget-me-nots, moss campion, and paintbrush wildflowers. Scents and colors filled the air. The hieroglyphics on the cliffs blended in perfectly with the tiny, hidden forest.

Mesmerized, Money stood staring blankly into space like he had forgotten where he was. "I've never seen a place so beautiful." It was like every pretty place on Bear Tooth Mountain packed into one little spot.

Potak pressed his lips into a tight smile as he watched his friends' heart rates accelerate. He had never dared to take anyone there before for fear of ruining it for all time. But the reaction he saw from his White friends was so strong that he instantly knew he could trust them with his secret. He nodded knowingly.

"What did I tell you, Rusty? What do you think now? Like I said, we are about ten miles from the compound. It almost seems impossible, doesn't it?"

"What I wanna know is, how in the world did you find it. The entrance is all but invisible, and that's after you climb over a dangerous cliff. Are you part mountain goat, or what?

"I must admit it's the most beautiful place I've ever seen, bar none. It's obvious it exists because it is a secret. Man would ruin this place in days, especially if they were White men from back East.

"The Indians don't like this area because they think it is cursed. They believe the cliff calls its victims to it and lures them into the void. Of course, that's nonsense. Man will always be more reckless than warranted. That is why some fall to their deaths on the path. Nothing more. Fear has helped keep this place sacred."

"When did you discover it, Potak?" Money asked.

"A better question is, how did you find it?" Rusty added.

"It was twenty years ago today. That was seven thousand three-hundred-five suns ago." Potak said, unfazed by the number of days he recalled. Time was nothing to him.

"And how did you find it, Potak?" Money asked.

"In a dream, a turtle told me where it was." Potak smiled. "He is ancient, you know. More than three hundred years. The turtle is the keeper."

Rusty didn't know if the medicine man was pulling their legs or if he really expected them to believe that a turtle revealed the secret spot. He wondered why people said that he talked to animals and, more incredibly still, that they talked back.

Rusty was never able to figure out what went on in an American Indian's mind, let alone a medicine man's. He pushed his hand into his pocket and fingered his rabbit's foot, a silver four-leaf clover, and the tiny box with the ladybug inside. He wore his grizzly bear necklace to ward off another bear attack, just like the native people of the mountains.

When he realized how superstitious he was, he began to think that maybe Potak wasn't all that crazy. Levi whispered to his horse. Who's to say if he understands or not?

Finally, Rusty shook his head and chuckled to himself. The old shaman had almost convinced him he spoke the truth. No, Rusty had his head set square on his shoulders. He knew better.

Fallen leaves lay like golden paper on the ground as the sun fell through the trees like rain. It glowed warm on the little mountain man apprentice's face as the earth floated off in a long curve to the end of the world. Money was so stunned by the beauty, he had to remind himself to breathe.

Ancient paintings with bright colors from a thousand years before covered the cliff walls. How the colors stayed so bright was as much a mystery as who it was that painted them. Some were too tall for a man to have made without a sophisticated series of ladders, but how would they get such a thing there? The mere existence of the secret garden was baffling. How did it remain a secret for decades, if not centuries?

THE FIRST THING they did when they reached the garden's floor was build a sizable fire and put a kettle on to percolate after Rusty made a show of grinding the coffee beans. They also put on a pot of black beans and hung some salted meat over the fire to heat. Sparks ran downwind as the fire sawed in the light breeze. Since the little piece of paradise was unknown and impossible to see from outside, they burned their fire day and night to keep the coffee hot and themselves warm during the ever-cool evenings in the Rocky Mountains.

"Look, Rusty. There's a freshwater spring over there in that stand of trees. I've never seen a place so lush and green. It's even greener than down in Yellowstone Valley," Money said, drawn toward the still water. He walked toward it as though he was enchanted.

High above were straw nests lodged into crevices. Bald eagles used their towering perches to spy on prey below. A mountain goat standing by the water's edge bucked its head and sniffed the air. It must have climbed over the cliffs to get to the long green grass. As soon as it sensed human presence, it climbed the vertical rock wall on hidden steps that only a goat could follow.

Smaller game animals scurried into the brush and scattered at the sight of their presence. Potak's secret spot was full of life. Swallowtail, monarch, and painted lady butterflies, some with wingspreads of five inches, fluttered through the fresh-smelling air. Dragonflies hovered over the glass-like cover of water as fish swam below the surface, which was undisturbed, without a single ripple.

Money walked up to the edge of the water, pulled off his moccasins, and tested the temperature with his big toe. "Why, it's as warm as bathwater!" he declared. As he wiggled his toes, tadpoles darted around his feet, nibbling on his skin. The three humans discarded their buckskins and, one by one, descended into the warm spring. Their chest and legs were lighter and paler than their arms and faces.

Great puckered scars lay scattered on Rusty's body like tracks of millipedes. Money saw two round, puffy spots that looked like gunshot wounds. He stared at his battle scars until he caught himself and looked down as his neck turned a fiery red with embarrassment. He hoped his temporary mentor hadn't seen him staring.

That night, the medicine man's face shone pale like the moon. The lobe-shaped white orb stood frozen on the horizon, over the mountains so high that it dimmed the stars. Money looked up and stared until his neck hurt. Cloudbanks stood at the edge of the lower peaks. He wondered if it rained in paradise.

Fort Hall

After Billy Rooster and Buster Balls roared into Fort Hall with five more wagons behind them, they thanked their lucky stars they made it to cover before the outlaws could kill them and steal the cargo. The problem was that four of those six wagons were destined for Fort Boise. They knew the outlaws would be waiting for them when they resumed their journey. With six wagons, they had twelve men to ward off the thieves, but only eight would accompany four wagons. That meant that they would be seriously outnumbered by the outlaws, who probably had reinforcements hidden along the trail.

Of course, when under duress, the bullwhackers had to focus all their attention on their job, ensuring the animals pulling the wagons didn't run away or the carriages tip over. They also had to be careful not to run their horses to death. Therefore, four out of eight men would be too busy to return fire, making their defense questionable. All the outlaws had to do was set an ambush, stop the lead wagon, and block the trail for the rest. Then, they could open fire from good cover and seize the cargo.

The shotgun guards could hide behind wooden boxes and barrels full of supplies, but the bullwhackers were easy targets with no cover at all. They had to rely on their guards' expertise and their own diversion tactics to stay alive. The outlaws' other option would be to shoot the horses, but then they would be left with no way to cart off the stolen valuables. Their only alternative would be to remove the drivers and guards without harming the animals.

Of course, the Oregon Trail was sometimes too wide to judge. Such heavy wagons could not stray too far off the main trail for fear of busting an axle or getting stuck, risking the lives of the men in the other wagons. So, finding alternative routes wasn't an option. Their best chance was to drive the six-horse teams hard, trying to bust through any defense of the outlaws.

None of the cargomen fancied dying in an effort to deliver the goods. They would rather take on wild Indians than professional gunmen. Native war parties would break off if they lost too many warriors. White outlaws would fight to the last man.

When they roared past the fort's open gates and heard them slam shut after the last wagon passed, Rooster breathed a sigh of relief. He was the head wagon master and in charge of the whole shebang. Now, he had to figure out how to finish the last leg of their journey, successfully deliver the other four wagons, and get paid. That was going to be the tricky part with the bandits waiting somewhere not too far away.

When they arrived, they expected to find the usual security in the form of guards or hired gunmen from the British Hudson's Bay Company. They left when the Americans raised Old Glory, the red, white, and blue, forthwith, and forever on.

"Whatcha think we should do, Rooster?" Balls asked. "We can't let those folks in Fort Boise go without these supplies. I doubt that they'll be in dire straits yet, but there are hundreds of wagons passing through here every week. They all need supplies for the last miles to their destination. I imagine, by now, wagon trains are lined up for ten miles, and more of the same is coming. Every wagon train that comes through here stops there, too, unless they get lost or killed first."

There were only three forts on the route across the vast Western wilderness: Fort Laramie, Fort Hall, and Old Fort Boise. After them, the next stop was Oregon. But the overlanders needed supplies to make the final cross and for the Fort Boise settlement to survive. Without these required stocks, they wouldn't make it and would end up dying there if they weren't murdered by mutineers first.

Two gunshots rang out, alerting everyone to the main gate, which had remained shut since the cargo train made it to the security of the fort's walls. A pair of soldiers opened one of the gates as two riders stormed to safety. They pulled their horses to a sliding stop as the gates quickly banged closed behind them. Both riders sprang from their saddles and gobbled air. The horses' lungs sounded like broken bellows.

Wagon master Rooster and his partner met the soldiers as they dismounted.

Corporal Shane Holmes managed to speak, "We need supplies as soon as possible in Fort Boise. Hundreds of wagons are piled up, and more are comin'!

The overlanders are about to turn on the townsfolk to take what they need. I don't know how much longer the fort can hold out. It's startin' to get ugly.

"Captain Harvey Crow told me to inform you that he's sending three hired men. He doesn't have a single soldier to spare after the departure of the British. But I reckon the fellas he's sending are the best. I hope they get here in time."

Holmes's partner, Private Joe Riley, grabbed a wooden bucket off the porch, dipped it into the watering trough, and hand-fed water to the horses, making sure they didn't drink too much and too fast. He tied them to a hitching post in the shade on the side of the building, then returned to the watering trough and ducked his head underwater. When he pulled it out, he shook his head like a dog, his hair spraying water everywhere.

"That was one hell of a ride. We liked to kill our horses. We didn't see any Indians, though. I reckon if they saw us flat out like that, they'd have been so surprised by seeing us alone in the middle of Indian territory, they just let us go on by."

"What are your orders now, Corporal?" Rooster asked. There was an urgency in his voice, and he was hoping for some good news.

"To send those wagons back to the fort as soon as Levi Johnson, Captain Forrester, and Marshal Walker arrive here to help with the escort. Our orders are to stay here and fill in for the lack of soldiers. We also need every gun-for-hire in town. The settlement of Fort Boise is prepared to pay top dollar.

"The goods stored in those wagons are worth a fortune and are becoming more valuable every day.

That's why we need to protect their transport. Who's in charge here?"

"The British lieutenant and manager for the Hudson Bay folks rode out three days ago and left us with US Army Sergeant Bud Burns in charge until reinforcements arrive. As you can imagine, he's pretty busy keeping the peace. There's slim pickings as far as security is concerned," Rooster reported. "These wagons were lucky to make it to the fort. Outlaws tried to ambush us not far from here."

"So, who do we have to help us get those wagons over to Fort Boise?" Corporal Holmes asked.

"You're lookin' at us," Rooster replied. "Buster and me got the lead wagon, and there are three whackers and one guard per wagon. That's eight in all. I'm Billy Rooster, but everybody calls me Rooster. Buster Balls here works with me on my wagon, and we ride point. Jimmy Johnson over there rides drag along with his shotgun guard, Red Hawkens. They nearly got shot before we got to the gates. I know for a fact that there are at least eight outlaws out there waiting for us to leave. They've got more guns on 'em than my dog has fleas. By the looks of their hardware, I reckon they know how to shoot, too."

"I think we're gonna need a better plan than what you've got, fellas," the soldier added. He had heard the discussion as he walked up. "I hope Levi and the captain can come up with something, or I don't see this cargo making it to Fort Boise without everybody getting shot all to hell."

A uniformed man who looked like he had just woken up came running toward the bullwhackers, stuffing his shirt into his pants and thumbing his suspenders over his shoulders. He wore a pair of Colt revolvers in cross-draw holsters and had a pockmarked face, short hair, and broad shoulders. At five-foot-six, he looked as sturdy as a hitching rail. They were surprised when his big smile showed a mouthful of white teeth. He walked right up, adjusted his gun belt, and said, "I figured at some point or other, Captain Crow would send messengers. How ya doin', fellas? I'm Sergeant Bud Burns. Have you got any news on reinforcements? What's the captain got to say?"

"Everybody is waitin' on Washington for orders. It looks like they pulled the trigger on the deal with the British border agreement before they had things organized. Now, we're all short of gun hands and soldiers. That's just like Washington, though. They're too far away to know or care what's really going on this far west.

"Here we have the fort settlers ready if the outlaws run out of patience and decide to attack the fort," Burns said. "Most of them were already armed, and I supplied guns for those who weren't. We don't have a man to spare. For now, it's three privates and me."

"It's that bad, huh?" Holmes asked with a shocked look on his face.

"WELL, we can't stand around here all day," Captain Forrester said. "We have folks in need of our services. So, we'd better get on our way. That cargo isn't going to get here by itself. We're going to have to go and get it and fight our way back."

"Do you think you can handle things here until we

get back, Sheriff Hand?" Levi asked. "I've never seen such a long line of wagons outside, and I reckon it's just gonna get longer. Things are bordering on chaos. Garbage is strewn here to the river, and the whole place stinks."

"To be honest, I don't really know," Hand replied. "It all depends on how long you boys take to get those cargo wagons here, and how desperate the overlanders get. After crossing two-thirds of the Oregon Trail, we've got some hard men out there. Once folks start starvin', things are gonna get mighty ugly fast. Half of these people can't even speak English, for Pete's sake. At the moment, we're sittin' on a powder keg with no idea of when it's gonna blow. I've even heard rumors that some of the European folks are talkin' about goin' out and huntin' Indians to eat. If something that crazy happens, we'll have the local tribes after us, too. That's why you don't see an Indian anywhere in sight. All the teepees vanished days ago, and the Crow, Nez Pierce, and Bannock. And the friendly Blackfeet went with 'em."

"We'll need three extra horses," Levi said. "We'll stay here, rest for a few hours, and get something to eat. That'll give you boys time to find us replacement mounts. Throw in some bullets, too, if you have any to spare. I don't foresee trouble riding east, but you never know. Once we get to Fort Hall, we can resupply before we turn around to head back. I figure if we ride flat out, we can get there in three or four days, but it's gonna be hard on us and the horses."

"The return trip will be considerably slower since we'll be driving wagons," Captain Forrester said. "If we have outlaws on our tails, it should speed us up, though."

Will almost cracked a smile as though he was going to enjoy the grueling gauntlet. He said it like it was no big thing. The concern on the faces of Joseph and Levi told the true story. The escapade was not going to be a piece of cake, and some of them might get shot for their efforts.

"I figure we've got a fifty-fifty chance of making it," Marshal Walker said. "I reckon if we try hard enough, and Lady Luck rides with us, we just might pull it off before the whole territory blows up. We're gonna have to plan carefully and not make a single mistake."

"Let's go have one last hot meal at McKay's Saloon before we go. I don't know about you and the marshal, but I don't run on air," Levi demanded. He had two hundred twenty pounds of muscle to feed, and he was always hungry.

"I've never seen a man think about food as much as you, Levi," Will said, shaking his head. "You go ahead while I get a quick shave."

The mountain man chuckled to himself over the irony of the captain's words. He had never met a man so obsessed with his stubble. At least food was imperative to living.

Levi smiled, shook his head, and said, "Come on, Joseph. Maybe they'll have freshly baked peach pie. I hate riding off on a dangerous mission with an empty stomach. It puts me in a bad mood."

"Well, come on then," Joseph replied. "I'm already in a bad mood. Beware of any men who step in our paths and try to stop us. If I have anything to do with it, I'll send them to their graves."

———

TEN MINUTES LATER, Joseph and Levi were sitting at a table piled high with food. Since Charlie Fox knew what they were about to do, he gave them everything in the kitchen but the stove, and it was all on the house. The saloon needed stock just as much as the other businesses in the settlement. The owner was eager and willing to do his part in hastening the arrival of the cargo wagons.

Soon, the captain arrived, brushing his newly trimmed mustache with his knuckles. When he rubbed his smooth face with his hand, he smiled. It was the simple things in life that the captain loved, and having a good shave was at the top of the list. His empty sleeve trailed behind him as he rushed to the table.

"You almost came too late," said Levi, who grinned like he had just won a pie-eating contest. "But not to worry. We saved you enough to fill you up. Be advised, we did eat all of the peach pie."

"We had our dessert first," Marshal Walker said as he swiped syrupy leftovers from his lips. "Levi ate a whole pie and half of mine. Had you come a few minutes later, all the food would have been gone."

Will laughed, well aware of his partner's insatiable appetite.

Ten minutes later, Sheriff Tom Hand busted his way through the batwing doors, leaving them swishing behind him. "I've got your horses ready to go, Levi. They're tied up out front at the hitching post. Your horses and three strong spares. They're the best we've got, so they should get you to the fort quickly."

"I'm not worried about gettin' there. I'm worried about getting back," the blond-haired mountain man replied.

Fifteen minutes later, the three friends rode out of the main gate leading a string of replacement horses. Sheriff Hand had changed their pack mule for a fast draft horse so it wouldn't slow them down. The town was pulling out all the stops to get them the best supplies and horseflesh available. The mountain men were focused on the thousand dollars they would get paid upon the arrival with cargo wagons.

One thousand dollars was a handsome sum in 1846. Back East, or someplace like San Francisco, it wasn't so much. In the wilderness, it was considered a fortune, enough money for some men to risk life and limb.

The Oregon Trail

Sheriff Hand stood on the fort's wall-walk, or *chemin de ronde,* as the Vancouver British called it. He shaded his eyes with the flat of his hand as he peered into the distance. He saw a dust cloud following three riders and seven horses. Levi, the captain, and the marshal were moving fast and soon would disappear over the horizon. It was anyone's guess as to what would happen next.

The sheriff turned his head toward the front gate and scoured the land between the fort and the banks of the Snake River. Every available space was occupied by wagons, carriages, and even sleds. There were mules, donkeys, oxen, and draft horses scrounging for the few tufts of grass that remained. Others stood belly-deep in the water, cooling off and refreshing themselves as the mud tugged at their feet.

Over a hundred men, women, and boys dipped cane fishing poles into the water, but not a single float bobbed, disappeared, or showed the slightest nibble. The river had been overfished for weeks, and much of the sewage from so many people and animals was disposed of right there. Strong currents prevented contamination. But if more people arrive, continue to flood into the region, the water would be poisoned.

As Sheriff Hand watched the children from the wagon trains splash and play in the shallows, he wondered if diseases would form and sweep through the community like an unchecked wildfire. Such a thing could wipe out all the overlanders in a matter of days, not to mention the residents. There was little a single sheriff could do to prevent it. His lone deputy had worked for the British Hudson's Bay Company. He, too, left for Vancouver.

Hand turned his gaze west again, but the mountain men had already disappeared over a distant ridge. Only their dust clouds remained visible.

Pollution from overpopulation and contaminated drinking water was a big worry. Everyone had to make long treks to collect potable water far upstream. The odor outside the fort's wall was becoming overwhelming, but there was little they could do in such heat. The travelers couldn't proceed without the much-needed supplies, and every day more wagons showed up, making a long line along the trail leading to Fort Boise. Every day, more wagons joined the queue.

The livestock that many of the overlanders brought with them had been eaten by their owners or stolen and devoured by others. People were guarding their food with loaded weapons, and more than one thief had been shot and killed. The last one was a young, innocent boy with an empty stomach. Now he lay under a plain stone marker in the massive yet growing graveyard outside the fort.

The travelers were so accustomed to the loss of lives that they didn't bother to mark the graves. Only those from Fort Boise had permanent gravestones or painted crosses that displayed names and dates. By 1846, over one hundred and forty thousand pilgrims had died on the Oregon Trail. Many more would follow. It was estimated that over ten percent of the travelers lost their lives for one reason or another during the massive westward migration.

That winter, the Donner Party would be tragically lost. Forty-one of eighty-nine overlanders survived. The rest died from snakebites, disease, exhaustion, outlaws, bandits, and hostile Indians. Some of the wagon trains were luckier than others, and some had no luck at all.

Inside the fort courtyard, it was another story. Every town citizen, including the women and teenage children, was armed to the teeth. For them, the new enemy could come from right outside the fort's double gates, the only thing that kept chaos at bay. For the moment, the sheriff had ordered no one to enter or exit the fortified compound until further notice.

Armed citizens stood on the allure, making note of the happenings among the wagons parked right outside their homes. At any moment, their would-be customers could turn into raging mobs if things became more dire.

Disease had a profound impact on the pioneers crossing the Oregon Trail. Nine of ten who died were due to illnesses rather than accidents or attacks. The deadly result was due to poor sanitation, limited diets, exhaustion, and often contaminated water. These conditions made the travelers more susceptible to typhoid fever, flu, tuberculosis, mumps, measles, dysentery, and last but not least, cholera.

Cholera was known as the unseen destroyer, spread rapidly via contaminated water sources, and could kill a healthy person in twenty-four hours or less. During rough river crossings, wagon trains lost two-thirds of their travelers.

Child mortality was even higher, and diphtheria was the most common culprit. Most rudimentary treatment and medication came in the form of castor oil, rum, and quinine. Fort Boise, sitting on the banks of the Snake River, was a time bomb waiting to explode.

The only precautions the overlanders could take were boiling their water before consumption, repeatedly washing their hands and bodies, isolating sick individuals from the rest of the party, and carefully disposing of human waste. They also used homemade remedies and basic antiseptics such as alcohol and vinegar as cure-alls.

Fort Boise's small military community, supporting businesses, and tiny residential population prayed for relief. If conditions continued to deteriorate, the sheriff worried they all might perish.

LEVI LEANED over his paint's head and whispered soothing words into his ear as the marshal gave him an odd look. Will knew Beaver's skills were second to none, but now he wondered if his horse understood him, too, or was it his tone of voice that settled the animal's nervous behavior? After riding with the mountain man from north of the Ohio River for over six years, Will still found Levi unusual and mysterious in certain ways.

"Sometimes, the wildcat needs to show the jackals

who he is," Captain Forrester said. His concern for the outlaws heightened as they got closer to Fort Hall.

"Maybe one of us should try to find out where that gang is before we approach Fort Hall, let them know we're around. Maybe we can discover what we're up against before all hell breaks loose. Once we get twenty miles or so from the settlement, I can break off and see if I can locate where they're hiding or maybe even where they're planning to launch an ambush."

"That's not a bad idea, Will," Levi replied. "I doubt it'll be too hard to track down twenty reckless outlaws. There will be no way you can miss their tracks. From what we've heard, they don't seem to be scared or hiding from anybody. The part we don't know is where they are between here and Fort Hall, but my guess would be they're probably close. I wouldn't be surprised if they didn't have spies inside the walls and all. At least that's what I'd do."

"Maybe I should be the one to go," Marshal Walker said. "I might get a chance to winge or kill a couple before we leave the fort with the cargo wagons. I ain't gonna be shy about it. There's no doubt that these ruffians mean business. I'm the only one of us here with a badge. I have the legal right to shoot and ask questions later."

THE CLATTER of trotting horses beat across the trail nearly all day and all night. The three blended with the eastern horizon like black images of marionettes with the sun bright on their faces in the morning and at their back at night. They raced along, adjusting their eyes to the dimming light. Behind them, fractured light colored the sky as the vanishing orb sought refuge on the mountain horizon.

When the yellow disk neared the earth's rim, squatting and pulsating with malevolence, they took a much-needed break. Sparks from their campfire rose over the plain as another day came and went. A carpet of stars rolled out from east to west, twinkling like little lamps millions of light-years away. The first glow of soft light broke the western horizon as the moon rose. When it reached its majestic height, it appeared as though they could reach out and touch it.

The marshal spat out the stub of a cigar and ground it under his boot heel. Then he climbed into his saddle and forked his legs around his horse. With tight lips, he tipped his hat to his friends and wheeled his mount into the night. There wasn't anything more to say. Everything had been said. It was time to get to work.

AS SOON AS Marshal Walker rode out of sight, Levi and the captain went silent. There were no questions that hadn't been answered. Now was the time for action. Soon, the marshal's guns would bark and growl.

Will and Levi framed in their minds what was to come as they stared blindly into the fire. They listened in the night as the sound of the lawman's galloping horse slowly vanished into the distance. Woe to the outlaws who crossed the territorial marshal's path. They silently relaxed around the fire, a yellow, flickering circle of light. Levi eased back with his shoulders to his saddle and his hands behind his head. He stared into the flickering flames. The captain pulled his hat over his eyes and listened to the night birds chattering in the dark.

The following morning, when the first sign of red spread across the skyline, they knew their surroundings would be bathed in light within minutes. Will scraped his boot along crumby earth, kicking dirt onto the fire. It hissed as smoke rose thick and heavy. In minutes, they were off again, disappearing into the coming dawn.

The soft blue of a cloudless sky was the only redeeming factor in the ragged, wild-looking country. To the north, the sky was a dismal gray, dark and depressing, but they saw a break in the clouds in the eastern sky. Fort Hall would only be another day's ride.

Levi was past his mid-twenties, and his eyes were beginning to redden, but the fire in them belonged to a younger man. He neck-reined his stallion toward the trees. The captain followed. Levi's long hair hung down his back, and his beard covered his chest. He hadn't shaved since he was a child back in Indiana, although his Crow wife, Dahteste, did trim both. The two men were buckskin-clad, except for the captain's Army riding boots and beige hat, making them look more like Indians than White men in the wilderness.

Levi and his horse had formed a kinship. Often, the horse licked salty perspiration from Levi's hand when he rubbed his nose. Beaver gently flicked the reins against Trigger's neck, easing him forward.

As the country yawned wide, the captain's spyglass inched over the expanse. His eyes continued to crawl out into the distance from them and the settlement. He carefully pinpointed the path they would choose to follow. They urged their horses with a sharp rowel to their flanks, making them burst forward, kicking up dust.

The captain's face needed the brim's shadows to soften his sharp, gaunt features and hard lines. Strangers often believed he was angry. Narrow hips, sun-darkened, thin-lined features beneath the turned-up brim of a faded Stetson. He spoke like a man much wiser than his twenty-some years. Will's beard was stubbled. He rubbed his face, brushed his blond mustache, and frowned. He hated it when he didn't get a chance to shave, even though it was only a few days old and hardly noticeable, especially when sitting beside the long-haired and bearded Levi Johnson.

They pressed their horses through the day, occasionally standing in their stirrups to peer into the distance. They looked out at the never-ending wilderness before them. Levi pressed his moccasin-clad heels into his paint's flanks, his mouth no more than a hard line. Their heads swiveled from one side to the other, taking in everything around them, while calculating the path they would follow next.

MARSHAL WALKER PAUSED to catch his breath. He wiped the sweat from his face with a grimy hand. His gut told him that the outlaws weren't far. Joseph believed he could smell wrongdoers. After twenty years of chasing bad guys, he had developed something like a sixth sense. His face glistened with oily preparation as the hair on the back of his neck stood on end.

The marshal's face was a bronzed, hard mask matured beyond his age. When he removed his broadband hat, thick brown hair hung close to his skull. When he finally caught sight of the gang, a scowl grew on his bearded face. He neck-reined his horse toward some trees, which he could use as a blind. The sun glared, and Joseph felt its heat rise over his face.

Marshal Walker stepped out of the saddle, letting his reins trail. Iron-willed anger was reflected in the tight line of his jaw. He hobbled his horse with a ready-made loop of rope, then pulled down his loaned Sharps rifle. He laid the nine-and-a-half-pound long gun on his bedroll perched on a boulder and stared into the distance.

Christian Sharps had been kind enough to provide Rusty and his gang with several prototype rifles to test for problems before putting them into mass production during the following two years, but to date, they had done their job and then some. There was no rifle on the market to match its shooting power for both impact and distance. They would be a game-changer when they were released to the public in 1848.

After hearing about Rusty Steel's and Levi Johnson's marksmanship during the Rendezvous shooting matches and later their exploits in the far stretches of the West, he sent them a shipment from Windsor, Vermont. Five high-powered rifles with cases of ammunition arrived. The inventor believed that if anyone could test his weapons in the harshest conditions, it was the mountain men.

Joseph pushed his hat from his forehead and ran the back of his hand across his mouth. A wad of tobacco bulged in his cheek. He suddenly sensed the tenseness in his breast, and his ears felt tingly, making every muscle instantly tighten. He believed the robbers were just over the subsequent rise and were about to show themselves. Joseph sniffed the air and noted the odor of cheroot smoke. Obviously, they weren't being careful about their movements. The marshal pushed his hands into his back to ease the stiffness of riding day and night and sighed. His eyes narrowed and focused to a pinpoint.

The sweltering, rock-strewn country was burned and gouged, leaving the marshal's face chiseled and expressionless. The flat dry land began to buckle into rock-strewn hills. Even the trees were sparse across the barren land. Those that did grow were short and wind-swept. It was a depressing, glaring panorama of rock, with few shade trees or kindly features to soften its squat ugliness.

The marshal's eyes were caged white and red with fury, as his blood began to boil with violent intent. He impatiently waited for the riders to breach the next rise and come into sight. He stared down the barrel-length scope and released the safety trigger as he breathed out and squinted down the barrel of the Sharps with his right eye.

His first target rode over the ridge and started down the narrow trail. The rest followed in a single file. If he shot the second man, he would see the first man cut off and an easy target, blocking his retreat. The marshal hoped to whittle down the odds some. He didn't have time to wait to see how many there were in total. If he wanted to take his shots and get away unscathed, he knew he had to act quickly. He had enough time for one shot or maybe two at most. Joseph aimed to make them count.

The grizzled lawman opened the fifty-two-caliber

chamber, inserted a round, and levered it home. Then, rested his finger on the safety trigger as he focused on his distant target. As they rode down the grade, he led his targets slightly, noting that they rode slowly down the awkward hill. Joseph stuck his finger in his mouth and held it up to feel the direction and intensity of the wind. He nodded and returned his eye to the rifle's scope.

The heavy-caliber long gun spat fire, bucking hard into his shoulder. The high-powered bullet roared out of the barrel and closed the distance between the gun and the target. When the bullet hit its target, it shattered bone and ripped through the second outlaw's heart. Joseph quickly slipped another 50-90 cartridge into the chamber and slammed the bolt home.

The second shot knocked the lead rider off his saddle. His horse ran wildly down the steep trail, slipping halfway and rolling the rest. The broken-legged animal lay struggling at the end of the steep grade.

Joseph was happy with both shots. One rider lay dead. A mounted robber frantically helped the lead outlaw onto a horse, but he was gut-shot and in pain. Joseph knew he wouldn't make it. He would slow them down, which was precisely what the lawman wanted. His shooting skills had just bought them a little more time, and he had an idea of what kind of gang they were up against.

Joseph snickered, happy his marksmanship hadn't suffered from age. The marshal grabbed his bedroll and rifle, jumped back onto his horse, and bolted for Fort Hall. If he rode as hard as he dared, he calculated he would be reunited with his friends just about the same time they arrived at the fort. If there had been up to twenty riders originally, there were now only eighteen. He didn't linger to confirm that number.

Whoever they were, they certainly were bold. The marshal slowed, picking his way through briars and brambles. Once out and in the open, he put the spurs to his horse. They shot off like a charging bull.

THE SUN WAS ALMOST OVERHEAD, crowding the sky with its bright, white light, when Levi and the captain neared the Fort Hall gates. The huge double doors were closed, and a line of armed men manned the parapets. Rifle barrels protruded like sticks from overhead. All eyes were on the cloud of dust kicked up by the two approaching riders, and every weapon was loaded and cocked.

Suddenly, riding flat out, another horse burst from cover. The rider was low in the saddle, his horse chased by another dust cloud. Several men took a bead on a fast-running newcomer. It appeared like he was making a beeline for the pair coming to rescue the cargo train. Hammers clicked along the line of defenders. Maybe it was an ambush. Thirty guns said he didn't have a chance.

"Wait, don't shoot!" Corporal Holmes shouted. "That's Marshal Walker! He's one of us! Man the gates, boys. We've got three men comin' in hot, and it looks like they got here in the nick of time."

The gate hinges groaned when two men on the ground pushed one open just enough for the three riders to rush in. As soon as they passed through the entrance, the gate closed again. Of course, they didn't expect the outlaw gang to attack the fort, but they weren't taking any chances. They, too, had locked down the compound until the outlaws' location could be established.

Sergeant Burns didn't want one or two of them to sneak in and sabotage the cargo wagons before they left. Nobody was getting in or out but Levi, Will, and Joseph. Unless one of the outlaws was already inside. There were so many strangers milling around that it was difficult to tell. A spy could have easily infiltrated the settlement with so many unknown faces.

The three mountain men dismounted. Private Joe Riley and a civilian rushed to tend to the exhausted horses. Their lungs sounded like steam engines. The men were covered in trail dust. It stuck to their skin from all the sweat. They looked like mud figures on horses.

A burly sergeant introduced himself. "I'm Sergeant Bud Burns, and the temporary commander of Fort Hall. You must be Levi Johnson."

"Captain Forrester," Will said as he offered his hand.

"And I'm Marshal Joseph Walker." He was breathing so hard he could hardly speak. He rested his hands on his knees as he struggled to slow his pounding heart and fill his lungs. He was twenty years older than Beaver and Will. For once in his life, he noticed his age.

"Well, let's get these men to the barracks and somewhere to wash up and get something to eat," Burns said. "From a distance, you two almost look like Indians in your buckskins. Running around like that, you're lucky you ain't been shot."

"Who's in charge of the cargo wagon train?" Levi asked, all business. He wasn't here for chitchat and felt there was no time to waste. "We don't want to linger long. Things are getting dire in Fort Boise. By now, the locals will be completely out of supplies. There's an angry mob between the fort and the Snake River. It's just a matter of time until some of the overlanders try to break inside. People are gonna start starvin' soon. There are no game animals in a radius of fifty miles, and I know for a fact that part of the river is fished out."

"Slow down, Levi. We don't want to kill ourselves in the process either," Marshal Walker replied. "If we push too hard, none of us will make it, Levi. We've got to keep a level head about this. Not too slow, but not too fast either. If we don't make it, it will have all been for nothing."

"He's right, Mr. Johnson. You have another hard ride in front of you. You don't want to make it halfway only to have your horses or one of your partners give out." Burns didn't mean to, but he was staring at the marshal, whose age was evident as he stood next to the two young men. He quickly turned his eyes back to Johnson.

"You get us plenty of food, and we'll worry about our stamina," Levi replied. "We've got a job to do. There's no time for slackers." His smile sagged, and he added, "It's time to get to work. That'll be enough negative talk. It's gonna be hard enough as it is."

Garden of Dreams

Money stretched out his arms and dove under the water, launching himself through the crystal-clear pond. He swam through a school of fish, but they didn't startle. It was a magical moment for the young boy. He let his body's buoyancy float him up until his head broke through the surface. Again, paradise greeted his eyes.

Dragonflies bounced on puffs of air as bullfrogs croaked at the water's edge. Golden fins made little wakes on the flat surface. One frog got too close to its neighbor, and in the blink of an eye, it gobbled him up. The nine-year-old's blue eyes reflected in the liquid mirror as he observed the micro-world around the natural spring.

Tiger and springtail beetles clung to the plants on the water's banks. Flies buzzed around Money's head. A colony of ants, in the thousands, harvested cuts of leaves from a nearby tree. One column marched up the trunk and the other down and to a nearby anthill and disappeared inside, carrying loads several times their size.

The sun made the surface shine like a mirror, creating star-like twinkles on the glass.

When Money looked down, he saw something significant and round at the bottom. At first, he paid little attention. When it moved and started to surface, Money gulped a lungful of air and paddled as quickly as possible back to the nearby shore. Rusty reached out and pulled him up the steep bank, chuckling the whole while.

"There's something in there with me!" Money huffed with wide-spread eyes. "And it looks to be as big as me, maybe bigger."

Potak smiled but waited as he watched the boy closely for what was to come. A massive snapping turtle surfaced, showing its large head and long neck. Its eyes scanned the landscape and settled on them. Its rhamphotheca beak was huge, and traces of meat were lodged in its hinges. It looked like it could snap one of Money's small wrists in two with one chomp.

"That's the biggest snapping turtle I've ever seen," Money exclaimed. "I ain't goin back into that little pond. There ain't enough room for both of us. It might take me to the bottom where it lives and have me for dinner."

"I've seen alligator turtles much larger, but they don't exist here in the Rocky Mountains," Potak replied, eyeing the boy. "Some grow up to a hundred fifty pounds and live for one hundred years. Snapping turtles live up to their name. They are far more aggressive and can survive for up to forty years. I reckon the one that lives in this spring is that old, if not older. Maybe he's been here in my secret spot forever. Who is to say what is and what is not possible in such an isolated place? Here, most of nature has no predator."

"That turtle's so ugly he could scare termites off rotten wood," Money huffed. "I admit, it sure does scare me. Why, I wouldn't have a chance if that old snapper got hold of me."

"What would you do if you got the likes of that critter on the end of your fishing line, Money?" Rusty asked and laughed. "I bet he'll eat just about anything we put on a hook. Maybe we should give it a try. It might make for some tasty turtle soup."

"Are you kidding, Rusty? That thing would pull me into the water if I hooked him up. Hopefully, the string will break first. We'd need a horse or mule to pull him out. He might swallow me whole. I think I'll stick to the fish."

Both man and boy went silent as Potak began to speak to the turtle in a strange language they had never heard before. When they looked over their shoulders, the medicine man was smiling as he seemed to lock eyes with the king of the freshwater pond. It even opened and closed its beak, as though replying to the shaman. Rusty and Money knew that wasn't possible, though. Or was it?

"What language is that, Potak?" Rusty asked, puzzled. "I don't think I've heard anything like it. I know you're a showman, I mean a shaman. But don't tell me you're talking to that turtle. Do you think we're fools?"

Potak sighed patiently, looked at Rusty, and flatly stated, "I didn't say I was talking to him, you did. You said it, not me."

The Tonkawa Indian turned his eyes back to the turtle and smiled. He nodded, and it disappeared again below the surface. They could see a large black shadow slowly making its way back to the bottom, as though swimming through glass. Potak claimed that the pond was some ninety feet deep. The turtle lived at the depths, where colors like red, orange, and yellow vanished. The only colors visible at sixty feet were the green and blue hues of deeper water.

"Tossin' your rope before buildin' the loop don't catch the calf," Rusty chided. He had to admit, he felt a little like a kid himself. "We've gotta throw a hook with some bait on it if we want a bite. Come on, it's time for a spot of fishin'. Don't you worry about that old turtle. I reckon he's too old and tired to bother us."

"But what about Potak's friend?" Money whispered into Rusty's ear. "What'll we do if we find it on the other end of our line? I ain't so convinced that he won't bite. I ain't wantin' to tangle with it."

"Then, there'll be more for us to eat." Rusty laughed until he had to hold his side. Surprisingly, Potak joined in. For minutes, they continued to chuckle and snicker. Of course, Money didn't understand what was so funny.

"Be decisive," Rusty said. "Right or wrong, go for it and stick to it. The trail is full of flat squirrels and dead mice. So, do ya wanna catch that snapper first thing tomorrow morning, or not? Now, don't worry. I'm just kiddin', but I *would* like some fish for breakfast."

Money didn't answer but sat there wide-eyed. His Adam's apple bobbed up and down. It was hard to swallow. Beads of sweat popped up on his brow, and his hair stuck to his head.

The blazing sun hung overhead like a fire, casting everything into shadows. Thunder muttered somewhere in the distance as heat wavered on the horizon, but the sky remained as blue as Money's eyes.

When they looked around, they saw Potak sitting

perched on the topmost rim of the anthill like a misflown bird, but not a single insect touched his body. Smoke from the ever-present eucalyptus stick snaked skyward from the shaman's grasp. Money stared wide-eyed and could hardly believe his eyes.

Potak studied the scene stoically beneath an impassive glare. It was almost like Potak was a statue. Rusty wondered if he was still in control of his own mind, or if he and Money had been transported to another realm by the shaman.

AFTER THE SUN SET, the flames yawned in the night winds. A retinue of wolves cast long shadows in the silvery moonlight. The night was beclamored with yapping coyotes and the screech of owls as small animals rustled in the grass. Potak's secret spot was jumping with wildlife. It was so isolated that the animals didn't seem afraid.

The following morning, the dawn-broached sky was a hellish red. The shaman remained perched on the anthill, as if hypnotized by the ants below. Rusty ignored the medicine man and his strange ways. He was accustomed to his odd behavior. He had seen his fair share of shaman-showmen in his time living in the wilderness. He felt once you saw one, you had seen them all. He didn't find Potak so different from the others. The Tonkawan was brighter than most of the rest.

"Who wants some fish for breakfast?" Rusty asked. When Money awoke, the mountain man mentor was already up, making morning coffee.

"I need some strong java, first," Money replied as he used his fists to rub away the sleep. "Did we really see that big turtle yesterday, or was it just a dream? It seemed real enough to me."

Potak began to blink. He looked as though their presence came as a surprise to him. Money stared at the shaman with a funny expression. He didn't believe he would ever figure him out. He still sat squatting on the anthill like he had spent the night there in a trance.

Potak did the strangest things, but always acted like his actions were completely normal. Rusty hardly ever seemed to be surprised by his actions, but Money was constantly thrown off balance. At times, the Tonkawa medicine man did the opposite of what he expected.

Money yawned wide as spittle sprang, arching from his mouth. He blinked and smiled when he again took in the beauty around them. At first, he had thought it was all a dream. When he saw the warm water pond, he remembered the school of fish he swam with. He smacked his lips and smiled as his heart began to beat like a drum. There was nothing like catching a fish to liven up the day.

Fifteen minutes later, they were sitting on the bank with fishing lines and cork floats bobbing in the water. Below, hooks dangled from ten-foot strings. Worms, dug fresh from the soft dirt, wiggled from the hooks in an effort to attract a hungry fish. Water-loving species, such as cottonwoods and willow, surrounded them. They circled the small pond.

Money looked down worriedly at the deep bottom as steam rolled from the tops of their coffee cups. Potak had finally stepped down from his perch and sat beside his friends in comfortable silence. The shaman nursed coffee from his gourd cup.

Suddenly, Rusty's line seized tighter than a fiddle string. Water dripped like tiny bombs from the tip of his pole, which suddenly came alive. A massive fish crashed through the surface, splashing on its side. Rusty struggled with the fish until it was out of oxygen and gave up the fight. It was the biggest carp they had ever seen. It was twenty pounds and nearly a yard long.

"Lucky for us that turtle didn't have a go at your bait," Money said, relieved. The flesh on the back of Money's neck tingled with excitement. His smile grew so big it felt like his face would break.

Suddenly, a restless urge to move came over him. Now that Rusty had landed the first fish, Money couldn't wait for his chance. He was still wary of the turtle. He couldn't get the thought of the ancient beast out of his mind.

It would be just my luck not to get a nibble, let alone a hard strike like Rusty got, young Penny thought. *Then again, that big old turtle might be waitin' down there for me.*

Again, the corks floated on the surface, hardly moving. Despite the quick bite Rusty got, the fish didn't appear hungry. They could see them circling the small pond a few feet under their bait, but none of them neared.

Maybe Rusty scared them off catching that first fish, Money thought.

As soon as the young boy turned his head to say something to Rusty, he felt the line tug hard.

"I've got a bite!" he shouted.

A hint of a smile softened the straight lips of Potak's mouth as soon as he heard Money yelp with joy. Tiny curls formed at the edges of his mouth as a sparkle lit up his eyes.

Suddenly, Money's amusement was gone, and his mouth tightened as he sat. From the start, he knew it was going to be a struggle, and he didn't dare fail before two of his heroes. He knew this was just another test to see whether he was prepared to live in the wilderness.

Money's line tugged so hard it snapped his pole in two. So, the boy grabbed the line in his fists. The power of the heavy catfish caused the fishing line to cut where it was wrapped around four fingers. It was all Money could do not to be pulled into the water. The old mentor laughed and grabbed him by the belt and pulled him back just in the nick of time. In minutes, both fish were flapping their tails on the dusty bank, trying fruitlessly to get away as their mouths opened and closed. Money landed a giant.

Without hesitation, the boy slipped the hook from the dying fish's mouth, careful not to stab himself with the sharp barbs on its dorsal and anal fins. He hooked another nightcrawler and tossed it into the water again. As soon as the bait hit the surface, hook, line, and floater disappeared.

This time, he didn't have the chance to settle down. The tug was so hard that it nearly pulled Money into the water. He could see the large black shadow under the surface and knew he had hooked the old snapping turtle that Potak seemed to speak with.

Money didn't want to fight the beast from the deep. It was too big. When he glanced at Rusty and Potak, Money instantly knew what was expected of him. He bit his lip, forced the fear aside, and dug his heels in. He pulled with all his might. That was when the string broke, sending Money sailing backward. He landed in a puff of dust.

The snapping turtle's beak bit it in two like a sharp knife, and the monster slowly swam back to its home on the bottom. Apparently, its curiosity had gotten the best of him. Money was just happy that the line broke, and he didn't have to come face-to-face with such a monster.

Everyone went silent for a moment, then Money laughed to fill the void and ease the tension. "It was only the turtle. Maybe I'll get lucky and land him next time." The boy laughed, but he knew the gesture lacked confidence. He was glad the line snapped and saved him from who knows what.

Later, Potak rekindled the fire, leaving a bed of orange, glowing coals shining brightly. They cut branches from the weeping willow tree above them and skewered the carp on the sharp points Rusty made with his knife. They had enough for breakfast and lunch, too. They lazed around the still water as they feasted on their catch.

Rusty twisted his mouth into a smile, but his eyes belied his true feelings. Worry for Will and Levi filled his thoughts. He pushed it from his mind and focused on the time at hand. Money and the medicine man were drenched with the excitement of the moment. It helped wash away the nervous tension and worries about their friends who were alone on the Great Plains.

Deep lines across his brow scarred Rusty's old face. Crow's feet stretched around the corners of his eyes. His skin was like worn leather, and his mouth was in a broad smile.

That evening, stillness held heavy over the men sitting along the hot spring and willow grove. Tin cups clinked as their boots scraped the ground. The campfire in the center glowed orange. As night deepened, the Tonkawa shaman pulled his blanket tight across his shoulders as the evening chill began to set in. When Rusty saw Potak smile, it softened his face, reaching his eyes. Despite his strange ways, he felt like Potak was an old friend, even though they hadn't known each other for too long. There was something about him that made him seem familiar.

A dozen falling stars left vapor trails streaking toward Earth and then burned out in midair. Overhead, the heavens swung counterclockwise on their nightly course as the Big Bear turned and Earendel winked in the farthest distance. The evening's cool air rustled the leaves in the trees and drove away the hot air that came with the daytime sun.

Rusty sat up the remainder of the night, pondering his thoughts as they flashed through his mind at lightning speed. A pleasant smile was frozen on his face. He turned to Money. He watched his chest rise and fall. A contented smile graced the boy's lips.

The following morning, the sky burst into a pink, rose, and crimson prism as it stretched to the western horizon. The dusk thickened into light when the first rays of the sun reflected in the sky.

Ambushed From Afar

When Andy Irons was knocked off his horse, the outlaw gang pulled their mounts to a sliding halt. Panic seized the outlaws. They drew their guns, looking for telltale signs of gun smoke. Then they heard the boom of a heavy-caliber rifle, but it appeared to be too far away for them to determine the shooter's location.

Tommy Verde panicked as he tried to steer his horse around the carnage and race back up the grade. Halfway through his turn, he felt the impact. The 50-90 round slammed into his stomach, knocking him off his horse. Again, a distant boom followed. Still, they didn't see the shooter.

Tommy staggered to his feet, and Garrott Sneed, the gang's leader, pulled him up behind his saddle. Blood streamed down his pant legs and onto the gang leader's horse as he began to bleed out. The outlaws spurred their horses out of danger and back up the trail they had come down. One by one, they breached the summit and disappeared over the other side. The only sound remaining was the hammering of their horses' hooves as they made their escape from sudden death. Not only was someone waiting for them, but they knew how to strike fear of reprisal. It was something Garrott had never experienced.

"Somebody knows we are here and intends to stop us," Garrott spat as they raced over the ridge at the top of the trail. "I wonder who it is. How are you holdin' up, Tommy? Whoever did this, I'll get that son-of-a-bitch. I promise you that, here and now."

A horse and a man lay dead behind them, and the other was dying. Howey Dundurn swore under his breath. "We're gonna have to stop for Tommy here and wait for him to die."

Garrott gave his right-hand man a sharp look, and Howey snapped his mouth shut. "Don't you pay Howey no mind, Tommy. You're gonna be just fine once we get you to the doc back at Fort Hall."

"Whatcha mean, Howey?" Tommy asked, blinking. "Am I gonna die? You ain't gonna leave me, are ya? Please don't leave me behind, boss. I can ride. Just give me a horse. I'll show ya."

As Tommy talked, the life slowly drained from the hole in his gut. His lips went pale as his eyes bulged from their sockets. They were full of fear as he lay on his back before his friends. A dark puddle formed under his body.

Nobody said a word while they all watched and patiently waited for Tommy to pass. By the time his eyes rolled back into his head, the men were nervous and ready to ride. Nobody wanted to think about what might befall them next. They were a gang of thieves, and these were the first men they had lost.

When times became difficult, hard men became

reckless, and some eventually lost their lives. Now all the outlaws were on their toes and paid more attention to what they were doing. They knew that somebody was out there trying to stop them. They wouldn't be caught off guard so easily the next time.

Even though they had lost two men in the blink of an eye, not one of them considered walking away. With each passing day, all knew the cargo wagons were becoming more and more valuable as overlanders piled up in Fort Boise. Of course, none of them gave the danger they were putting both forts in a second thought. Their focus was on the task at hand and the reward it promised.

They intended to kill every one of the Tornado employees and then send anonymous couriers to Fort Boise and Fort Hall to sell the stolen goods to the very people they had stolen them from. What they didn't know was that three additional men had been added to the cargo train. They were not only frontiersmen but three of the most dangerous men in the West. They had no idea of the challenge they presented.

They had a warning, though, and two men were dead. Still, it didn't slow them down or alter their course. Even as they watched their friend slowly die from a massive gunshot to the belly, quitting was not an option. There was so much money involved that none of them had second thoughts. The loaded supply wagons were so desperately needed, robbing them was like money in the bank.

Garrott ordered the men to tie the bodies across the back of one of the horses, so they could flee before the shooting started again. They did as they were told and then hightailed it back the way they had come.

Garrott originally thought that stealing the cargo wagons would be a piece of cake, but it was proving to be more complicated than expected. He wasn't worried about the men he lost, even though he didn't like losing old friends. His concern was that the cargo teamsters knew they were waiting for them to leave the fort, and he had lost the element of surprise. Therefore, he would need to devise a new plan entirely. What appeared to be a simple job was becoming increasingly difficult, but that didn't deter the outlaw boss or his gang. All were more determined than ever.

Garrott had plans for the money from this heist. He secretly intended to get out of the highwayman business he had practiced successfully for so long. Even back East, he robbed carriages along the roadside and the occasional cargo wagon if he found the freight to be valuable enough.

When he heard that it was easy pickings along the Oregon Trail, he and his men rode west. So far, they had gotten away with robbing isolated family wagons that had gone astray or couldn't keep up with the larger groups. Now, they set their sights on the large cargo train, the big prize. Even though they didn't successfully rob the Tornado Express train en route to Fort Hall, he knew better opportunities would materialize along the trail to Fort Boise.

Despite his men's discomfort, the gang leader made a show of respect by not abandoning the bodies of their friends. Everyone would know their lives were valued, even in death. With Tommy and Andy gone, each outlaw would get a bigger share. The prize would be cut eight ways rather than ten.

Evil men always found something fortunate in

horrible situations. Still, to date, the gang leader had treated all his men fairly, and he planned to bury their friends as soon as they were a safe distance away from where the shooting occurred. Garrott, who calculated every move as if it were a chess game, knew that this small gesture would ensure the loyalty of the others. He was playing for keeps.

Garrott never considered the enemy would be bold enough to ride out and take on the entire gang. He didn't even know how many men stalked them. Or was there just one shooter with a high-powered rifle? He had never seen men shoot so accurately from such a distance. Still, he brushed off the element of danger and continued to focus on the objective. If nothing else, the outlaw gang leader was methodical.

When he signaled for the fleeing band of outlaws to halt, there was little banter among the gang members. They knew this was as good a place as any to bury their friends. Verde didn't wait for Garrott's order. He got to it immediately.

"Let's get 'er done, men. We need to bury our friends and move on," he ordered.

"Where should they be buried, Garrott?" Howey asked.

"Wherever you can find soft dirt. Maybe over there in the shade of that canyon wall. Make the hole deep so the varmints don't dig them up. Grab that red stone over there to use as a marker so we can tell their folks where they're buried if they are so inclined to visit their graves."

Even though Slim tried to hold Garrott's gaze, he looked away after a few seconds. He had noticed that not many men locked eyes with the outlaw gang leader, especially now that they had lost two friends. Everyone felt strangely detached. The only one really grieving was their boss. The rest of them were biting at the bit to get on their way. Then again, if it were their time that came, they wanted the same respect from their fellow men.

The boss smiled. When the graves were dug, he added, "They were good hands who never shied away from danger. A man can't ask more from a friend."

Garrott grabbed a handful of dirt, let it slip through his fingers, and solemnly said. "Ashes to ashes, dust to dust."

When the stones cover the gravesite, Garrott said, "We might as well make camp right here for the night. There's good cover over in that gorge. Whoever's out there with a rifle won't have a shot from there. Nobody is gonna get away now. They know we're here, and they're charging hard. Boys, keep in mind, those wagons are no match for our horses. It's not a question of if we overrun that cargo train, it's a question of when and where it happens."

"I figure the fella who took that shot is employed by the cargo wagon train to locate us and back us down if he could. If there were more, they'd have gotten more of us. I figure it was a single shooter, and he only dared two shots to guarantee his escape," one of the outlaws theorized.

Sometimes, in the distance, they saw Indians with drapes of ghostly black hair. They had no idea what tribes they came from, but assumed that they were hostile. So far, due to their numbers, the Indians hadn't bothered them. Nonetheless, they kept a sharp eye on them.

That night, as they sat around the fire, pondering what had happened, their eyes reflected the fiery coals.

"Tomorrow you boys will ride out like nothing happened," Garrott said in a low voice. "The cargo train will be a ways ahead of us by now. Ride their drag until I get back. I'm gonna sneak off before daylight and find out if I can see what we're up against. Maybe I'll get lucky and find that rascal who shot Tommy and Andy, and I can return the favor. Maybe we should use their tactics and start to whittle them down before we make our final strike.

"Four of those six wagons are destined for Fort Boise. That means it's all of us against their eight, considering each wagon has a bullwhacker and shotgun guard. I wanna find out if there are more hired guns out there protecting the valuable cargo. That's what I'd do if I were them. It's a damned shame that we didn't catch them before they hit Fort Hall. Now, we've lost the element of surprise."

Back at the Compound

Money was exhausted from the tension of the day, especially his confrontation with the giant snapping turtle. He sat looking into the fire while listening to the stories of the medicine man. For a moment, the young boy's mind drifted to his family and what once was. Although he missed them, he knew that fretting over them did him no good. He pushed the negative thoughts from his mind like Potak had told him to do. In a flash, his sorrowful reflection passed, and he again listened to the shaman's tale.

Everybody there gathered around the large table on the main cabin's porch. A gallon kettle of coffee sat in the middle beside a ceramic jug of corn liquor. All the men, except for money, had added a dash to their coffee. They had let Money try the whiskey, but when he took his first sip, he had to run outside and spit it out. He found it so vile that it nearly made him vomit. Rusty told him that it was an acquired taste, but he didn't quite know what that meant. As far as Money was concerned, if he never had another drop, it would still be too soon.

Money noticed that all the men drank, although not to excess, with the occasional exception of his father, Marshal Walker. The only woman in the compound who had even as much as a sip was Betty, the captain's wife. Of course, she was from the Tennessee hills and a part of the famous Crocket clan before marrying Will. Her uncle was Davy Crockett, the famous frontiersman and legislator who died at the Alamo.

Everyone ate their fill of freshly caught fish. A pile of bones continued to grow in the middle of a large tin pie pan. The perpetual bowl of black beans and another of mush sat before them, steam rising from the tops. Huckleberries, wild berries, and bearberries, known as Kinnikinnick, filled little baskets. They even had a sparse supply of buffalo berries and serviceberries, or saskatoons. Of course, with Levi, Will, and Joseph gone, Angus made half the food. Beaver and the marshal were the biggest eaters of the bunch.

Since Angus made the meals, the others helped clear the table and wash the dishes outside in the water barrel beside the porch. Towels and scrub brushes hung from elk horns. American crows cawed loudly as they watched the humans eat. Some jumped across the ground, daring to get close enough to steal a few scraps. Dusky Grouse hooted and gobbled.

After a while, Dog got back to his feet and sniffed and licked the planks under the table, cleaning up any scraps. Cigar smoke floated a foot from the ceiling as night birds chattered and owls howled in the trees as dusk neared. Crickets began their racket, then stopped, only to start all over again as fireflies blinked yellow-green light in one place, only to appear at another.

"Well, I'm ready to turn in," Virgil said as he stepped off the porch and headed down the worn path to the next cabin. "I don't know why, but I'm plumb worn out."

One by one, the lights in the buildings and teepees went out as the lightning bugs continued to blink their tails off and on to attract their mates.

ANGUS STRETCHED STIFFLY on his straw mattress. He yawned so wide that anyone looking could almost see his stomach. He passed his tongue over dry and cracked lips as he blinked his eyes awake. It was still dark outside. The aging mountain man always got up an hour or two before the others to prepare food for that day's meals. But first, he listened for Rusty's snoring. He shook his head when he heard the house was as quiet as a church. So, he was still gone. He sighed as his lips moved in a silent prayer. Dog lay curled up beside the dying embers. He didn't stir when the old mountain man did.

Angus was lean and beginning to stoop slightly. Before, he wore a raccoon cap, but as he aged, he favored flat-brimmed hats that provided plenty of shade. Curtains of white hair flowed past his shoulders, and a white beard covered his chest. With age, his buckskin clothing seemed loose-fitting because he had shrunken some over the years.

In the next cabin, Virgil walked to the door, flipped the latch, and pulled it open, as wind swept across the porch. He blocked it open with a piece of cast iron. The breeze raced through the cabin, festooning the curtains in the open windows. After a long winter, it was time to air out the cabins and teepees. He sniffed the air, but he had yet to smell Angus's coffee, so he knew he had a few minutes.

He strode across the porch and headed down the worn path to the outhouses. He pulled the spring-loaded door open, and it shut behind him with a bang. He began to whistle. The notes floated through the trees.

Smoke began to stream out of the small chimney in the main cabin. The building was built into a hill, protecting three sides and providing additional warmth during the freezing-cold winters. In the summer, it was covered in so many vines and plants that it was nearly invisible to the untrained eye.

On the front wall was a single double-shuttered window and a heavy timber door, both leading to a large, covered porch. A long table with a dozen chairs stood empty as the first light of a new day had yet to come. Even the chicken house was still quiet. The roosters had yet to stir.

When Virgil stepped out of the outhouse, the door banged shut again. The noise echoed across the mountain in the cool early morning air. This time, when he raised his nose and sniffed, he smiled. The aroma of freshly perked coffee floated on puffs of crisp morning air.

The old, dust-covered Dog, finally awake, barked dispiritedly and then lazily disappeared into the crawlspace under the cabin. Dog was usually the first on the porch for breakfast. They all fed him scraps under the table when Angus wasn't watching. No wonder there were never any leftovers.

Today, the table slowly filled as the light crawled across the eastern horizon, and the first sign of a yellow, blazing sun peeked over the end of the world. They knew that in minutes, shadows would grow as the earth was bathed in light.

Money tried to reject the fear stirred by some of Potak's stories, but as a nine-year-old boy, it was hard to do. He knew that now he couldn't act like a frightened little kid. Then again, Rusty had told him not to believe everything the aging shaman said. To Money, he seemed almost as wise as Rusty himself. Even Levi, his mentor, didn't know all the secrets that the Tonkawa Indian did. They wondered if he really did talk to the animals, even though he never admitted it was true.

"So, who is gonna tell the next story?" the medicine man asked. "And not you, Rusty. You've already had your turn. You repeat the same things over and over again. At least my tales are original. How about you, Money?" Potak said, glancing at his White friend with mischievous eyes. "I know you're young, but I'll bet you've experienced a lot more than most adults have. Sometimes the most truthful story comes from young, innocent eyes. Adult thoughts are distorted by all the things that have influenced us during our lifetimes."

The boy snapped out of his daze. He was surprised. Money stood for a moment, chewing on what the medicine man asked. Still, to follow such a person as Potak with a poorly told tale was something that he didn't quite feel up to yet. Young Penny feared he would make a fool of himself. "Why don't Angus tell us a story? Every time he starts one, Rusty butts in with another of his own. You sure do like to talk," Money said, shooting a glance at the old man beside him. Angus was sound asleep in his chair. He nudged McFarlin with his elbow, jarring him from his after-meal nap.

"Angus, wake up. Didn't you hear what I said?" Money was direct with what he said because he was too young to know better than to say exactly what he thought.

When Angus heard someone say his name, the old mountain man was startled awake. For a moment, he stared at them all, baggy-eyed and confused. He had just been stirred from his first siesta of the day and had yet to get his bearings. He shook his white-haired head as curtains of hair swirled across his shoulders. His snow-white beard swayed across his chest.

"You know me. I ain't much at telling stories," Angus replied.

"Oh, come on, Angus. Tell us one of your stories. You've been here the longest. You must have a whopper or two to tell. You can't shrug it off like that. Go on and give us a treat," Money encouraged.

"Why, you're only nine, and you already have more stories to tell than you can shake a stick at. You've won every battle that's come your way and survived. My stories are of the old times nobody remembers anymore. Anything of any interest, Rusty had said a hundred times anyway. We've been runnin' with each other for more than a decade and a half."

He could see the light in Money's eyes grow brighter with the compliment, but it was mixed with disappointment, too. Finally, he jutted out his chin and puffed up his chest in response. He appeared almost manic with excitement. He fantasized about doing everything Angus and Rusty had done.

Then, when he thought about Potak's stories, Money wasn't so sure. The shaman was always talking about Indian spirits, and Money wasn't so sure exactly what they were. Rusty said they didn't really exist. Who was he to believe?

Money's mother had educated him as a child. That was the way of the poor and often isolated. *Brenda Penny, where are you now?* he thought as his mind wandered. The youngster snorted and pushed all those thoughts aside. They couldn't do anything but hurt. That much he believed Potak was right. He said live for the moment because yesterday is past and no longer relevant. Tomorrow is still on the other side of the world. No matter what you thought, no one could change it anyway. That is, if it ever came.

When Potak talked about such things, it confused the boy, but he listened intently anyway, trying to piece together the riddle-like puzzles that came out of the shaman's mouth.

When they all continued to stare at him and saw he had no way out, he said exactly what he thought, without even trying to make it an interesting story. He just told his new family the truth.

"To be honest, before I came here, I was scared stiff most of the time. I reckon I just did things without thinking, but it did work out in the end. Sitting here with my new family proves that. What do you want me to tell you about? My mother and I got kidnapped. Should I tell you how I felt when they sold her to an Indian named Acha?" Money remembered when Potak showed him his mother living in a cave with a wolf, so he knew the truth, that she had gone mad. Potak had also heard that she howled with her pack when they ran through the night on the hunt. Of course, these were things heard from the Indian gossip, so he didn't know if they were true or not. The Tonakwas medicine man thought it was better if the boy didn't know and had some closure in the mess, which could compromise his young life were he to know the whole truth. He might try to find her again and he wouldn't like what he discovered.

The boy's mind was buzzing with all the stories he had heard from this strange Tonkawa Indian and Rusty, and he believed that his stories would be boring next to theirs. Both Rusty and Potak prided themselves on being reputable yarn stretchers.

"Be careful now, or I'll sic Dog on ya," Rusty chided and laughed. His dog was already old when the mentor adopted him along the trail after it saved his life. Now, he allowed Dog to laze around the compound and tolerated his noisy barking sessions when the canine decided it was time to earn its keep. The mountain man believed he deserved to spend his last days lazing in the shade.

When Dog opened one eye and looked, everybody laughed. Then it promptly shut, and Dog fell back to sleep. When he breathed out, his loose lips fluttered and flopped. Then he sighed deeply as he regained deep slumber.

Tornado Express Company

Contemporary travelers described the trip from Fort Hall to Fort Boise as daunting and foreboding. Deep canyons and swift rivers formed natural barriers to easy passage. Other sections were relatively open valleys or prairies, dissected by countless smaller streams and creeks, slowing things down even more. For overlanders, the voyage could take anywhere from a few days to three or four weeks, depending on the weather and hostile Indians and outlaws, as was the current situation.

The great Snake River was both a lifeline and a hazard, at times making the trek even more difficult. Volcanic rock and old lava beds complicated travel farther west, especially along Goodale's Cutoff. Travelers' views were of distant snowcapped mountains and the mighty chasm of the Snake River. The trail between the frontier forts was wild, rugged, and unforgiving, offering both the stark beauty of the region and dangerous obstacles.

In some spots, the trail was wide enough for eight

wagons to travel side by side. Often, these trails were damaged or washed out by torrential rains, forcing wagons to seek alternative routes in some places. The sagebrush-covered land usually offered no comfort, devoid of natural shade or relief. To the north lay volcanic country. This rocky, rough, and arid ground often damaged wagon wheels, creating breakdowns. The stretches away from the Snake River were frequently devoid of water. With the hot, dry conditions, the journey punished both the overlanders and their livestock.

The travelers alternated between pleasant campsites along the river's banks and long segments of desert, dusty and dry, where the wind seemed never to stop. At times, the only relief came when they forded streams or water-filled ravines. The canyons were gloomy and dark when compared to the open, desolate plains. The Oregon Trail was a nightmare of hardships, but it was the only way to reach what many called the land of milk and honey, the heart of lifelong dreams.

After leaving Fort Hall, they were required to ford the Snake River to reach the north side, where the going was easier. This site was located four miles west of the military stronghold. They would crisscross the Snake several times when the terrain got impassable. The last of the trail to Fort Boise was on the south side of the river. Then, they could avoid dangerous crossings like those at Shoshone Falls or Cauldron Linn due to their treacherous rapids and high canyon walls.

The last major crossing would be near the confluence of the Boise and Snake Rivers. Sometimes stock and wagons were floated or ferried while teams of animals were chained together for safer crossings.

These crossings would dictate the success of any journey. It would determine the success of the Tornado Cargo Company, too. Billy Rooster was in charge of the wagons, and Will, Levi, and Joseph were charged with getting them to Fort Boise safely.

Some of the overlanders had Native American guides to help them decide which paths were more suitable for their current weather conditions and the types of wagons in the train. When not available, the travelers had to rely on their own judgment, which was a toss of a coin for those unaccustomed to the western wilderness. Marshall Walker was one of the experienced wagon train guides in the early days of the Oregon Trail. That was before the wilderness highway got its name. Back then, Beaver and the captain had accompanied him. Such scouts directed them to the best fording points, wagon spacing, and how to lash rigs together for greater safety when crossing dangerous streams or vast stretches of water.

They used any place where the river's canyons allowed easy crossing. The first recorded crossing was in 1834. There was also an early private ferry near the mouth of the Blackfoot River, which also supported traffic. No matter how you looked at it, it was a treacherous trail between Fort Hall and Fort Boise.

THE MORNING OF THEIR DEPARTURE, Levi, Will, and Joseph dined with Rooster and Buster. Tables near them were filled with the other six teamsters who would be traveling with the mountain men. They had gotten up an hour before dawn. Unfortunately, the kitchen wasn't open. Levi refused to leave on an empty stomach. In the end, he had eaten everything they put on the table and all the extras that the others couldn't finish. He popped the last piece of cornbread into his mouth, grinned, and let out a deep sigh of satisfaction.

The bartender wiped his hands back and forth on his apron and asked, "Will you boys be needin' anything else, or are you all done here? I swear, I've never seen a man eat so much."

Dirty coffee cups and glasses strung out the bar's length. On the table were empty plates stacked ten high.

"The good news is the sergeant says the Army will foot the bill, boys. They don't have any soldiers to spare, but they have extra cash on hand this month. I reckon it's well spent. How about a snort before you go?"

Sergeant Burns lit a cheroot, inhaled deeply, and tried to figure out what to do once the wagons left the fort. He was understaffed and worried about an attack. The local hostile Indians had to have seen all the Brits leave. God only knew when replacements would arrive from Washington. The country's politicians seemed to live in another world, one where they were unaware of anything happening in the West. They had been promised extra soldiers before the Forty-Ninth Parallel treaty was signed, but so far, they hadn't heard of or seen any new arrivals. More troops were needed at both forts.

Levi pushed himself away from the breakfast table and said with a big grin, "I don't think I can eat another bite." He rubbed his belly and chuckled. The smell of bacon, ham, and eggs filled the air along with the aroma of freshly perked coffee. He turned his tin cup up and savored the last drop.

"You ate everything but the kitchen sink, Beaver." Will laughed. "It's been daylight for nearly thirty minutes, boys. I believe it's time we headed for the stables and those four wagons. I don't like to hold folks up. That is, unless Mr. Johnson here wants to have lunch before we leave."

"Mark my words, we won't be the last ones ready to go. I hate to hurry up and wait, but it's always the same," Levi replied. He didn't seem to be bothered or in a hurry at all. The smile on his face said his belly was full, and that was the primary objective at the moment.

Joseph was still on his second helping, and the captain had finished eating and was impatiently waiting for the others to go. All eight teamsters sat around the dining hall. Rooster and Buster were sitting with the mountain men. They, too, had finished their meals and were nervously nursing their whiskeys. They thought about what was ahead of them and took another sip.

Their hard, leather-like faces said they weren't new to this work. It took a particular type of man to drive wagons across the frontier to supply the forts. It was much more dangerous than it was for the wagon trains full of overlanders. Sometimes they numbered in the hundreds. Indians weren't dumb and never attacked impossible targets—they preferred to pick them off one at a time and not risk their lives when they were outnumbered.

In 1846, Fort Hall focused on its role as a fur-trading post and supply station on the trail west before reaching Fort Boise, another point of resupply for migrating hordes. These frontier forts were the bloodline of the trail west, and without them, everything stopped. Without supplies in such a harsh land, the travelers would be doomed—all the more reason for this cargo to get to its destination. Lives, the forts, livelihood, and peace in general depended on it.

Wagons were loaded full of staples like flour, dried beans, rice, salted pork, and dried fruit, plus countless other necessities for the brave people crossing from east to west across the American frontier. At times, the shipments were more valuable and sought after even more than gold or silver. If a man had no food, money had no meaning.

Levi wiped his mouth with the back of his hand and burped, then he giggled like a little kid. His muscles rippled up and down his arms and back. The veins in his neck looked like mooring lines, ridged and hard. He pushed his chair back as he stretched out his long legs. Finally, he stood, buried his fists into the small of his back, and arched away stiffness.

The Army sergeant exhaled a blast of cigarette smoke as he wiped the sweat from his brow. His eyes were full of concern, and his jaw hurt from grinding his teeth. He drummed his fingers on his holstered gun. He felt like he was sitting on top of a time bomb that was about to go off. "My mouth is as dry as a corn bin after a drought. I think that the worst part is waitin' for somethin' to happen. I've got a bad feeling about all this. Too many of the people we relied on for security have vanished," he said.

"A man needs always to plan carefully and act decisively. There are no exceptions," the captain said dryly. "We don't have to overreact either. We'd better take this one step at a time. The first thing we need to do is cross the river. That's where we'll be most vulnerable. Then again, the outlaws will be expecting us to be ready at the cross. Maybe they'll wait, hoping to catch us off guard and surprise us somewhere we won't expect it. We need to figure out where that might be."

"I believe we'll be best served if we ride alongside the wagons and not on top. We're used to fighting from horseback and not on a bumpy carriage. The trail is full of potholes and bumps. If we need to move fast, it'll be hard to hold on up there. Joseph, you had better ride drag. Will can ride point, and I'll scout ahead of us to ensure the coast is clear. Once we're a good way down the trail, we'll need to be alert to trouble."

"And what if they're behind us, Levi?" the captain asked.

"I'll swing back every once in a while to make sure nobody's tailing us," the marshal said. "If I get the chance, I'll try to take another one or two out. If we can whittle them down as we go, they might change their minds and run off."

"I doubt these boys are gonna walk away when they're this far along. I figure it's just a question of time before they make their first move. They aren't gonna quit after they almost stopped the cargo wagon train outside of Fort Hall. They made that mistake once. I doubt it'll happen again."

Marshal Walker's mouth bulged, a tobacco wad accentuating the creases in his ruddy face, surrounded by unruly brown hair and beard. Despite the large wad in his cheek, he continued to sip his whiskey-laced coffee. He turned his head to the side and spat a stream of brown juice into a spittoon, then wiped his mouth with the back of his hand.

When Levi was finally ready to depart, he asked, "Is everybody ready to go?" His eyes swept the room full of teamsters. "Come on then, boys. We're burnin' daylight. The sooner we leave, the sooner we're gonna get there. We don't wanna disappoint them outlaws waitin' either."

THE BULLWHACKERS and shotgun guards all looked tired and curious. The wrinkles in their faces showed concern. They all had a week's beard. Their ill-fitting clothing had buttons missing and was covered with grime from the trail. One used a rope for a belt to keep his britches up. Double-barreled shotguns were slung across their backs, and braces of Colt Patterson revolvers hung from their waists. Long looped bullwhips were in the teamsters' hands. Their appearance might resemble a ragtag outfit, but when it came time to use their weapons, they were all business. Determination filled their eyes, knowing they didn't get paid if they didn't deliver the goods.

Once they were outside and ready to go, Rooster asked, "You don't scare easily, do you, @Captain Forrester? It almost looks like you're having fun. Or do you always have that confident air about ya?"

The cargo wagon train master wasn't shy. The captain's attitude put most people off, but Rooster appeared to have no fear of the famous Indian fighter.

Forrester flashed his fiery blue eyes at the bullwhacker and replied, "I never saw much sense in it. It's just another job, as far as I'm concerned. And you gentlemen can call me Will. This isn't an Army job, so we're all equals here."

"Did you hear that, Buster? Now we're gentlemen

and all. I'm takin' a likin' to you already, Captain," Rooster said, finishing his whiskey-laced coffee, and poured another. "What did you and the captain do before you left the territories, Levi?"

"We fought Comanche and a few Kiowa back before we ran into serious trouble, changed our plans, and headed for the mountains," Levi added. "We were lucky and caught the last Rendezvous before the beaver was trapped out, and them top hats went out of fashion. That's where we met the famous mountain man Rusty Steel. He made us his apprentices after I beat him at the yearly shootin' contest."

Levi went on to detail the sheer terror of the Indian raids and also described their enjoyable time at the yearly trappers' meet held by the British fur trading company.

"The Indians we fought were called the *Lords of the Plains*, you know. I'll never forget them whooping their war cries and firing their rifles and bows like demons of the apocalypse."

Despite the violent nature of his tales, Levi's face came alive with excitement, even amid the losses they suffered. As old memories were rekindled, the fire in his eyes glowed like hot coals.

Bringing up old memories like that wasn't something that Captain Forrester liked, especially when the expedition the Comanche wiped out was under his command. He lost almost his entire entourage of soldiers, scientists, and explorers. Levi was only a hired scout. In the end, they luckily survived. Four others lived through the big battle and decided to return to their original post. Later, they learned, the four soldiers never made it. They probably fell to the same hostile Indians who killed their fellow soldiers.

Levi chuckled, shaking his long, light-brown hair and beard. He acted like they were the good old times as he thought back to when they had nearly lost their lives. Afterward, he and Will abandoned their old lives and sought new ones as frontiersmen on Bear Tooth Mountain in the Rockies.

Suddenly, they heard the loud discharge. Everybody scattered as though the blast marked the start of a horse race. In a way, it was. Eleven men pushed their way through the batwing doors as boots hammered the porch. Levi stood beside the door with a smoking gun in his hand, the barrel pointing at the ground. The lead slug dug a neat line in the hard surface as he grinned like a kid in a candy store. It was Johnson's way of telling everyone the time for action was at hand. He and the Tornado crew were as ready as they would ever be to depart.

"Where's my drag wagon?" Rooster asked. "Let's get this show on the road, boys. Line the wagons up in the center of the courtyard so we can all ride out at once in a neat, tight line. I don't want any slaggers on this trip.

"Levi, you and the captain can ride up front beside us, and like you said, the marshal can ride beside the last wagon. My boys are good shots, but nothing like you men. Especially with your fancy and new, long rifles. I doubt the outlaws will be counting on that."

"I'm afraid that ship has already sailed," Marshal Walker said. "I shot two of 'em from long range before we rode into the fort. So, they already know we have special rifles. I didn't get a head count, though, but I figure there are more of them than there are of us. I doubt it'll be anything we can't handle. They won't be makin' it easy, either. Men don't ride onto the frontier expectin' anything but a bumpy road. Difficulties are generally the order of the day. That much I've learned from livin' up on Bear Tooth Mountain."

"They have the advantage of mobility," the captain reminded everyone with a frown. "That's the part that I don't like. I've seen a dozen cavalrymen on horseback turn back a hundred soldiers on foot using Indian guerrilla tactics. At least they could hide behind rocks, but those wagons are going to be sitting ducks. We'd need to be quick to respond. Don't hesitate. Deal with anyone who crosses our path, and do it quickly. We need to get to them before they get to us."

When Jimmy Johnson and Red Hawkens arrived, they were breathless, their lungs wheezed, and their eyes were full of fire. "Are we too late?" Both were bent over, hands on their knees, as they tried to catch their breath.

"No, there are two more wagons left to pull out. The horses are already rigged and harnessed. Your team is over there, ready to go," Rooster replied. "All you gotta do is hook 'em up to the tongue and yolk. Well, don't just stand there like noon half-struck, get a move on. All these wagons gotta push across the prairie, and we don't get paid until we reach Fort Boise. Any questions?"

No one spoke.

"That's what I thought," Rooster said. The likable bullwhacker was all business.

Johnson slapped his hand across his forehead and said, "I plumb forgot we were last. We weren't late after all. Maybe we've got time to go back to the saloon and get another stiff drink. I know I could use a double shot right about now."

Red cocked a brow and looked at his partner like he was crazy. "Get a hold of yourself, man. We've got this. If I thought otherwise, we wouldn't go. I know all you boys are on edge about this last stretch, but we have three of the best guns on this side of Missouri, and they know the country like the back of their hands. If we stick together like we always have, we'll all get through this in one piece. All you've gotta do is follow orders, and this thing will move right along, and before you know it, we'll be driving our teams through the Fort Boise gates."

The captain raised the pistol, cocking the hammer. Marshal Walker heard the metallic click, making his head swing back. Then came the second blast, and the Fort Hall gates were quickly thrown open as the wagons' horses burst into a charge.

Levi's paint reared up, his front hooves kicking at air. The mountain man's eyes shot all around, making sure everything was moving as planned. As soon as all four hooves hit the dirt, he shot off like a bullet, leaving everyone behind.

THEY RODE with the sun at their backs, their shadows standing long before them as they raced west toward their destination. There were three hundred and thirty miles between them and a big payday.

The wagons started their journey from Fort Laramie, where they had initially been loaded with supplies for both western forts. They felt a deep responsibility to the overlanders who relied on their ability to deliver the goods.

"Lookee there, fresh horse droppings on the trail, and there ain't no wagon tracks around here," Joseph said. "I didn't expect to see hide nor hair of these outlaws so soon. It appears they're being reckless, which will work in our favor."

The marshal's fourteen-hundred-pound gelding munched on grass tucked up to a rock. His mount had a shotgun blast of brown and white with a long, white strip down its long face. The animal's mane was white and wild. The horse lifted its head, staring at the marshal, bright-eyed and intelligent. The horse neighed and shook its head, appreciative of the nourishment.

When they looked through their spyglasses, they saw Shoshone Indians staring at them like hungry wolves. They maintained their distance before skulking away into the brush. Most of the tribes feared soldiers and men with badges. A few still resisted. They were poor, dirty, and ragged. They dragged their feet when they walked, like the defeated men they were. Strangers stole their land and erased their history. The wagons rolled right by without giving them a second glance. They were no longer a threat.

"I believe these boys are the garden variety of outlaws," Levi suggested. "I wouldn't worry too much about 'em. Their boss is another matter altogether. He's obviously reckless to a fault. Otherwise, he wouldn't try to pull off such a stunt. I reckon they must know this ain't gonna be a walk in the park."

"An honest man this far west is as rare as hen's teeth," Marshal Walker said. "Levi, you and Will put these deputy marshals' badges on. If you've gotta kill anyone in an unsightly manner, this'll make it legal. The badges will help scare off the Indians, too. They know if they kill a lawman, more will come to seek revenge."

The middle-aged marshal handed each of them a shiny piece of tin. The badges made the difference between working as a scout and the law having their backs.

Levi chuckled. He huffed on the shiny tin star and then rubbed it on his shirt and promptly pinned it on his chest. He wiggled his eyebrow in jest. The captain looked at the badge as if it were distasteful, but pinned it to his shirt just the same. As usual, he wasn't in a joking mood.

Levi didn't say a word but stared into the distance like a sharp-eyed vulture ready to swoop down for its next meal. Before they knew it, the day drew toward its apex as the sun grew brighter, and their shadows disappeared. Heat wavered in the distance. A dry wind blew from the north across the valley, influenced by the Treasure Valley System. The mountain-valley relationship caused constant winds, at times creating dusty conditions.

Somebody out of sight sent a shrill whistle from across the clearing. The eyes of the mountain men snapped toward the sound like branding irons. In an instant, the marshal's eyes turned dark and dangerous. Everyone drew their weapons, ready to fire at the first thing they saw move.

Will's face darkened as he spoke. "Well, they aren't whistling Dixie. I believe it's time to go to work. Either we heard them whistling at each other, or they were taunting us. Either way, they will be digging their own graves."

When the clouds shifted, Levi saw sunlight flashing off something metallic. "That must be where that whistle came from. Those boys are just over that ridge, and I'd say they'll be waitin' on us."

"Yep, one madman and a dozen and a half fools who follow him," the captain replied dryly. "I've seen village Indians that scare me more than this bunch. So, don't get your shorts in a knot."

The three frontiersmen rode out of sight for the remainder of the day, waiting to see if the outlaws showed themselves. They didn't believe they could outrun them if they decided to charge the wagon train while they were out scouting. Night suddenly came as a creek gurgled before them. They sat around the fire, dozing off and on, waiting for first light to come.

They knew the wagons would follow not too far away. If they parked the wagons in a tight square, they would have good cover from behind the wagons at night. The livestock, picketed in the center, would be safe, too.

"I doubt they intend to kill the horses, anyway," Levi said. "They'll be planning to use them to pull the wagons. So, Rooster only needs to worry about his men."

"Yeah, but if they steal them draft horses, we're stuck here, and this is where we'll have to make a stand," the marshal said. "I wanna do things my way and not some fool outlaw's way. Maybe one of us should go back and keep an eye on things until first light. Those wagons aren't but a half an hour or so away."

Hell Bent for Leather

Four heavy wagons roared down the bumpy trail. They were moving so face, the spokes of the wheels appeared to spin backward while churning up dust. On the sideboards, *TORNADO CARGO CO.* was painted in bright red letters. The heavy-duty beds were stacked with wooden boxes and barrels of various sizes, all tied down with heavy rope, so the cargo didn't shift while running at breakneck speeds. Guns, black powder, lead balls, cartridges, nails, along with axels, shovels, saws, and lumber were among the costly cargo. To cover breakdowns, they had three extra wheels, so they didn't have to waste time repairing broken ones.

Barrels were filled with rice, sugar, grain, cooking oil, and whiskey. A new variety of sparsely available canned goods was also on the wagons. All would be sold at a high price. In the far reaches of the country, folks didn't mind paying extra to enjoy items like canned oysters, fruits, and vegetables. The vast majority of the stock heading for Fort Boise were staples to their diets and hardware to meet their customers' needs.

"If we go out and look for the highwaymen, we'll probably have a chance to get their real numbers and pick off a few while we're at it," Joseph suggested. "We suspect there are more of them than there are of us. That would mean twenty guns or more are waiting to take target practice, and we're in the bull's eye."

Levi and the captain had just ridden toward the top of a hill. Before they reached the summit, they dismounted and crawled on their bellies to the top. They were surprised to see the highwaymen's camp not half a mile below them. The mountain men pulled their hats off and hugged the grassy ground as they reached for their spyglasses.

They sat in a tight circle as the leader appeared to speak, gesturing with his hands. Cigarettes and cheroots glowed in the dark. There was still an hour before first light.

Captain Forrester put his telescope to his eye, edging it along the distance. His mouth moved as he counted.

"Whatcha see down there?" Levi asked.

"The same nothing as you, only bigger."

Levi frowned as he carefully inspected each man and their weapons. He also examined their campsite with his collapsible telescope.

"Have you noticed how they're dressed?" Will whispered. "I haven't seen coats like those for a long time. You must remember them as well as I do."

"They look like those outlaws we saw back by Folsom before we headed out. We'd better get back and tell Marshal Walker about this. He might have an idea of who they are. Did you get a count? These boys look more organized than I expected."

Their inspection saw thin-lipped, sun-darkened men in range clothing, dark leather chaps, and brown dusters. These were cowpunchers who intended to rob the wagon train.

"I count twenty-one now. Like I thought, they had replacements ready somewhere along the trail."

"Yep. There are twenty-one men and forty horses in all. That includes the cook, and he's armed too. Everyone is wearing the same brown dusters. This looks like an unusually organized gang, and there are twice as many of them as there are of us."

"Let's back out of here before one of those highwaymen spots us up here on this barren hill."

The mountain men carefully backed down, making sure not to dislodge loose stone or make too much racket. They were as quiet as wildcats stalking prey through the forest.

Unfortunately, they found little cover along the Oregon Trail. Parts of the trail near the rivers and creeks were lush and green, but the rest was barren rock and dead weeds. Their clothing blended into their surroundings, making them harder to spot, as long as the captain didn't put on his dark cavalry cap. Levi had changed from the beaver hat with a fox tail he used during the winter to a wide-brimmed covering to keep the sun off.

"PSHAW," Rooster said when Levi reported what he and Will discovered. He spat a stream of brown juice into the dirt. "I ain't ever heard of nothin' like that." A long cheroot was clamped in his sneer.

"Well, believe it or not. I take it as an insult to try and doubt what I saw with my own eyes," Will said. "Those fellows were wearing brown dusters. Levi saw them, too. They might wear ragtag clothing, but those coats set them apart. They're armed with rifles and Colt Patterson revolvers, and it looks like they have plenty of supplies. Two of their mounts are draft horses, and I saw aparejos stacked with their kit. These boys know what they're doin', and they are prepared to wait us out."

"He's right. They all wore identical brown coats. I've never seen anything like it, except when I scouted for the Army. I rarely saw that many of them coats in one place. It means they're used to working together, I think. Anyway, there are over twenty gun hands out there. They are well-supplied and have good horses and spare mounts. I'd say they're ready to do some hard riding if needed. This won't be a bunch of clowns this time. It looks like we're up against the real deal—professionals."

Joseph's face turned red as he shook with rage. When he looked into the captain's eyes, he knew he wasn't kidding. Blood drained from his face. He remembered confronting a similar outfit. They ran in large numbers and robbed and killed everything in sight. If it were the same bunch, he knew that they were about to meet their matches.

"I remember an outlaw gang that wore such gear back in my marshaling days in the territories near Folsom. They were called the Long Riders. I wonder if it is the same bunch. That would put them around my age. Then again, it would be rare for them to survive so long in such a profession. That's unless they were in prison for several years. Maybe then, it might be possible. If it is the same outlaws, we're gonna have our hands full. Yep, I've seen my share of dusters, but it was back when I was posted as a Missouri Territorial Marshal. I grew up not far from there."

"They won't panic," the captain said. "They're a bunch of killers and professional thieves. They're not freedom fighters, that much is for sure. They're here for the cargo, and they won't leave until they get it." He spoke through gritted teeth.

Marshal Walker's eyes flicked from one shadow to another, looking for signs of an ambush. As soon as he heard they wore dusters, he was captivated. Back in the day, there was an outlaw gang that even he couldn't deal with, and they dressed just like the crew his friends spotted. Could it be the same outfit? Brown dusters were sold across the West. The men wearing them could be just about anybody.

Rooster and Buster sat listening with concern etched on their faces, but they didn't say a word despite their situation going from bad to worse. If Marshal Walker was concerned, they knew that things would get even riskier than they thought.

They all knew that America's future lay in the development of the West, and the very people who dared to cross the Oregon Trail. Their lives and safety were paramount. Despite the danger, they knew they had to get the supplies to Fort Boise, no matter the price. But the ante suddenly soared. The danger they faced just increased tenfold.

Marshal Walker wasn't so worried about the heat, but he was nervous about the Indians. Everywhere they rode, they saw signs of pony tracks, abandoned cookfires, and carcasses from animals they hunted and ate.

Hundreds of Shoshone Indians were nearby. He knew how to deal with outlaws and thieves, but he wasn't the Indian fighter that Will or Levi were.

Finally, Rooster suggested, "Maybe we should turn back and wait them out. They'll have to run out of supplies at some point. The folks at Fort Boise will just have to hold on for a while longer.

"Hell, no!" Joseph said with a voice full of iron. It was clear he wouldn't be deterred. "If they get tired of waiting or think we've decided not to go, they might raid Fort Boise, which is understaffed, too. They might not get much from the overlanders, but if they breach the fort's fifteen-foot walls, they could roust the locals. They'll have money and valuables.

"Keep in mind, those wagon trains are looking for supplies to get them to Oregon. I figure one way or another, these boys intend to make a haul and walk away wealthy."

Sometimes Marshal Walker seemed to enjoy—and even invite—heated arguments, discourse, and even an occasional fistfight. A fire was beginning to build within. When he finally got a chance to go after the outlaws, they had better watch out.

"I hope we don't die out here on this barren God-forsaken land," Rooster huffed.

"Wherever you die, it's still the same distance to hell," Joseph growled. "If you're worried, you're in the wrong business, friend."

"Just because you have a crazy notion, doesn't mean that we've gotta go with ya and get shot all the hell," Rooster replied. "Mind ya now, I ain't sayin' we won't go. I ain't no coward.

"Go ahead and tell us what you've got planned.

Then, I'll let you know what I think. After all, these wagons are in my charge. You boys are just the guards. Don't take that the wrong way. I know you're the best, but I still have to get my mind around the idea of setting a dangerous trap. My question is: Who is in the most danger?"

"I say we leave enough men to guard the wagons," Levi said. "When they're boxed up, it's nearly like a small fort. That will cut their odds of putting one of us down, and for them to attack, they'll have to ride directly into your line of fire. Meanwhile, Rooster, Buster, Will, Joseph, and I can see if we can't capture one or two gang members so we can question them. We need to find out what their plans are. Only then can we move ahead confidently. Whatever we find out, we'll plan accordingly."

"Or better yet, why don't we set a trap. Maybe we can get 'em to attack the wagons at night. Then we hit them hard where they least expect us to attack," Captain Forrester suggested. "I figure a few outlaws are keeping an eye on us right now."

"Do you think you can get your men down into that arroyo that we saw just before we pull up for the night?" Levi asked. "And do it while making as little noise as possible?"

"I reckon if we wander off one at a time, we can make it look like the men are going out for a leak before turning in," Rooster said. "That way, it don't matter how much noise we make. Yeah, I reckon that Buster here and me can organize that for ya."

"Stuff somethin' under your blankets," Marshal Walker said. "That way, if there is a spy, they'll figure we're all asleep. Make up a dummy with a poncho and a hat and lean a gun against that tree where the firelight flickers out. They won't know it's a ruse until they're too close. Then it'll be too late."

"When I give the signal, we can hit them fast and hard," Levi instructed. "Captain Forrester, Marshal Walker, and I can find somewhere to hide up close. If they fall for the ruse, they won't get away before you boys are on them. Whatcha think, Rooster? Depending on how many come, keep in mind we don't wanna kill 'em all. Do you think we can pull this off?"

"It'll be daylight soon, so if they have somebody watching with a spyglass from afar, we don't have time to waste. Once the sun's up, they won't risk approaching the camp because they'll have no cover. Yeah, sure, we can pull it off."

"Joseph, Will, and I will make a big show of leaving the camp on horseback, so they'll think we've gone off to scout ahead. We'll ride out in five minutes. We'll stash our horses somewhere where they won't be seen and hightail it back here to see what happens. I agree, they'll probably have one, two, or even three men keeping an eye on us from a safe distance. We can't even try to hide the wagons. All we can do is circle up and try to ward them off."

Joseph removed his cover, raked his fingers through his hair, and down his weathered, bearded face. The marshal passed his shirt sleeve across his forehead and pulled the hat's brim low over his fiery eyes. The way he huffed and puffed, they knew he was gnawing at the bit to go to work.

THEY MOUNTED up and wheeled their horses away under the great bowl of a sky in sober silence, not knowing what to expect next. All they knew was that they had to lure the outlaws to the wagons before they discovered they were spying on them. Hopefully, they would have a chance for a couple of shots too. Maybe even more. It depended on how many took the bait and breached the circled wagons. They knew they wouldn't come alone. Still, there wouldn't be too many, or they would be easily spotted.

The outlaws weren't counting on the extra gun hands. When they attacked the first time, they surely counted numbers and knew precisely what they were up against. At least they thought they did.

The wind whispered through the grass. Owls hooted in the darkness as coyotes howled at the moon. Levi lay waiting there, looking up at countless stars in the heavens above. He wasn't the type of man to worry about what was about to go down in the next few minutes. He stared at the endless blanket of stars that would soon disappear with the rising sun.

Beaver acted like he didn't have a care in the world. No matter how it went, they couldn't do anything about it anyway. That was the way of life in the wilderness. Some made it, and others didn't. And just because you made a good plan didn't mean it would work.

Levi heard and smelled the outlaws before he got them in his sights. He could hear the faint sound of horses nickering in the distance. Three highwaymen stepped onto the circle of light, expecting to find the bullwhackers and their guards lying around the fire and asleep. The fire snapped and crackled as cinders soared into the night, disappearing a few yards away. It was almost comical how they tiptoed to avoid making a sound.

The barrel-chested marshal snapped his head in their direction as soon as he heard the voices. They rang clear through the cool of the predawn morning. He slowly levered a round into his rifle without making a sound. His well-oiled weapon was in perfect condition.

Little did they know that Beaver smelled their fancy store-bought soap long before he heard their footsteps. It was difficult to hide the sound of stiff boots compared to the supple moccasins Levi wore. Even though the outlaws believed they were being quiet, they sounded like a herd of buffalo and smelled almost as strong to Levi.

When their Sharps rifles cracked, the slug sang through the stillness and made a zipping sound while traveling at three thousand feet per second. Hands clawed at their wounds as the bandits dropped to the ground. They were so close that the reports were almost simultaneous.

Will spotted a fourth shooter and brought his gun around. When he aimed and fired, his round was intended to slow the outlaw down, not kill him. When the heavy-caliber round hit his shoulder, it spun him around like a top before he fell to the ground. He stared at the sky, blinking, like he was trying to figure out where he was. The outlaw couldn't move from the shock of the impact. He shook his head and looked at his arm, but it was only a graze. When he looked up again, it was into the barrel of a revolver, held by a man with a US Marshal's badge in clear view.

Walker knew they needed him alive. When the outlaw jumped up and made a run for it, he didn't fire.

Levi grabbed the nearest horse, jumped astride it bareback, and dug his heels into its flanks. He slammed into the outlaw, knocking him and his horse to the ground and leaving them dazed.

When the dust settled, they counted the bodies of the dead and wounded. There were four in all, one of them was already gone, and the other was bleeding out. The other two were still alive per their plan. Dead men didn't talk.

Levi slid out of his saddle and grabbed his captive by the hair. He was screaming with his eyes spread wide. "You were sent to spy on us, weren't you?" He shook him so hard that Levi came away with a handful of his hair.

"Let me drag that other bastard over here so we can see what he has to say," Marshal Walker spat. "If I cut his throat here and now, I bet his buddy is gonna wanna talk. Well, whatcha got to say for yourself, fool?"

"I say, if he doesn't want to talk, we string him up to that tree over there and quit wasting our time," Rooster said. "It's not much, but it's the only tree I see. If we make the noose short, I doubt his feet touch the ground. If not, we can do it Texan style."

"Texan style?" Levi asked. "What's that?"

"We'll put a noose around the outlaw's neck and drag him across the desert with a horse. From what I've heard, most times their heads pop right off."

"Why in the world would a man do that?" Levi asked, shocked.

"Because they don't have the luxury of a tree to hang 'em from. In some places, it's all flat desert."

Both outlaws backed away from the bullwhacker's violent words. Levi still sat with his mouth open.

Marshal Walker nodded like he had already known of such practices.

Captain Forrester smiled. “Well, those Texans sure are inventive, aren’t they? What do you say, outlaw? Do you want to take a ride from the back of a racing horse, or would you rather talk? You’d be surprised how friendly we can be if you’re fair with us.”

The gang members in their brown dusters stared at the frontiersmen and the marshal like they were specimens from another world. They had never seen buckskin-clad men like these. The smug look froze on the outlaws’ faces, but that changed as soon as Joseph hammered the closest one with his massive fist. When the highwayman grimaced, his teeth were covered in blood.

“Oh, I see how it is now.” Marshal Walker smiled. “You boys think you’re hard, don’t ya. You watch carefully because I’m gonna show you what hard is all about.”

Rooster grabbed the reins close to the bit rings. Once the team was hooked up, he glanced at his tarnished gold watch. “It’s time for us to get on our way again. In ten minutes or so, it’ll turn daylight.” He pulled out his watch again and popped the cover. Will wondered if he could see in the dark, or if he fiddled with his timepiece out of habit. It was apparent that he wasn’t used to seeing men tortured for information. He turned away as soon as the punishment began in earnest.

Rooster saw that for Levi and Will, it was difficult too, but the marshal appeared to have no problem with beating the outlaws until they talked. Maybe he had lived more challenging times than they had. Then again, somebody had to do it. A chill ran up his back as he realized how menacing Marshal Walker was.

Joseph took three steps to the man he shot and poked his gun barrel into the bullet hole in his shoulder. When he began to scream, the blood drained from the man's face, and he nearly passed out. The lawman patiently waited until his voice gave out.

"*Xinga tu madre*," the outlaw spat in Spanish.

"Why, this one must be Mexican. It looks like your boss recruits men from all around, don't he? All right then, tell me who it is you two miserable fools work for. Or are ya gonna make me stick my gun barrel back into that bullet hole? You already know how that feels. If I were you, I'd fess up. You can see that I ain't gonna change my mind."

"We work for Garrott Sneed and Howey Dundurn. I've been riding with them for neigh-on a decade, if not more. You'll never beat the boss. He'll eat you all up and spit you out. You don't know what you've got yourself into. There are twice as many of us as there are of you. You're all gonna die. You're nothing but buzzard bait."

Two gunshots rang out, two seconds apart. Smoke squirreled out of the marshal's pistol barrel as his arm hung limp at his side. Joseph moved his tobacco chew from one side of his mouth to the other, then spat a stream of brown juice on each of the men's heads.

"Ride like an outlaw, die like an outlaw," the marshal said before he turned and walked away in a huff.

"It's gonna be a hell of a three-day journey to Fort Boise even if we run day and night," the captain said. "We only stop for meals and to give the horses a rest. We've gotta make sure our animals don't die on us."

"That's just one of the hundreds of things you don't

know about bullwhackers," Rooster said. He grinned despite the situation. "I've never had a horse die on me in all my years driving wagons. You've gotta know the signs when the horse is tired, but first you've gotta have the right kind of horseflesh. We'll rest them in short spells as we travel. These are my horses, and I picked them special for this kind of work."

Joseph looked at the teamster out of the corner of his eye and wondered if he was as brave as he acted.

WHEN THE SUN CAME UP, they stared across the far-stretching plains and to the mountains on the other side.

Levi could see Joseph finally relax the hard line of his jaw. His face was rugged and leathery until he looked at Will. Then, a smile crossed his lips.

"I told you that I'd come in handy. I'm here to do the dirty work you two don't wanna do," the marshal said. "Bein' a marshal for so long will do that to ya. It takes a hard lawman to survive the territories as long as I did."

As they traveled west toward Fort Boise, Levi counted the hoofprints of seventeen riders. Two were packed with supplies, and they were all shod. Behind them ran a string of spares. These were the same men who had a go at the wagon train before it hit Fort Hall. They rode fast but with apparent ease, trailed by a cloud of dust. All the while, they stayed out of pistol range. Even with a rifle, they would be hard to hit as they raced by. As the men waited with their rifles in their hands, nobody cracked a smile.

By now, Sneed and Dundurn would suspect that the

four men he sent to spy on the cargo train were killed. It was clear that the men they had nearly waylaid outside the fort had hired guns for the last leg of the journey, and they were formidable enemies.

FROM 1846 ONWARD, the mountain wave of emigrant wagon trains had a significant impact on Fort Hall's native communities. Both the Oregon and California Trails brought a drastic increase in the number of wagons passing through the region. Fort Hall and Fort Boise grew in importance.

The overlanders overtaxed the trail's natural resources, wild game, fish, fruits, and berries, depriving the locals of natural food sources. These trails cut right through vital grazing land, making it harder for the Bannock and Shoshone to sustain themselves. Eventually, this led to the Army's military presence on Indian land. They were sent there to protect the migrants, resulting in the deaths of many Native Americans.

The two tribes were peaceful until they felt they were about to lose everything their ancestors had left them centuries earlier. Ancient cultures were vanishing right before their eyes. Some Shoshone began to trade heavily with travelers, offering food, horses, and services in exchange for metal tools, materials, flour, and coffee. Of course, this only worked for a few. Some of the remaining warriors rebelled and began demanding exorbitant tolls to cross their land in peace. They threatened them with their lives if they didn't pay.

This created an uproar from some of the travelers, although others opted to pay and continue, knowing they wouldn't be fallen upon by a hostile war party. When the deer, elk, and antelope began to dwindle in numbers, some of the natives had to turn to violence to survive.

With the overgrazing by the overlanders' livestock and the disease brought on by the Whites, human and environmental destruction had already begun. Time would tell how the local tribe's future would work out. In other places across the vast stretches of the West, entire camps were abandoned or died out.

Mostly desperate men populated one poor camp that stood only twenty miles off the Oregon Trail. The children had gotten the measles, and many of the women were taken by opposing tribes. They were in a desperate situation. They had lowered themselves from honorable hunters and brave warriors to mere beggars and thieves. But there was one young man who gave them hope. Chief Pocatello sat patiently while, one by one, his people voiced their complaints.

Usually, the Shoshone people coexisted with the Whites, but now their game had been decimated, and their fishing holes fished out. If it didn't stop, their people would perish from starvation or be marched off to some reservation far from their homeland. Friends and family would vanish from the face of the earth.

Fed up with his people's struggle to find enough food to prevent starvation, the chief turned to the only choice left. He decided, his people would take what they wanted when the opportunity arose. The White travelers brought unheard riches to the local Indian tribes. Rather than bartering for what little they had, they would find stragglers or small wagon trains to attack and pillage.

Young Pocatello knew where such a path would eventually lead, but as the small band's leader, he had to do something, even if it was only a short-term patch. If they died tomorrow, it would make little difference anyway. So, they decided to go for broke and fight back. At least then they would be guaranteed a place in the spirit world when they perished. Death was unavoidable without some divine interaction from the spirit world to stop the advance of White men.

The chief hoped and prayed that other bands of warriors, those also struggling to survive, would join forces with him and his people. Maybe they could start a movement to stop the trespassing on their land. He had no idea of the enormity of what was heading their way. If they had known what the future held, they would have realized it was unstoppable, and they might have chosen another course of action.

The Sneed Gang

"Whatcha think happened to Todd, Smitty, Bill, and Sam?" Sneed asked, frowning. "I figure they should have been back by now. It ain't like them to be late unless something serious happened. They know I don't tolerate men who do not follow my orders. I told them to report back here."

"I reckon it was those scouts and the lawman who are responsible, if our spies inside Fort Hall can be trusted. The boys say one is an ornery old US Marshal from the Missouri territories near Leavenworth. He has quite a reputation. The other two are mountain men," said his lieutenant. "Still, I don't put much stake in a burned-out lawman and a couple of half-breed strays.

"Our inside men said the scouts dress like Indians, and I ain't ever seen an Injun I can't handle. I ain't too afraid of men who make a living shooting dumb beasts like those buffalo. Hell, they're too stupid to run when the shootin' starts. Don't worry, there are more men where those four came from. Lots of folks are without work and would do almost anything for a few dollars. If it's enough money to get them to California, they'll be glad to join us."

The countryside that surrounded the Oregon Trail between Fort Hall and Fort Boise contained rocky outcroppings that formed mysterious shapes and shadows, creating dark places for a man to hide. It held a dim, desolate beauty with pink bands and black rock. Travel on the rutted path was always exhausting, back-breaking, and dangerous. So, the gang was on its toes. They had let the cargo wagons get away once, costing them part of the shipment. They were not about to let it happen again.

A full moon shone brightly above them, casting shadows across the countryside. The sky was no longer completely dark. The riders breached a summit and slowly stood in their stirrups as they led their horses down the steep grade. They set up their camp in an arroyo so their campfire wouldn't be visible from afar. They ate and settled in for the night.

Sneed stirred at midnight and was checking on his perimeter guards when he spotted a shadow moving in the dim light. The outline of a single man on a horse was evident as he moved toward the encampment.

The lone rider emerged from a dark copse of wind-twisted trees. Sneed believed the stranger, whoever it was, would appear beyond the large boulder before he turned for their camp. From where Garrott stood with the spyglass, the distance between him and the stranger was several hundred feet.

His knuckles quickly turned white as he wrapped his fingers around the butt of his Colt. Sneed eased back the hammer on his revolver and stared down the barrel to the sight. He waited in dead silence for what seemed like an hour, but he knew it was no more than fifteen minutes. The smooth, hickory grip of his Colt Paterson was comfortable in his hand. He caressed the trigger with his finger and intended to fire as soon as the figure stepped around the boulder.

The intruder slid out of his saddle and pushed his back flat against the large stone. Sneed stood just outside the circle of campfire light in the shadows, but the countryside was alight with a silvery tinge. He saw the stranger point his gun at his sleeping men. When the gang leader pulled the trigger, he noticed he was a split-second too late as the silhouette dove for cover.

Immediately, Sneed knew he had given away his position. A bullet singed into the air as it ricocheted off the stone. Suddenly, a cacophony of gunfire erupted from his gang. Men fired blindly into the dark. The gunshot had awoken them all from their restless sleep, and they went for their guns. Suddenly, bullets whined and ricocheted off the stone walls in every direction.

The gang leader hugged the ground as bullets tattered the foliage above him. He saw the intruder's powder flash and fire, cocked his gun, and shot again. The gunfire stopped, but Garrott was unsure whether his shot found its mark. It took a brave man to open fire on a camp of seventeen heavily armed men. Right then, he knew it could only be a bounty hunter after the reward on his head. Five thousand dollars would make even the most conservative man take a chance and see if they got lucky. Many men in the far west had little to lose.

Stooping, Sneed made a mad dash for where he thought the assailant would be. He saw the surprise in the man's eyes when he popped up next to him. Sneed's revolver flashed when his finger applied four pounds of pressure on the trigger. The report launched the gunman against the boulder as one side of his bewildered face exploded. His legs buckled beneath him as he released a pneumatic sigh. He slouched to the ground and died on the spot.

Sneed suddenly felt tired, but it was a good feeling because he was still alive after a close call. His bone weariness was combined with a deep sense of relief. He had dodged another bullet. This wasn't the first bounty hunter to come for him, and it wouldn't be the last.

Foremost on his mind was the cargo wagon train, though.

"BUFFALO BOATS WILL GET us across the Snake River. It'll ford us and our horses to the other side," Jessy Crow said like nothing had happened. "They'll be waitin' at the end of the portage trail. We've got it all worked out."

The water vessels were made of raw buffalo skins. They were smaller and easier to hide than most of the ferries. They would be waiting behind the cane growing at the water's edge, just out of sight. Most of the boats on the Snake River were flatboats, constructed of rough-cut timber. They were made for shallow running to prevent them from getting hung up on sand barges, submerged tree trunks, and branches.

"How about some of that bull cheese?" Howey asked. He grabbed a piece of buffalo jerky and gnawed with what teeth he had left.

"It's nearly as good as buffalo cider." Jessy Crow grinned. The fluid found in the buffalo's stomach was a favorite thirst quencher among mountain men and Indians alike.

Despite the sudden appearance of a bounty hunter, nobody seemed to be upset. For a gang with their reputation, it wasn't unusual for them to be followed by the law or men looking to recover the rewards on their heads. One and all were wanted men in some part of America's West, but the big prize was for the outlaw gang's boss. If a man could kill and bring his body in, he would be rich by most men's standards.

"Let me fork this horse and let's get on our way," Hawkeye said, with urgency in his voice.

"Pass me that flask of tanglefoot," Sneed growled, ignoring him.

Howey reluctantly passed his personal stash of whiskey.

"After seein' that fugitive recovery agent out there in the middle of nowhere, it left a bad taste in my mouth."

"Don't you think we had best move on after the gunfire? Maybe he wasn't alone. We don't want those wagon train scouts to come snoopin' around, do we? That one was close, boss."

Sneed lit a hand-built, then sat unmoving for a while, ignoring Howey's urgent need to leave. He took another sip of whiskey and spat the remains into the dirt. He reloaded his weapon and jammed his pistol into his empty holster.

Three vultures hobbled out to pick at the dead with yellow beaks. The side of the dead man's head was swollen like a melon where a bullet exited. The imprint of Sneed's round was marked on his face in black and blue with puffy edges. Blood dribbled from his wound, nose, and mouth. Howey stared at the corpse with his sleepy eye. He smiled, displaying a mouth of yellow teeth.

Sneed was the undisputed leader of the cargo train robbery gang. At six-foot-three, he towered over his men. To enhance his height, he wore high-heeled cowboy boots. He loved it when he could look down on his opponents and gang members when he had to scold them for not doing their jobs. His silver hair was swept back on the sides of his head, and his cheeks were covered in stubble that matched his hair. Despite the location, he still dressed smartly like the professional gunslinger he was.

Howey Dundurn was the leader's right-hand man. He was lazy by nature, but he worshipped his boss unlike other men Sneed had met. Despite his grumbling, he would walk out into a field of fire or into a burning house if Sneed ordered him. If he were in need, he knew that Dundurn would save his life. He knew that most of the others would turn and run, trying to save their own lives. Howie was the man the boss trusted most among the ten permanent gang members.

The others were men hired for their guns, and most were untested. Time would tell how well they stood up against an aggressive enemy. Nobody expected attacking this wagon train would be anything but difficult, and it was inevitable that men would die. For them, the prize was too big to resist despite the inherent danger.

Tommy Verde was half Mexican and half Gringo. He was a good man with a gun, but was mostly silent. Nobody was ever sure what he was thinking because he hardly talked. Sneed thought this was his best attribute. He was dark-skinned, with a handlebar mustache, and wore a large Mexican sombrero to shield himself from the oppressive sun. When he was angry, he always answered in Spanish until he calmed down. Being Latin, he had the most explosive nature of the bunch and killed at the drop of a hat In the end, he was killed by Joseph's hand.

Jessy Crow was born and raised in Hazard, Kentucky, which was moonshine country. His family was well known at the Perry Courthouse. Sneed knew that the family clans stuck together like bees to a hive. Their ties were unbreakable. They all hated the law that harassed them at their home, generating intense hostility. Tucked away in the mountains were countless unregistered whiskey stills, of which none paid tax. So, the law was the enemy of the entire community.

Another character of the Sneed gang was Jessy Crow. He was born and raised in Hazard, Kentucky, which was moonshiner country, and Sneed knew that the family clans stuck together like bees to honey and were extremely loyal because they all hated the law that suppressed them ever since they arrived in their mountains with great hostility despite the difficult access.

His quick handiwork and his lack of reluctance to use his guns made him an essential tool for the gang. He was reckless to a fault and too young to be afraid.

The most belligerent of the gang was Lenny Gabbert, a red-haired, second-generation Irishman with a temper like a ticking time bomb. He had a stubble of red hair growing on his chin and just enough of a mustache to create the slightest shadow. He suffered from an inferiority complex with men who were smarter than he, which was just about everyone—especially Sneed and his second in command. Although he would never admit it out loud, he despised them both for their brains and cunning. Even Howey was smarter than him.

Secretly, once this job was over and he got his cut, he planned to kill them both. He hated men who gave him orders and treated him like an inferior, which, in fact, he was. Sneed could think circles around the foolish man. Still, he knew what he planned to do once the cargo was in their hands. He had no intention of allowing Garrott to execute his plan before shooting him dead. Men of reckless blood filled the gang's ranks.

Tod Zillow was a quiet man who was full of pent-up violence. If you met him in a saloon, you would never be the wiser. He was known for allowing insults to simmer for weeks before catching the culprit asleep in his bunk late at night. Then, he would remove his ears. He always accused the Indians of this despicable act of revenge, a common practice in the Indian Nations. His boss could never pin it on him despite his suspicions.

Slim Parkins was an aging outlaw with a permanent limp from a gunshot wound to the hip. He didn't let it slow him down. He was shot in the upper leg during a prison escape. He wasn't much in a foot race, but he was hell on wheels on a horse. Only Sneed could outride him, and, in a pinch, he wasn't so sure of that. Despite his handicap, he was the best horseman of the bunch. He was tall and gaunt, wearing torn, tattered clothing. He had long ago disregarded how he looked. When given the chance, he robbed innocents whenever convenient.

Every outlaw in the Sneed gang was rotten to the bone, and all had black souls. Slim had been with Sneed for as long as anyone could remember, and he had never let him down to date. The gang leader was the only man who treated him for his worth and not for how he looked.

Danny Ramrod was an ex-rancher who had fallen on hard times and turned to rustling horses and cattle to survive. He was their go-to man when it came to selecting horseflesh. For a serious outlaw, having quality horses was paramount. Whenever they had to buy or rustle a new animal, Ramrod was Sneed's go-to man. He was bowlegged, of medium height, and wore a beige Stetson he claimed to have stolen from a Texas Ranger he shot and killed.

He was also a first-class bullwhacker, which they would soon need once they had secured the remaining wagons headed for Fort Boise. He seemed to always have a whip in his hand or within reach. He also used the cat-o'-nine-tails on his opponents whenever they had to extract information.

Joey *Jaw* Morgan was known for relentless scraps, whether it be with fists, knives, or guns. The mild-mannered, unassuming outlaw in a black suit was almost unnoticeable. But when provoked, he was like a rabid dog, thus his name, Jaws. He got it from biting his opponents and ripping their ears or noses off. He was a psychopath in sheep's clothing. He, too, blended in everywhere and was sometimes used to spy inside Fort Hall. He tended to get into trouble if he didn't have the gang leader watching over him. Lank, greasy hair fell around large butterfly ears.

The ten men had been with Sneed for a decade, but the other thirteen men were guns for hire and could only be trusted as far as he could throw them. Still, Sneed kept the fear factor prevalent, and nobody dared try to get the drop on the boss. How things would go once they secured the valuable cargo, Sneed knew, would surely change. But he felt he could depend on his eight men.

"This bounty hunter fella must have been crazier than a dog humpin' a pig to come into our camp all on his own," Howey said with a chuckle. He never seemed bothered after a man was killed.

"Maybe he thought he was meaner than he really was or just wanted to chip down the odds. I hope he don't have some friends waiting nearby. I doubt it. He looked like a loner to me. When men like him come around, I kill 'em on the spot," Sneed bragged.

"Maybe you need to control your temper a bit, boss. It would have been a good idea to question him some," Howey huffed.

"I don't need to control my temper. I need people to stop pissin' me off!" Sneed replied.

Fear kicked up a notch in Howey as his boss got his full attention. After it was all said and done, Sneed looked relieved as he let out a breath he felt like he'd been holding for hours.

"This time, the law meddled with a serious fighter, and we showed them just how ready to fight we are. I'm not leaving these plains without that cargo, even if we've gotta kill every man on those wagons and half the people in the fort. I don't care who they are. I didn't come this far for nothing."

Howey swallowed grudgingly. He knew how his boss was when he was in this kind of mood. He might have a mind to shoot the first man who mouthed off, so he walked like he was treading on glass.

The attack fueled Sneed's resolve and made his

blood race faster, and his nerves began to fray, making him even more edgy.

"It's time to separate the chaff from the wheat," Sneed growled.

The gang seemed to be descending into malice and self-destruction even before their final encounter with the remaining cargo wagons. They all knew they would meet resistance because most of their encounters were violent. For them, it was just part of outlaw life.

The boss harrumphed and curled a sly grin. "Their time is gonna come, and it'll be real soon."

Howey Dundurn got up, grumbling under his breath, looked over his shoulder, and stormed away from the campfire. A tooth-clenched curse followed. He wasn't happy that his boss wasn't being more careful. Usually, he wasn't so reckless about their jobs. He felt the bullwhackers had gotten under his skin when they escaped into Fort Hall. Now, his anger seemed to blur his vision.

"The day a bunch of teamsters outsmarts me will be the day monkeys fly out of my ass," Sneed growled. His men knew him too well and kept their eyes locked on the flickering flames in the fire. When he was in an ugly mood, one just never knew what he might do.

They had spent days riding where few white souls ventured, save the now seventeen outlaws. All eyes focused on the money the valuable cargo would bring. Now, they found themselves in the middle of nowhere, and there were signs of Indians everywhere they looked. The first bounty hunter found them, and they hadn't even finished the job.

THAT NIGHT, Sneed put out extra guards as he lay on his back with his head perched on his saddle as he looked up at the millions of stars twinkling overhead, but his mind wasn't on the beauty. All he could think about was making the cargo teamsters pay for their stubbornness. It ticked him off to no end that they had lost part of the cargo, and he didn't intend to let it happen again.

He watched as Howey busied himself with checking every guard post, making sure they had sufficient ammunition. He unloaded his pistols and rifles and reloaded them. The routine helped settle his nerves.

"What a fool. Howey scampers just like a racehorse," Slim said. "He'll wear himself out before we even get to the wagons."

"Maybe," he said, shrugging. "Then again, maybe not. It's good to have a paranoid man among the gang to keep us on our toes. It allows me to have a peaceful sleep at night," Lenny said.

The wind moaned like a distant beast. Lenny turned his head and pinched his nose with thumb and finger and blew twin strings of snot onto the dirt. He wiped his fingers on his cotton shirt.

THE NEXT MORNING, the fiery disk rose with the color of molten steel and sprayed orange rays of light across the eastern horizon. Sneed was the last to rise as he couldn't sleep and spent half the night staring at the sky. He felt he had gone over every detail ten times, but their first failure stuck in his craw. He didn't know if they would have another chance after the next attempt. If not, it could turn into a running battle all the way to Fort

Boise, and then it was anyone's guess what might happen.

"Maybe it's best if we try to split the wagons up. At least we can secure some of the cargo and let the fools know we mean business," Howey suggested.

"No, we're gonna go after them all at once," Sneed growled. "I don't want to lose any more cargo. We've already lost enough. I don't wanna hear another word about it. We'd better keep sharp, or things could go to blazes in a handbasket."

"You're about as frank as a two-dollar funeral," Slim said. "All right then, all of them at once it is. You're the boss, and so far, you haven't steered us wrong."

"That first attempt was poorly planned, to say the least," Howey said, and regretted it as soon as the words left his mouth. The backhand from Sneed came lightning quick. One thing the boss didn't tolerate was sass.

LATE THAT NIGHT, a pack of wild dogs shied and backed away, save one. It stood its ground and uttered a deep growl at the strangers before running off. The night guards listened until the last of the yapping died in the distance. There must have been a dozen of them hunting for their next meal. They smelled food cooking, but the outlaws were far too dangerous to steal food from. Even the wild canines instinctively knew this.

"If you're wrong, you're gonna be sittin' down when you take a leak for the rest of your life," Slim Parkins said. "Maybe you had best consider it. If they only lose a wagon, I doubt they'd take chase. We've already lost six men, and we ain't even laid eyes on 'em. Sometimes I think your mother mated with a scorpion, Sneed. I know you're pissed off because they got away the first time, but now, we'd better use our heads. There are seventeen of us. Still, they'll have the advantage of cover, and we can't take a chance of killing the horses. Now, we've got Injuns to worry about. We'd best hope they don't catch us with our pants down out here on these damned plains."

"If I wanted your advice, Slim, I'd have asked. You had better remember back on the last time you sassed me like that. You trouble me like an old woman," Sneed said. "I figure a gang member who's always unhappy might turn on us one day. Are you unhappy, Mr. Parkins? Is that what you're tryin' to say?"

"Sorry, boss. I didn't mean no offense," Parkins said and pulled on his brown duster. The dusters were the outlaw gang's trademark. Sneed liked people to know who they were. He believed it intimidated his enemies, which included just about everyone but his chosen few, and he wasn't so sure about all of them.

When the outlaws passed the dead body on their way out of their camp, little birds chattered in the wind. Vultures rose from the ground with bony wings: whoop, whoop, whooping like children's puppets on a string. Bloody beaks already held scraps of meat from the recently deceased bounty hunter, but nobody seemed to care.

Shoshone Warriors

Tethered dogs howled at the edge of the Indian camp as they bared their teeth and snapped at one another as the war party silently departed. Wives walked to the beginning of the trail to see their husbands off. Not one shed a tear, nor did they embarrass the warriors, even though they knew that some of them might not return. Shadows of the horses and riders were painted black on the ground. Small puffs of dust followed the horses' hooves.

It was the meridian of the day when they departed. Dozens of teepees were scattered across land cleared next to a quick-flowing stream. Fish nibbled at the water's surface, feeding on bugs. Dozens of Indian women squatted on the banks, washing their clothing. They laid their wash out to dry on sun-warmed rocks. Upstream, old men and young boys cast lines and hooks into the water, hoping to catch some bass or trout, but there were far fewer gamefish available than in years prior. The same went for the game animals. With each passing wagon train, wild game diminished.

They climbed the rolling hills, clopping over stone as they passed through rifts of cool shade. The riders' shapes were stenciled on canyon walls as the sun glared, flashing off the water, making them squint. They knew the oven-like heat wouldn't relent with the setting sun but would continue into the night. The bone-dry wind on the plains never stopped.

Shoshone Chief Pocatello stared at the ground and sniffed the air. "Those tracks are from wolves," he said, kneeling and touching the footprints with his fingertips.

"What are timber wolves doing so close to humans?" War Chief Sagwitch asked. "Maybe they're after scraps from the White men. Indians leave no scraps. That means the people we are looking for are close. They are the same ones that tried to capture the cargo wagon train before Fort Hall and failed."

"And those tracks over there? Those are unshod horses, but they aren't Indian ponies. Only heavy horses make tracks that deep. It looks like we have more company than just the men looking to rob the wagons. In the smaller group, there appear to be only three. Unlike the thieves, they hide well. I wonder if they are after us or the men who tried to rob the wagons only to be fended off. There was no mention of these three buckskin-clad men in the smoke signals. I don't know whether they are alone or with the cargo wagons headed for Fort Boise. If they plan to take on the group of outlaws, they *are* bold, I'll give them that. Of course, that doesn't mean that they are smart."

"There are too many white men for us to attack, but if we wait, we might see an opportunity as they focus on the cargo wagons. Now, we will have to watch our backs," Sagwitch whispered. "There might be somebody else watching who is as good at hiding as us. There is more going on here than meets the eye. We must proceed with the utmost caution."

Aboriginal people hunted the Great Western Plains for thousands of years. The original inhabitants witnessed the glaciers recede as the land began to warm. The changing environment accelerated the demise of the saber-toothed tiger, the great mastodons, and the hippo. They hunted the same land when it was densely forested, and now it was a sea of grass. Through all these changes, native people continued to live as nomadic hunters on the vast stretches of land. As Levi, Will, and the marshal watched the highwaymen, the Indians watched them all.

Nineteenth-century Indians were colorful, mystical, and warlike. The antiquity of their rituals and the intricate organization of their many tribes were unique. They were a hunting society built around the horse, even though the four-legged animals were only introduced into North America by the Spanish three hundred years earlier.

A small waterfall thundered out of the nearing dusk and into a large pond, spilling off downhill in several quick-moving streams. The flow trickled over the rocks, turning the Oregon Trail green and lush along the Snake River. The farther one traveled from the water, the drier and more barren it became.

A stark silence came over them as the full moon rose over the first flat stretch of land they came to. On the other side of the world, the sun closed its eye and disappeared over the horizon, leaving a rainbow of colorful light. Fireflies flashed here and there as crickets began to chirp. The war party stopped for a brief rest, then mounted up again and rode into the night.

As the war party traveled deeper into the countryside, the prairie lay around them like a big plate, wavering in the moonlight. The soft white light created long shadows that came alive in the wind-swept landscape. The Indians quietly rode with their rifles across their thighs and bows and quivers of arrows strapped to their backs.

They made no more noise than alighting birds. The veins of their temples pulsated like fuses as the file of warriors continued to walk their mounts beneath the slow wheel of stars in the heavens above. All that was heard was the occasional nicker or whinny of their ponies. The unshod hooves hardly made a sound on the soft earth.

They stopped by a stream to refresh their ponies. The Shoshone chief slipped off his pony and dropped to his hands and knees, putting his ear to the ground. The animals dapped their hooves in the water, rose, and lowered their dripping heads. They drank deeply from the crystal clear stream, beads of water running down and off their chins.

Another Shoshone warrior came running into sight, beating his pony into a whirlwind. He abruptly stopped, jumped off his mount, and struggled to talk as he caught his breath. "A lone man is stalking the White men at their campfire. We had better stop and wait to see what happens. He looks like he might be a White lawman."

"That makes two groups of White men and one stray. We can assume they are all after the same thing.

What was the lone man doing? He must be mad to be wandering around here in the wilderness alone."

"It looks like he plans on sneaking up on the outlaws. At the moment, they still don't know he's there. What he thinks he can do alone makes me wonder. Then again, some White men will do anything to acquire gold and silver coins. Maybe even risk their lives against daunting odds."

It was nearly dusk when they saw a faint wisp of black smoke from a campfire curling skyward in a line so thin it was almost invisible under the moonlight. When the war party got closer, they could see yellow flickering flames in the distance. It was apparent that the White men weren't being as careful as they should. If they could so easily locate them, the others could do the same, especially three men who wore moccasins and left little or no track at all.

That night, the warrior braves carefully circled the gang's campsite, taking advantage of the cluster of trees. The outlaws thought the location provided protection, but it was a double-edged sword. They knew farther west, they wouldn't have the luxury of dense vegetation. They used the opportunity to recount their numbers and to inspect their possessions. It turned out that the outlaws had exactly what the warriors wanted most.

The Shoshone coveted their large arsenal of weapons and ammunition, both rifles and revolvers. The young war chief needed the firearms to make his mark and to seek revenge on those responsible for taking their land, game, and freedom. If they killed enough of the overlanders, maybe they might retreat and not come back.

The war party carefully sought cover while they

watched the churlish-looking White men sucked their teeth and look around with crazy eyes. Their shadows shrank as the moon moved directly overhead. The following day, whirlwinds stood like smoke in the distance as dust swirled across the ground. That was when they got their first good look at the riders who chased the wagon train.

As soon as first light broke, and without warning, arrows lofted across a blue sky that was void of clouds. They whistled like ducks flying through the air. They thudded when they hit their targets, and four of the White thieves went down. When a cloud of arrows fell all around the outlaw gang, they scattered like roaches suddenly caught by a bright light in a dark room.

As they retreated, taking the best cover they could find, the gang returned fire with a barrage of bullets, but none found their mark. Once the rest of the gang fled, the warriors removed the four dead outlaws' scalps, leaving them raw-skulled, red, and bloody.

"They should have known better than to go snooping around on our land," Chief Pocatello said. "Maybe if we can whittle them down to a reasonable number, we can attack them and take their guns. They won't run far for fear of losing sight of the cargo wagons. All we have to do is patiently wait for our moment. With a gang this reckless, we won't have to wait long."

"I figure they only ran because we caught them by surprise," Sagwitch said. "We also must remember to watch out for the three lone riders. I have no idea where they went. They are good at covering their tracks, unlike the thieving fools around the campfire. They were advertising where they were. Still, we need those guns much more than anything. With such weapons, maybe we can scare the overlanders away and take our land back."

An old Indian appeared naked save for his blanket. He rode a bone-tale mule. They didn't know where he came from, but he clearly was a shaman or medicine man. So, the warrior band held their ground and waited for him to approach. He slid off his mouth, acting like he was alone. But the old Indian knew exactly where they were hiding. He appeared to be too old to be dangerous. When he kneeled beside the stream, he lost their interest. Wizened and honed by age, he hardly moved when an arrow whined past his ear, bringing a round of chuckles from the Shoshone men. They weren't interested in old shamans, especially this one who appeared to be deaf.

The Indians crept across the distance like animals, slow and with their backs arched. They copied the movements of animals to go unperceived as they resumed their pursuit of the White men, who had yet to see the Shoshone warriors.

"EVERYTHING SEEMS TOO quiet for my liking," Howey said as they sat around the crackling fire, as heat wavered from the flames. The orange glow of coals reflected in their eyes. All the gang members were on edge. They had to keep focused on the target, or the other four cargo wagons could slip their grasp, meaning that they would have made a long, hard ride for nothing. They hadn't counted on missing their first opportunity. The bullwhackers drove the six-horse teams much faster than expected and caught them off guard, but Sneed wasn't about to allow that to happen again.

Sneed sat listening to the boring chitchat of his men as they bragged about jobs they had pulled off in the past and displayed brave faces in the current situation. None of them was afraid of the wagon drivers or their guards. In the back of their minds, the Indian attack remained alive. They knew they didn't have the skills to track them or effectively hide from them if they were nearby. They were an unknown element that made everyone nervous.

"I don't doubt we'll get those wagons," Todd Zillow said. "We'll be fine as long as them Shoshone Injuns don't find us again."

"You don't think a small war party would attack the likes of us, do you, boss? There'd have to be a bunch of them, wouldn't there?" Lenny asked. "You saw how they hit us and ran. That means that they have inferior numbers."

"You never know what a bunch of Indians, hopped-up on who knows what, might or might not do. It's best if we're ready for anything, though. I have no idea what runs through an Injun's mind at any given point. Right now, I'm not gonna let anything get in the way of those other four wagons. Not even if all the Indians on the plains come after us. One way or another, we'll have that cargo in our possession in the next two days or so. It's a three-day ride to Fort Boise. We've hung back so they think we've given up. Now, we have the element of surprise."

"Is that rustling I hear in the bushes?" Sneed asked. He forced his eyelids to lower slightly until he was peering through slits with bullet eyes. The moonlight made things waver in the dark. A long shadow ran across the distance in a crouch.

"Uh-huh, boss," Howey replied, wide-eyed. "There's somebody out there all right."

Suddenly, a Shoshone Indian appeared right in front of the outlaw gang, holding a pogamoggan—a three-pound stone attached to the two-foot-long leather-covered handle. If you got hit on the head with that, it would be all she wrote.

Danny Ramrod said, "He doesn't look like he's in the mood to palaver, does he? But I must admit, he has balls coming here like that."

"To me, he looks like he's come to raise our hair," Slim replied. An amused smile crept onto his face. "Did you see those scalp-locks sewn into his shirt. He's challenging us to take him on. He's taunting us, Sneed. It looks like he's ready to kill a few White men." He snickered at the thought.

Howey went from nervous to irritated, his mouth puckering into a childish pout. He felt his patience quickly wearing away. He didn't have as bad a temper as Sneed, but he wouldn't have had the job as second if he were a daisy.

When the first arrows landed, Sneed raised his pistol as he drew back the hammer, swinging it to the side and firing wildly without aiming. They all made a mad dash for safety and out of reach of the Shoshone arrows, firing blindly over their shoulders. Now they saw he was so brave because he wasn't alone.

"Oh God," Howey huffed while others cursed and prayed. Two men lay behind them with arrows poking from their chests. The gang knew what would happen to their dying friends after they fled, but they had no choice.

Howie felt like Indians surrounded them, yet he didn't know exactly where they were. After the barrage of arrows, they all turned and frantically ran for their lives. Now, it was clear to everyone that the Indians were after their guns.

They all knew that Garrott Sneed was hard-shelled and mean, but they also knew that when the going got rough, he didn't flinch. He faced the danger head-on. At least with everybody but the Indians, who they all seemed to fear. Of course, most of the outlaws came from Comanche country, where everybody feared the most ruthless tribe of the Great Plains.

Levi Johnson

Most of this part of the country was composed of rolling hills. The teamsters struggled to rein their horses down a long grade, using their foot brakes to ease down the incline. The bone-dry dust added a thickness to the air as dusk approached.

As the sun neared the western horizon, the glaring ball made them pull their hats lower, shadowing their eyes. It was almost time to stop for the night again. Their horses were covered in sweat, and their lungs sounded like billows. The wagons were ready to circle up. The mountain men rode out into the darkness to look for a safe place to spend the night and keep watch on their surroundings. They wanted their presence to remain unknown to the outlaws until the last moment.

The teamsters expertly swung the wagons into a tight, square configuration, then unhitched the horses before dragging the wagons' tongues to the plank tail-gates. The space left was only wide enough for a man to squeeze through. When they went out to do their business, they went in twos, one man to do his business and the other to stand guard. At this point in the game, nobody was taking any chances. They were on the last stretch of the trail to Fort Boise. The closer they got to the end, the farther away it seemed.

In the old days, after making their delivery, the teamsters would have reloaded the wagons to the brims again with valuable beaver pelts and exotic furs. This time, when they were done, they would return with smelly buffalo skins. So many buffalo hunters were coming west that the prices plummeted due to the large volume. Smelly, bloody hides meant they would have to fight off the vultures, and it would take weeks for the smell of dead buffalo skins to fade from their persons.

Sweat rolled off Captain Forrester's brow like he had a fever, but Levi knew better. It dripped into his eyes, making him blink repeatedly. Then he had another look through his spyglass under the twilight of countless blinking stars. Despite the night, the wind was warm, at times even hot. They could hear it whistling through the prairie grass. As he traced the telescope across the distance, he saw no signs of trouble even though they knew it was there.

Levi watched the world turn from a distance, his eyes half-closed in the glaring moonlight. He leaned back onto his saddle with his boots near the small fire. From the arroyo they were hiding in, the flames were only visible from directly above, and at night, the smoke was no more than a sliver of black. It looked like another shadow. All three men were deep in thought. From the tracks they had seen, they knew that a Shoshone war party was also tracking the thieves and maybe even the cargo train. A game of cat and mouse loomed. Time would tell who caught who first.

The marshal's dark mustache curled around the sides of his mouth and down, tangling in his beard, contrasting with the clean-shaven cheeks of the captain. The flames reflected in his dark eyes. He had already gone to that violent place that some embraced before a dangerous mission. Walker's face bore the battle scars of decades as a lawman. He was a no-nonsense type who did what he felt he had to do to keep the innocent population safe, or at least try.

Levi watched Will, his best friend, closely. He remembered their years riding together, and he could see it in his mind's eye. He imagined Captain Forrester returning from the Indian Wars, having lost an arm. He knew that he would never return home after all that had happened. He also knew that Will would somehow always feel the scorn of his prosperous family if he did return. Somehow, the captain thought he dishonored his family's military tradition, but that was far from the truth.

When he ran away with Levi to the Rendezvous and the Rocky Mountains, it was his way of proving to himself, and eventually to others, that he was just as much a man without his arm as he was with it. In the end, Beaver felt that he had done more running than proving. Just the fact that he ignored the loss meant that the pain was still buried deep inside. Will wasn't a man to express his feelings, even if it was with Beaver. Still, he knew the bitterness continued to simmer somewhere buried in his soul.

The captain drank some of the corn liquor, then fiddled with his tin cup, rolling it between two fingers of his only hand. His eyes lifted, and Levi filled his cup again and nodded like he knew exactly what Will was thinking. They had been riding as a team for six years and had spent most of that time together. Most times, they traveled alone through the wilderness, putting themselves in harm's way and doing whatever they had to do to survive.

"I guess a man without all his parts can use a stiff drink of whiskey once in a while," the captain whispered, with a barely perceptible nod. "Do you believe it's held me back, Beaver?"

Levi couldn't believe he asked the question, but there it was. Nobody replied. The marshal stared at the fire like he was a million miles away. If he noticed what Will had said was anybody's guess. Little did they know he had heard every word, but he kept his silence. Such things deserved some respect, and Will lost his arm a long time before the marshal joined up with Rusty Steel's team. He kept his opinion to himself. He had enough skeletons in *his* closet as it was.

"Don't talk foolishness. After all this time, why are you bringing up the missing arm? You've never mentioned it before today. Even right after it happened, you refused to talk about it. It was as if you were ignoring it, hoping it might go away. How's that workin' out for ya, Will? Don't you think you've proven your point, and then some? You have Joseph and me, along with our family and friends, not to mention those in the Crow stronghold who respect you. You have proved to us many times that you are just as much a man as any other and more so than most. What else do you believe you have to do to make it right?

"I think you're more of a man without it than you were with it. You're always the first to volunteer, and you never shy from a skirmish, and we've seen plenty—

especially against the Comanche in the territories, and the Blackfeet back on Bear Tooth Mountain."

Will punched the empty shell casings out of his pistols, replacing them with new bullets. He nodded, then he slipped his Colt Walkers back into his holsters. At times like this, he slept with his guns on and his rifle by his side. This was no time to take chances. Marshal Walker and Levi did the same. Joseph lay with his rifle wrapped in his arms like a lover, cuddling his cheek into the thirty-inch barrel. He knew it would be his lifeline if things turned south.

AS USUAL, they took turns at guard duty, each working three-hour shifts. It provided the horses and the men with enough rest to endure another day racing across the Oregon Trail at neck-breaking speeds, stopping only to water the horses so they didn't collapse or die.

Everyone was near exhaustion by the end of the day and was soon nodding off. In minutes, Levi heard the marshal begin to snore. His barrel chest rose with each breath. Soon it would be his turn to keep watch, so he got as much sleep as possible. A silence surrounded them, broken only by the occasional stirring horse as it blew and shifted its hooves.

The moon claimed it was three o'clock. Levi stretched his neck and gulped cool mountain air. He insisted that he take the last watch. Inside, he had a bad feeling, but he couldn't put a finger on why. It wasn't like him to be on edge, even in similar situations. Nor was it like him to worry. When he turned his head, he thought he saw a shadow shift through the dark. He knew no

White man could move like with such stealth. He was sure it wasn't one of the outlaws. Of course, the Shoshone would have their spies out there, too.

It made his watch more critical. He circled the perimeter of the camp for three hours, making sure nobody penetrated their ring of safety.

When he returned to the campsite, Will was already making breakfast. He saw the marshal with a shotgun in his hands and his holstered pistols at his sides. They were already tooled up to go to work.

The frontiersmen from Bear Tooth Mountain made camp at a safe distance from the cargo wagons but close enough to detect anyone who might be snooping. If one or two gang members took a chance to sneak up to the circled wagons, they would be unaware of the three mountain men.

Levi and the others had no idea that a Shoshone war party was whittling down the gang's numbers. They knew the marshal shot and killed two. Then they killed the four that were sent to spy on them.

They saw the sliver of red in the blackness to the east and knew it would soon be daylight, giving them a sense of urgency. Everybody seemed to have the same thing in mind. Armies didn't run on empty stomachs.

"Well, don't just sit there like you're expecting me to serve ya, Levi," Marshal Walker growled. "Grab a coffee and scoop up some of that bacon and eggs. At least we could get some good supplies before he left Fort Hall. We're eating well, even if it isn't Angus's cooking. Soon, it'll be time to get this show on the road. Those bull-whackers will have the wagons ready to go any minute now. We've got to be ready to leave at a moment's notice."

AFTER BREAKFAST, they saddled up and started to ride toward the cargo wagons. They knew they didn't have to worry about an ambush when they had the cover of the circled wagons to shoot from. With eight rifles, they could hold off a small army if they picked a spot with little cover three hundred sixty degrees around. It was an impossible position to approach ruthless White men or Indians alike, especially with so many long guns in their defense.

The camp of the mountain men was behind a cluster of boulders so they could keep watch on the wagons. Levi sniffed the air for suspicious scents and used his keen hearing as a radar. He had been alerted since he heard the rustling bushes earlier. He discounted it to the never-ending wind.

Levi stared at his friends, his thumbs hooked in his gun belt. "The marshal's right. We'd best be on our way. Those bullwhackers don't look like the types that wait for much of anything."

Pounding wood, iron, and hammering hooves came racing toward them. It looked like Rooster wanted to get an early start. He only knew one way to travel—full speed ahead.

Levi stepped out from behind a boulder and raised his hand to slow down Rooster, but the driver didn't immediately attempt to stop. Suddenly, though, he was up and using his weight to pull back on the reins and apply the front wheel brakes. The bullwhacker wove the reins through his fingers as his boot continued to push on the lever. The mountain men wheeled their horses to the lead wagon where Rooster and Buster waited.

"What is it you want?" Buster said. "We don't have time to linger."

"Come on, swing your gear up here," Rooster said. "Tie your pack horse to the drag wagon. That way, you won't have to worry about the horse's lead when you need to use your guns, heaven forbid. Let's hope we don't have to fight our way across the trail. We're gonna be movin' mighty fast. You men can ride atop those cargo boxes in the back. How do you boys wanna do this? I'm all ears."

"We'll fight best from horseback," Captain Forrester said. "You already have shotgun guards with scatter-guns, but we'll be using rifles and revolvers. I can shoot better from a horse than a bouncing wagon."

The horses stirred impatiently as their hooves kicked up dust. Then, just as suddenly as they stopped, the teamsters cracked their whips and were on their way again. They tried to squint through the darkness as they returned to the Oregon Trail. Long strides took the mountain men to their waiting horses. The marshal had them saddled up and ready to go. When there was a job to be done, Joseph was a bundle of nerves unless he was on the trail of whoever he was chasing.

In seconds, the horses found their pace, and the wagons sped up. When the trail smoothed out, the drivers pushed the teams harder, as the captain and Levi rode alongside the lead wagon at a gallop. Marshal Walker rode drag, eating dust.

Levi was lean and tall, deeply tanned from living and working outside his entire life. His Sharps rifle lay across his lap as he forced his eyes to penetrate the hazy light of a new, fresh dawn. He looked down at the rutted trail below that went curving out of sight and over rolling hills. Like the captain, a brace of heavy Colt Walkers, in cross-draw holsters, hung from his waist.

When they saw vultures in the distance, they wheeled their horses and veered away from the racing wagons. The buzzards made lazy circles in the sky, then folded their wings and dove. As they neared food, they opened their seven-foot wings and floated to the ground, landing at a run. Soon, their yellow beaks were pecking at the dead White men as crows lined the tree branches, waiting for their turn.

The mountain men backed their horses down to a trot as they neared the carnage. Their rifles pointed up with their stocks resting on their thighs, ready to drop them and fire at the slightest sign of danger. The bodies were as stiff as boards and had been dead for a while. Still, they advanced with caution. Levi and the captain slid out of their saddles to the ground. Forrester walked up and nudged each one with the toe of his boot as the captain gave them cover. After a thorough inspection, they deduced what had happened.

The marshal gripped his hands over the other, leaning on the saddle horn as he impatiently waited. He pushed his hat back from his forehead, easing the hot tightness of the headband. A wave of uncertainty clouded Joseph's face. His voice got louder as his raw-boned face tightened. "Check these fellas out and let's get out of here. We came here to stop the wagon train robbers and not fight with the local tribes."

"Well, we know they were Indians by the red, bare skulls of the victims," Levi said as he watched the captain push his boot through the cold fire and shook his head. "They've been here for a spell, so the gang had plenty of time to escape. You can see the tracks heading for those bushes."

"It looks like the Shoshone surprised them in their night camp, and they managed to kill two. You can see where they busted through those bushes. They must have been scared. Hiding inside this stand of trees would usually be a good move, but this time it gave the Indians cover, and it looks like they won the day." Captain Forrester's blond mustache hid his upper lip. He unconsciously brushed it with his knuckles, then twisted the ends. His sky-blue eyes flashed all around with his revolver leveled, ready to fire.

"They picked a stand of trees that were too close together," Levi assumed. "That was their first mistake. It allowed the Shoshone to sneak up on them in numbers. Those are arrows broken off in their chests, or what's left of 'em. Then came their second mistake. Had they stood and fought, they would have easily turned the tide, but the hostiles caught them off guard, and they panicked and ran. At least now we know some of them are ill-prepared. Not all of them are hard asses. I reckon the gang leader has had to hire new strays to keep enough gunhands to pull this off. The ones that aren't from the gang might not be so willing to die like the fellas who've been ridin' together for years."

With the glaring light in their eyes, they couldn't see the man's features, but they could make out the silhouettes of revolvers and rifles.

Out of nowhere, they spotted a lone rider moving toward their spot.

"Quick, over to the other side of the trees for cover," Levi whispered. "It looks like one of 'em has come back for something. I must admit the man has balls to walk around here alone."

"You don't have to have balls if you're mud-stupid," Marshal Walker spat. "Most outlaws I've run into don't have the brains God gave an ant. That's why they always end up dead and in a pine coffin. That is, if they're lucky."

The three carefully watched as the solitary man walked right up to the dead men. He had a careful look around and then unstrapped a shovel and began to dig.

Levi looked at Will and whispered, "Why would he risk comin' back to bury the dead?"

"Maybe it's his brother or somethin'."

Levi could hear the man's hard breathing. He had no idea they were watching from no more than five yards away. Beaver's teeth shone white in the morning's dim light when he smiled. The captain shook his head at the stranger's stupidity.

Suddenly, the marshal jumped the gun. Hell, he didn't even tell Levi and Will what he planned to do. He slipped the thong off the revolver's hammer and wrapped his fingers around the walnut grip as he moved toward the target. Joseph's pistols hung in his fists at his sides.

The foolish outlaw looked down the muzzle of Marshal Walker's gun and stopped in his tracks. It was dark like the owner's soul. A broad grin creased his sun-scarred face. He was here to stomp out evil.

The granite-faced outlaw stared stonily at the lawmen, but he knew it was too late. He had been caught at his own game. He was sent to spy on the circled wagons to get a final headcount. When he got close to the scene of the Indian attack, he felt he had to bury his cousin despite the danger. Little did he know somebody was spying on him. Maybe someone was even spying on them all.

Marshal Walker walked right up to the outlaw and fired. The man's boot exploded and gushed red as the intruder grabbed his foot and screamed like a woman. The intruder didn't even have time to draw.

The gang member jumped around like a wounded bullfrog, screaming and hopping on one foot.

"Why'd you shoot my foot off? Now, how am I gonna walk?"

"Where you're going, you won't need your feet," Marshal Walker said, as suddenly as death.

The robber let breath pass his lips in a long sigh. He raised his hands into the air as he stood on one leg and said, "All right, I give up. Don't shoot me again, mister. How'd you get so close to me without me knowin', anyway?"

The pain in his voice was there, but so was the rebellious streak of a hardcore outlaw. Marshal Walker had met the type many times in the past, when he worked out of Folsom Prison, where they housed the worst criminals. It was risky business traveling with an outlaw or two for several days. The lawman had to keep sharp to remain alive. Often, the best option was to shoot the men where they caught them or hang them from the nearest tree.

Levi and Will looked the prisoner over with eye-squinting sternness. "Well, look who dragged a new dog into camp. Where'd ya catch this one, Joseph? Don't you think you should have waited for us?"

"He was snoopin' around the wagons. I have no doubt he is a spy. Then he came back here to check on his dead friends. I reckon they think that we're stupid. Is that what you think, fool?" Joseph roared.

"You don't have to let the whole world know we're out here keeping guard, Joseph," Captain Forrester said. "No need to shout. You never know, he might have some friends out there watching us right now."

"I'd have seen if he came with backup," Levi said. "The only prints around are his."

"You're either mighty brave or too damned stupid to know better. Then again, most outlaws I've jailed or hung weren't miracles of modern science," Marshal Walker growled. "Be that as it may, you're mine now. We can do this the easy way or the hard way. Please tell me you're going to pick the hard way. Yep, I reckon that'd make me happy."

"Why don't you kiss my ass, you motherless dog. Go ahead and shoot me in the other foot. Do I look like the man who's gonna talk to the law? I'm an outlaw first and foremost and would never rat out my friends."

When the heavy-caliber bullet hit, he worked his mouth into a scream, but all that came out was a moan. Before the pain came, he stared at the man who shot him and spat. Blood spewed across his shirt. His face was a mix of puzzlement and surprise. He apparently didn't think that Joseph was going to shoot. Obviously, he was wrong.

Violent conflicts were usually preceded by near silence, save for the dying. It didn't take the outlaw long to expire. The bullet hole in his chest made him wheeze as he struggled to breathe. The bold smile on his face disappeared over blood-covered lips, but defiance was still there. The man's attitude told the mountain men something they hadn't expected. At least some of the men after the cargo wagons were hardcore and determined. They weren't afraid to die for their cause. It was get-rich-quick or die-trying. Blood flowed from his chest as he wheezed his last breath.

Levi's voice was urgent when he said, "We'd better get back to the wagons. We don't want them to get too far out in front of us." Levi didn't even ask why the marshal shot the man. They would have had to hang him anyway. A bullet to the chest did the same thing. Drastic situations called for drastic measures, and this was no time for the faint of heart.

Running feet made muffled, scraping sounds as they moved over the dry land toward the mountain men. They thought another attack was imminent.

"This one is wearin' moccasins, so I doubt he'd be with the outlaw gang," Levi whispered, then sniffed the air. "I smell bear fat, so I reckon he's one of the Shoshone scouts. I think you made more noise than you should have, Joseph."

Flexing his index finger on the trigger of his rifle, Levi took in the slack. The safety clicked. He idly cuddled his cheek to the wooden stock, slipping his finger forward in the trigger guard. He peered down the scope and found his target. He recognized him as a Shoshone Indian right off. He took a breath and slipped his finger out of the trigger guard and laid it on the wood stock.

Beaver had no beef with the local Indians. They were trying to stop what every Native American was doing across the vast West. The outlaws were his enemies, but the Indians weren't. He and Marshal Walker had wives who were Crow after all.

Walker chewed on the end of a dead cheroot as his

sharp eyes grazed the distance. They galloped into a fast-falling gloom until the dimness clung close to the ground.

"I could have used a knife instead of my gun. I reckon my adrenaline got the best of me. Now, I know we've gotta get out of here."

Once they were a distance away, they pulled up to have a pow-wow.

"Well, by my count, they lost about nine men so far, including those killed by the Shoshone," Captain Forrester said. "And we still have forty hours to go. If we can whittle them down that much again, we can turn and take them head-on. There's no sense of us pussy-footing around when we could nip this in the bud before anybody on our side is killed. Then we can stop looking over our shoulders."

"Don't forget those Shoshone Indians are still tracking us all," Levi said. "I reckon they're after all those guns the outlaw gang have. We know they ain't interested enough in the cargo to risk their warriors' lives."

"If we leave them where they lay when we finally finish them off, maybe the hostiles will be satisfied with what they find," Levi said. "We don't need all that weight to weigh us down when we're ridin' fast."

"That's out of the question," Will said. "If the Indians get the guns, they'll use them on the overlanders, and we'll have a new and more serious problem to fix. We need to figure out how to finish off the outlaws, because we can't take them back to hang. It makes no sense and would be too dangerous, even if it were the right thing to do. We're not going by the book any longer, are we?"

"Sometimes goin' by the letter of the law doesn't work," the marshal replied. "When west of Leavenworth, you kind of have to figure out the law all by yourself and try to do the right thing, conditions permitting."

Then, he rode out. Riding drag left the wrinkles in his face and the folds in his clothing full of trail dust. It gave him a minute to get away and think about what he had done and what he still had to do.

Walker slouched in the saddle, one leg hooked over the saddle horn. When they caught up, he swung his boot back into the stirrup and nudged his stallion into a trot. His tongue slid over his cracked, dry lips from the endless wind and sun.

The mountain men yanked their reins to wheel their horses around sharply. They all tugged their rifles from their boots as they raced the same trail the wagons traveled. Suddenly, the captain raised his hand to halt their advance. Everyone pulled to a stop.

Levi cocked his ears to a sound that was still a whisper. As it became louder, he heard the familiar pitch to the clamor of cargo wagons. He saw the driver throw his boot at the brake lever, and the coach jackknifed to a stop again. The dust slowly began to settle.

They heard hooves pounding the packed, sunbaked dirt in the distance and knew that things were on track, but they all felt that it was going too smoothly and suspected they might be riding into a trap.

The Tornado Express wagons raced across the gravelly expanse at a gallop. When they turned the corner in the trial, they almost skidded sideways on the loose stones. They careened too close to the river until their horses got a foothold on solid ground. They wheeled their mounts toward safety along the dense timber-lined path.

All the mountain men were surprised at the speed at which they traveled. They were the most experienced bullwhackers they had seen. Of course, they suspected they were getting paid a pretty penny to get the last of the cargo to Fort Boise.

Rusty Steel

When the present members of the compound awoke the following morning, they found Potak sitting in the middle of the yard with a blanket over his head. From what they could see, he didn't move a muscle. They wondered if he had been there all night. Money had to admit that, although he felt safe with the medicine man and even admired him, he was the strangest man he had ever known in his nine years on the planet.

Rusty pondered as he took a sip of coffee before he spoke. "Potak's the only man I've seen sleep sitting up just as well as lying down. He's got more surprises than a jack-in-the-box."

"Don't let 'em fool ya. He's probably listening to everything we say." Angus chuckled. "Don't bother him now. He might be in a witch doctor's trance."

Money's eyes grew bigger as the others laughed. They all knew that Potak did strange things because, as a Tonkawa shaman, he was supposed to. If he were like everybody else, he couldn't claim he was special. The

Crow Indians believed he was a gift from the Indian spirits. He was a gem that they never wanted to part with. In many respects, he was the one who kept the tribe in line, especially since Bar-chee's brother, Wanata, had become the new chief. Alone, there was no way he could lead his people. Too many of them had seen him take questionable actions, but the shaman was solid as a rock and always gave them good advice.

"Don't listen to them, son," Rusty said. "He might be strange, but there's nothing harmful about him. Potak likes to make a show of bein' a medicine man is all."

"Who's that?" Angus asked with a ring of suspicion in his words. He squinted his eyes through the dawn. He walked out onto the porch, pushing his fists into the small of his back, arching away the stiffness. Angus wasn't a young man anymore, but he could still hold his own with the best. Lately, he had noticed his aching bones more and more. He was the oldest member of the compound and one of the first to arrive way back when. Still, when it came to intruders, he was as sharp as a tack.

They watched the black speck gradually grow as it came nearer. Finally, the speck turned into a horse and rider. Whoever it was, it was riding down the north trail to the upper entrance to the brick-and-rail fence surrounding the cabins.

"Wanata?" He said it as though it were a dirty word. Rusty felt the anger rise hot on his face, but he forced himself to calm down. Now wasn't the time to make rash decisions with the chief of the Crow approaching. He talked softer, but there was still an edge to his voice. With him coming alone and unannounced, Rusty knew that something serious was wrong. He usually stormed into camp with an escort of painted warriors.

Rusty softly called out, "Don't move." His suspicious eyes narrowed. "Chief Wanata's the kind of fella that walks under a flock of birds and doesn't expect to get shit on his face? Be careful what you say now. We don't want to start something we can't finish without Levi, Will, and Joseph around."

Wanata, Bar-chee's brother, had streaks of ochre paint down his face from top to bottom, making him blend in with the foliage.

Rusty looked at him like he was a dead tree: completely free of emotion. A knot tightened Rusty's mouth. Still, he forced a smile that didn't reach his eyes and hid his loathing for the man.

The brash unfriendliness of Wanata's voice turned cordially polite. "May I enter your compound?"

"I don't see why not," Rusty said. "You've never asked before. Your sister lives here, so you have every right in the world."

Rusty knew the chief would take his words as a challenge, even though they were technically living on Crow land. But the agreement to stay stretched back to the old chief whom many of the tribe still revered.

Suddenly, Potak was on his feet as he twirled his blanket through the air, bringing all eyes on him. One horse screamed, and the others began pawing the ground and neighing shrilly and straining at their dancing ropes. Others tried to jump the corral fence. All the while, the lips of the Tonkawa shaman curled at the edges, and his eyes filled with mischief.

"What brings you to Rusty Steel's home, Wanata? I was just about to tell my friends the secrets of life.

That's what I've been doing under that blanket all night. Summoning up the spirits."

Potak made the chief uncomfortable. Despite his dislike for the shaman, he knew Potak was more powerful. He believed in the Indian spirits, and Wanata knew not to cross a man with such spiritual connections.

"I, er, we need Potak, Rusty, and Betty, the captain's wife," Wanata said, expressionless. "My new wife suffers from fever, and I am afraid that she will die and lose our child. Dahteste, will you come and help me manage tribal affairs so I can spend time with my new family? I am afraid she is dying and will take my first son with her. You are still my head war chief after all."

Chief Wanata said it with such solemnity that most of them didn't doubt a word. The Crow chief was a tall, narrow-hipped man with large hands and broad shoulders.

Potak pointed a crooked, accusing finger at the stronghold leader. "You've brought this on yourself with your vain ways. I told you many times, the spirits never forget. Now you may be called on to pay the price."

"Are you saying you won't come with me?" Wanata huffed. He was so shocked he had to catch his breath.

The medicine man stared down his long nose, his skin was like old leather, and his eyes were sunken in their sockets. He wore his hair braided in many trances like snakes growing from his head. The tall Tonkawa Indian wore a studded, cured-hide vest and carried a perpetual pipe in his hand. White feathers hung from drooping earlobes. A heavy-caliber pistol was shoved in a leather belt, and a bow and arrows were strapped across his back. He was a shaman but, like most Tonkawa, knew how to fight, too.

The medicine man's square-jawed face looked as though it was chiseled from granite. He wasn't only powerful, he had a certain air of mystical superiority in his presence. He wasn't allowed to roam the lands of all of the Indian Nations unchallenged for no reason. Potak spoke many tribal languages, acted as an intermediary, and counseled many chiefs, including the recently deceased Chief Hachta.

Betty felt the war drums beating in his chest as her guts turned to ice water. Her back went rigid. "Why do you ask for me and not one of the others?" she asked. "Your sister, your war chief, or even Pine Needle, Angus's wife, are better choices."

"I have heard that sometimes the White man's medicine is better than Indian medicine," Wanata turned his head and said, "I mean no offense, Potak, but I want to give her every chance I can. Maybe it would be best if you all came to stay in the stronghold for a few days, until my wife's fever breaks. I guarantee your safety and promise you will be treated as our special guests."

"Livin' in the wilderness is a lot riskier than growin' corn in Oregon, as I once planned," Betty said. "All I can say is I'll do the best I can with what I've learned over our travels. I've birthed a child or two and have had a hand in several more. Maybe my experience will help a little. Of course, I'll do whatever I can to save the poor woman and child." Betty surprised herself when she said it.

Silvia wrapped her arms around Rusty like she would never let go. He held her back by the arms and looked her up and down to make sure she was all right. Then, he embraced her. She worried that if he rode off with the wicked chief, she would never see her husband again. Despite her months at the compound, Rusty's wife was still leery of certain Indians, and Wanata was at the top of her list. The things he had done in the past made her distrust him entirely. She couldn't believe what she was hearing after all the hardship Wanata had initiated to make life difficult in their mountain home.

For Rusty, it wasn't Silvia's pretty face, flowing black hair, and well-formed figure that made her so beautiful. There was something in her voice and the way she looked at him like he was the only other person in the whole world that won his heart. He didn't want to leave her any more than she did, but when duty called, he had to respond in kind.

Rusty was the blood brother of the late Chief Hachata and had always been considered an honored member of the Crow stronghold, despite the feelings of the new chief. Wanata was jealous of Rusty's reputation and refused to accept him for the man he was.

All the while, Wanata's sister, Marshal Jospeh Walker's wife, looked on like she wasn't even there. It was clear that her brother had asked her to come, too, but she was not his first choice. Sure, he had defended her in the past as any brother would. She knew that he had never had deep feelings for her, or their father and mother. He had always seemed to be an empty shell until he decided he would one day wear the Crow chief headdress of the biggest native strongholds. In the eyes of others, he was conniving, hateful, and untrustworthy.

"Who's going to take care of Money?" Bar-chee asked.

"Wanata, if you touch that boy, I'll knock you into next week," Rusty growled like a rabid dog, surprising everyone, including himself.

"My role is to stay and take care of my adopted son and your nephew. You have never needed me before. Why now? I have my job to do here, and you have yours, brother. Our worlds have changed." Everything was hazy as though Bar-chee's thoughts covered her eyes with a blindfold, but she refused to leave the side of her newfound child.

Knocked off balance, the chief hesitated.

"Do what you want with your wasted life," Wanata snapped. Then, he caught himself and softened his tongue. "Take care of your boy, and I will try to take care of mine. Maybe one day our sons will play together as we did as small children. Perhaps, deep down inside, I'm not the man you think I am. Maybe having a wife and, hopefully, a son has changed me."

Potak pulled a carrot from the pack mule, popped it into his mouth, and passed another one to Money.

"I agree, I think it is better if we *all* go. Angus can stay with his wife, Pine Needle, in their wigwam. Dahteste has her war chief's teepee. We have plenty of space, so you can all sleep in the shelter. There is room for you and your wife, too, Rusty Steel."

The chief smiled, but it was clear it was forced. Wanata knew if he wanted the help of the White man's medicine, he would have to be the perfect host.

Despite Bar-chee's dark Indian skin, she was pale and glistening with concern, both for Money and her brother. He was as unpredictable as the weather on Bear Tooth Mountain. The color came up over Bar-chee's face like she had been slapped. She kept her mouth shut tight, though. Wanata was grinning and shaking his head.

"Come, sister. I won't let anything happen to your son. He, like your husband, is one of us now, too."

Bar-chee looked like a frightened animal cowering at the end of a boxed-in canyon with nowhere to escape. It was clear how much she really feared her brother, she always had. She wrapped her arms around Money so tight he could hardly breathe. She shuddered. Money could feel it run through their bodies. Despite the kindness in her brother's eyes, Bar-chee's were icy and cold.

Rusty hid his emotions. He covered them with a mask of good-natured innocence. "Well, if we're needed, we must go. It's not like us to refuse a cry for help regardless of who's asking."

The Tonkawa Indian stepped around the side of the mule, careful not to get behind her, and tightened the cinch. He didn't say another word until they were on their horses, climbing the trail for the half-day ride up to the Crow stronghold.

Money was surprised when a low-hanging limb unseated him and knocked him off his horse. He sat on the ground, puzzled as he pushed through the pain. His face and neck reddened from shame. All the others began to laugh, which made it all the more embarrassing. Potak began to laugh at himself, too. He rubbed his head where a knot the size of a small egg was rising, making him flinch. His smile instantly returned. Money didn't know it, but he was learning more than he knew from the medicine man.

That afternoon, a blue haze clung over the mountain as the contingent climbed higher toward the Crow village. Per Wanata's invitation, everyone embarked on the six-hour journey to the stronghold.

Rusty struggled to mask his frustration and

contempt. He knew he had to do the right thing, but that didn't mean that he trusted Wanata any more than he did before. The chief had tried to kill him and his friends. Wanata was the Crow chief, and nothing could change that fact. So, they had to learn to live with it. For Rusty, the new chief would have to earn his respect, it was not given easily.

"Many men wiser than you say worrying is for fools and horses. It's the opposite of faith. So, how can you be a godly man if you worry all day?" Betty asked Rusty. "Worryin' is like you believe in a problem that might never come." She believed what she said, but the happy act she was putting on was just for show. She, like the others, knew Wanata's true nature and was shaken to her core that he had personally asked for help. She and most of her friends suspected there was something more to the emergency. Then again, love and children did change some men in unexpected ways.

"I've never much thought about the risk," Angus said. Despite his age, he hardly knew what fear was. "In my years as a mountain man, I've found it is unhealthy to worry, just like you, Betty."

Half an hour later, it began to rain. Of course, the mountain men were used to the constantly changing weather of the Rocky Mountains. It was like it had a microclimate of its own. Soon, mud puddles cover the trail, making it slippery. The clouds hung so low they felt like they were just above their heads. They continued to climb, ignoring the wet weather and cooling temperature.

Wanata and Rusty Steel, road lead, and the rest of the clan followed with Virgil Lovejoy taking up the rear. The Black buffalo hunter was a crack shot despite his deeply religious ways, and, if push came to shove, they knew he had their backs.

The mountain men knew Crow spies lurked along the trail. Even though they couldn't see them, they knew that they were there and in the encampment. The cloud cover dimmed the sun as the end of the day neared. Just before it got too dark to see, they arrived at their destination.

As soon as they arrived at the camp, all but Potak and Betty were led to the chief's lodge. Even Dahteste and Angus had an escort, which raised some suspicion, as they had been there for years. Maybe there was more going on than met the eye.

THE RAIN finally wore itself out, turning into a warmer drizzle. A break in the clouds brought the sun, which came as it disappeared over the horizon like a big red rubber ball. The cloud cover closed in around them again, and everything outside of the circles of light was pitch dark. They had a moonless night, so they all stayed gathered within the vicinity of the chief's spacious lodge.

Flames from a central fire flickered and licked the air as cinders swirled skyward, only to disappear into the night. Smaller campfires were scattered among more than one hundred teepees. When Chief Hachta was in charge, the population of the stronghold was larger. Under Wanata, the village had dwindled in size and numbers.

Rusty sat cross-legged and tented his fingers before his mouth, deep in thought. If it weren't for the color of his skin, he almost looked like an Indian with his buckskin clothing. The fire's flame made shadows dance on his aging face, but he was still as tough as railroad nails.

When Rusty pulled off his buckskin shirt and laid it beside the fire to dry, several terrible scars were revealed. Despite his age, muscles rippled across his arms and chest.

"Where did you get those scars from, Rusty?" Money asked. Like many young people, he didn't know it was rude to ask.

Rusty locked eyes with the young mountain man apprentice, somewhat shocked. He blinked his eyes, traced his fingers along a long scar over his heart, and said, "That one's from the grizzly bear that belonged to these here claws." He rattled the necklace around his neck. "And the puffy one across my belly I got when I was saving Chief Hachta, my blood brother and the old leader of this Crow camp. He and I were best friends. He was the one who let us live up here on Bear Tooth Mountain. Were it up to the current chief, I doubt he'd have let us stay, and maybe, to some degree, rightly so. Does that answer all your questions, young man? You sure are the inquisitive one, ain't ya?"

"I figure every man will have an arch enemy in his lifetime," Rusty mumbled. "After Chief Hachta died, I reckon mine is Wanata. He was always jealous of how close I was to the chief. I figure it irks him still today. Even though I find him insufferable, I believe we've gotta find a way to live together in peace. Maybe he'll change if we somehow save his wife and child."

"Wanata has a short memory, if I remember right," Angus grumbled. "We've done the stronghold favors in the past. As soon as they were done, he forgot all about it."

"If you don't make your life purposeful, you risk declining into vice and violence," Rusty said as he stared into the boy's eyes. "How's that lump on your head, son? I must say, you took it like a man." A grin crept onto his face.

"Like a man, huh?" Angus chuckled. "Why, you still have to learn what a man is, Money."

ANGUS HAD MADE supper for the members of the compound, and they all slept soundly on full bellies. Only Rusty lay awake late into the night, watching the smoke from the fire rise up and out of the teepee's vent.

For Money, everything in the Crow stronghold was exciting and beyond anything he imagined. It made him nervous because scores of questions riddled his brain.

"Here, put a dash of this in your coffee," Angus said as he uncorked the whiskey jug and poured a dash into the boy's coffee. When Money took a sip, he spat the bitter brew and nervously wiped his chin with the heel of his hand.

Late that night, Silvia twirled the gray hair on Rusty's chest as they lay and whispered secrets to each other. The small fire in the middle of the teepee and thick buffalo blankets were enough to keep them warm all night when the temperatures dropped. It was that time of year.

Just before drifting off to sleep, their blood chilled when light scratching was heard at the teepee's flap. After a day of tension, everybody was jumpy. Rusty and

Angus wrapped their fingers around the walnut grips of their Colt Walker single-action revolvers.

When they saw Potak poke his head inside, they all breathed a deep sigh of relief.

"Rusty Steel, come with me," he ordered and vanished into the dark.

"What in the world is he up to now?" Rusty grumbled. "If he's not careful, he's gonna get us into a shit storm that we'd best avoid."

"Potak knows what he's doing," Angus whispered. "I reckon he had more to do with runnin' the stronghold than Wanata does. I know these Crow people would do anything for the old Tonkawa."

Rusty swore under his breath as he, too, disappeared out the teepee flap.

He ran behind the shaman, half-crouched, even though there was no moon and he could hardly see. He was moving with little more than his instincts to guide him and the faint sound of the medicine man's feet. He stopped for a moment, pressed his back against a tree, and held his breath, listening. His heart pounded. For a moment, he lost sight of Potak. He was better than Rusty at shifting through the shadows and the hard places to see. Steel was the finest of the mountain, save one.

At the camp's boundary, they walked into the dark and made no more noise than a couple of birds. After ten minutes, they stopped. Potak put his finger to his lips while locking eyes with Rusty. The medicine man tilted his head and listened. The mountain man mentor heard it too. It sounded like muffled crying. Potak signaled for Rusty to close his eyes to adjust to the pitch dark. When they opened their eyes, Wanata was sitting on the ground with his shoulders slumped. The chief shuttered and mourned the future of his wife and son.

They exchanged looks. Potak clearly saw the surprise in Rusty's face. The shaman nodded his head and then was gone as Rusty struggled to keep up. They had seen a deep change in the tribe's chief. It appeared, despite their beliefs, he did have a heart.

First Strike

Wagon wheels rolled so fast they appeared to go in reverse. Vast clouds of dust rose fifty feet into the sky behind the four racing wagons. There was no way for them to hide. All they could do was push the six-horse teams to their limits and keep a sharp eye out for opportunity for ambush.

Since the outlaws knew their presence was known to the Tornado outfit and a Shoshone war party, they were being careful, too. As they watched the train from afar, they hoped the horses would collapse under the whips of the bullwhackers, making their job easier.

Men braced themselves as they stood in the wagons with bullwhips cracking overhead, and men shouting until they were hoarse. Flat reins slapped the horses' backs. Every time a whip cracked above their heads, the teams mustered another burst of energy. The only thing they had in mind was successfully getting their cargo to its destination and getting paid. From then on, it would be easy.

After hours of the nonstop charge toward Fort Boise,

they pulled to a stop at a small spring. The horses calmed, drinking deeply from the water and grazing on tufts of green grass. They were given limited food, just enough to keep them going, but not enough to make them lethargic or sick. The animals could withstand ten times the exertion of a normal horse.

It was Levi, the captain, and Marshal Walker's job to hold any threat at bay by force, if needed. They knew they couldn't outrun or outgun the enemy. They would have to be clever to keep them from robbing and killing everyone attached to the Tornado Express Company.

Nobody had any idea of what awaited them, but they knew a storm was brewing and nothing would stop it. At some point, they were going to have a go at them, and they knew it wouldn't be at night. That would be too hard a nut to crack. They would hit them along the trail, striking from an ambush with deadly intent.

Sneed's men had no qualms about their plan. They would stop the wagon train at any cost and grab the valuable cargo without harming the horses. They would shoot all the witnesses so that no one could testify against them. Dead men couldn't testify. Whoever died on the desolate plains would be left behind, the dust of their remains blown away by the endless wind.

On the way to Fort Boise, they crossed a herd of scraggly, skinny longhorns, distant descendants of herds abandoned by the Spanish a hundred years earlier. They had adapted to the radical weather and had somehow survived. Only them and the Indians were rugged enough to live in such barren lands.

Will nodded and sat silent for a spell. He was a moody man. On this job, in particular, he seemed to be more so than usual. Levi could only imagine that he was still dwelling on the past. All this time, Levi thought it was just his strange ways. He believed the difference between them was what made them get along so well. Most men didn't take to the captain at first. Sometimes, they didn't get a chance because Will put their lights out.

"One thing that I can promise fellas like these. If you steal somethin' in our presence, and don't surrender, you die," Levi said. "You'd better ride drag and give the marshal a breather. I reckon he's eaten enough dust for now."

The captain stared at his old friend with keen interest. "So now you're telling me what to do? Who's the boss here? I thought it was equal rights. Ain't that right, Marshal?"

"Why not? You're always bossin' me around when we go on a job," Levi snickered. "I doubt you even realize it, do ya? I got used to it when I was in your charge. I reckon some things never change." Levi laughed so hard he had to hold his side.

The captain nodded, indicating he and Levi should ride away from Joseph to have a private word. It was something that they didn't want him to hear.

"We'll be right back, Joseph. The captain here has gotta tend to his personals. Unfortunately, he can't hold a gun and do both. I'll stand guard. If we're not back in a few minutes, send out the posse."

Levi's buckskin shirt, stained by sweat, covered his massive chest. Unruly hair hung from the shadow of the wide-brimmed hat, thick and glistening from the heat.

"What is it, Levi? You're concerned about what Marshal Walker and I might do, aren't you?" Will asked.

"I've seen him angry before. For some reason, this

job is different for him. It's like it's personal or something. Why would that be? Do you think he suspects who the robbers are?"

"Knowing Joseph like I do, I'd say that's close to the mark. It looks like his plan is to shoot the outlaws on sight. That's not murder in my book. You don't understand the way of a lawman or a military man. You grew up in a happy home in the isolated forests near the Ohio River. What do you know about how a soldier's mind works?

"Sometimes, Levi, you're just too kind for your own good. Every one of these men intends to do us harm. All we're doing is beating them to the punch. Only a fool would do otherwise. Plus, what are we going to do with them if we capture them all? There are too many to take back to one of the forts to stand trial. We'll have to hang them anyway. Right now, we don't have much time for such a luxury. Let the marshal and me do what we do best, and we might all survive."

When they moseyed back to where Joseph waited, he stared at them like he was anticipating an explanation. Will and Levi brushed it off. Will fiddled with the buttons on his britches to make it more believable.

The marshal hooked his thumbs behind his suspenders as he looked at his friends questioningly. He nodded and let it slide. Then, he said, "I doubt these outlaws will have a go at us before the end of the day. Not with those Shoshone warriors snoopin' around. And we know they won't take a chance to move at night after losing nine men. They're sittin' ducks in the dark with a bunch of Shoshone warriors, not to mention us. I doubt there are twenty of them left if the hostiles haven't whittled them down even more. I figure that's what the hostiles are up to. Pick 'em off one or two at a time, steal their guns, and swoop in for the kill. With all those weapons, they wreak havoc on us and, most likely, the settlers. I imagine they have a mighty big hate for those people right about now. This job gets more complicated with every step we take."

"But we have one advantage that they don't," Levi said. "They don't have these prototype rifles that Christian Sharps gave Rusty. What we need to do is catch them as they make their move, and we can pick them off fast with three of us shootin'. Maybe we can get enough of 'em to make a difference."

"These fellas ain't the quittin' kind," Marshal Walker said. "Those brown dusters give me a sneaky suspicion that I might know who they are. I can't quite put my finger on it yet. There's something about one set of tracks and the way they chose a place to camp. Let 'em make a mistake or two more, and I'll figure out who we're up against. One thing is for sure, they ain't from around here. They heard about these valuable cargo wagons from back East. I reckon they read that the British traders were leaving and figured the forts would be understaffed, which they are."

"Once those long-range rifles hit the market in a year or two, the local Indians won't have a chance," the captain said. "Up until now, we've only advanced to repeater revolvers with the Cold Pattersons. As soon as these quick-loading, bolt-action, long-range rifles come into play, the game plan will change. I've also heard about a small startup named Winchester Repeating Arms bunch is working on a repeating rifle with up to fifteen rounds in the tubular magazine and with another in the chamber. Can you imagine that? Sixteen rounds without reloading. I imagine it'll be years before they get that one figured out."

"I believe it'll be at least a decade or so before guns like that are available," Levi added and frowned. "When they do arrive, the Indian Wars will abruptly end, and I guarantee you it'll be a bloody finish. There's too much bad blood on both sides of the fence for any other result. I reckon that'll mean the end of our lives in the Rockies, too."

"Aren't we bright and chipper today? All we've still gotta figure out what our enemy is gonna do before they do it, or we're all toast," Will said.

NEAR SUNSET, they saw antelope bounding across the hillside. On a distant ridge, shadows raced beside a pack of wolves. As the sun set and a blanket of stars rolled out across the sky, offering only limited light, the mountain men broke off from the circled wagons and headed off into the darkness. Levi led the way more by instinct and smell than anything else. Neither Will nor Joseph doubted who was the best tracker.

When Levi raised his hand to stop, they all waited silently as he cocked his ear and listened for what the other couldn't hear. "Can't you smell them? Every tribe has a different smell, just like humans who smell of soap. I figure the Shoshone party ain't but a spit away from us. Let's go and see what we're up against. They won't expect White men to sneak up on them in the dark before the moon rises."

In the distance, several campfires blazed, surrounded by numerous Indian ponies. The black silhouettes of four-legged figures wandered calmly grazing around the camp.

"Now that we know where the warriors are, all we've got to do is find where the outlaws are camped. We've got to do it before dawn, so we can warn Rooster and his men and get ourselves into position," Levi whispered like a breath of air. He pulled a tuft of dry grass and let it drop, watching the direction of the wind. Then he raised his head and sniffed.

"I smell meat cooking and coffee too, but it's quite some distance away. If it weren't for the damned wind, I would have noticed it sooner. At least we're downwind, and the horses won't smell us until it's too late. Unless these Indians have taken a likin' to coffee just as much as White folks, but most can only afford chicory. Still, what I smell is definitely coffee. The Indians must have robbed a lone wagon or two that lost their way."

As they traced their telescopes across the distance, the closest cold campfire they saw held the remains of a dog on a stick. Despite all the overlanders suffering from low food supplies, the Shoshone Indians were feeling the same due to the decimation of their wild game across the vast western frontier. They had resorted to eating dogs and mules when they couldn't find wild game.

"By their tracks, it looks like the number of thieves has swelled somewhat," Levi whispered as he kneeled and studied the trampled ground. "I count about twenty warriors, too. They look to be hell-bent on gettin' those guns. So, what'll it be, Will? Are we gonna do what we're paid to do and escort the wagons or see those Indians don't get their hand on all those weapons?"

"First things first," Marshal Walker said. "If we can

get to the outlaws in time, the guns will be in our hands, and we can transport them on the Tornado Express cargo wagons and not worry about the Indian threat."

"You're puttin' a lot of faith in your formula, Joseph," Levi obliged.

"When you've got a better idea, Beaver, let me know."

Marshal Walker pushed his gun belt lower on his hip as he tightened the buckle. He was ready to go to work. In seconds, the only sound was the squeak of leather saddles and the soft clopping of the unshod hooves of their horses.

DAYLIGHT CAME SUDDENLY, as if unexpectedly. One moment it was pitch dark, and the next the sun came racing from the other side of the world, bathing everything in light. At the crack of dawn, the whips cracked, and the rumble of wagons resumed.

As they rode through the day, the mountain men spread out wide, keeping a sharp eye on the wagons' flanks. Marshal Walker was back on drag. Strangely enough, he insisted on it. He seemed convinced that if they were attacked, it would again be from the rear. Levi was convinced they would have prepared something more elaborate after their first failure. Then again, if they were geniuses, they wouldn't be outlaws.

As the day wore on, it was more and more evident that today wasn't going to be the day. Levi nudged his fourteen-hundred-pound gelding and broke into a sprint to catch Rooster in time to make camp in the barren stretch of land they were currently crossing.

Once the wagons were in a tight circle, their small fortress would be all but impossible to breach.

Rooster was whirling a long bullwhip over his head, making it pop like a small-caliber revolver. When he saw Levi out of the corner of his eye, he raised his hand above his head to warn the other that the lead wagon was going to break. If not, with all the dust, they could run into each other and have a pileup.

"What's up, Levi? Have ya seen somethin' we haven't?" Rooster asked.

"Get those wagons circled up quick," Levi said as he removed his hat and wiped the sweat from his brow with his sleeve. "I figure that the outlaws won't be far from us now, and the Shoshone are right behind them."

"Truthfully, I doubt the hostiles will have a go at us tonight," Rooster replied.

"Truth is a byproduct of a man's character. Honest men reveal their truths with every breath they take," Captain Forrester said. "Dishonest men distort the same. When we do catch them, Levi, listen to me and don't believe a word they say. It'll be best if we shoot them on sight. This time, that soft spot in you could cost us our lives."

"I doubt they will with those Indians waitin' out there for them," Marshal Walker said.

"We're gonna wait until the sun sets. Then, we'll ride the perimeter. If we can find out exactly where both of our enemies are, we might be able to get a step ahead of them. I figure that's all it'll take."

AS SOON AS it was dark, Joseph, Levi, and Will slipped away from the cargo train, staying as low as possible while they walked their horses. Once again, Levi led his friends into harm's way. It was up to his sense of smell, hearing, and instinct to find the men they sought: one group to avoid and the other to kill.

Soon, Beaver held out his hand, and they suddenly stopped and silently slid from their saddles with guns in their hands. They heard the trickle of water over rocks. Levi moved all around the watering hole with his nose inches from the ground. He stopped and picked up a dirt clod, breaking it open and smelling it. Then he dropped it to the ground and searched some more.

"Both the Shoshone and the outlaws have been here not two hours ago," Levi said. "The Indians are right on the tail of the robbers. I'll bet that gang doesn't know exactly where they are, but they know they're still bein' followed."

Marshal Walker closed his eyes and listened and sniffed the air, as Levi did. All he heard was the moaning wind and water, and he smelled his own sweat.

GARROTT SNEED SMILED, showing his tobacco-stained teeth. After squinting at the horizon for a moment, he spat a long stream of brown juice onto the ground. He pinched his nose and blew twin strings of snot into the dirt and wiped his fingers on his shirt. He fished his tongue around his mouth and spat out his chew. Brown juice dripped off his lip.

Sneed poked Howey in the chest, but when he didn't

stand down, he poked him again, harder. Howey slapped his hand away.

"Don't start getting aggressive with me now, boss. I'm the only one here that you can really count on if we get into a pinch. Remember, now, half these men are hired guns and are only faithful to a fistful of dollars. They might get the idea that it might be more profitable to bushwhack us. I'm your second set of eyes. There's no honesty among thieves, but you and I are friends, Garrott. That makes all the difference."

Sneed got up and saddled his horse without a word. The men followed suit. Their voices crackled with expectations. You could see the men's interest spark as the gang leader jumped up, grabbed his horse, and prepared to depart.

Then, as sudden as rain, Howey's guts turned to water, and he got a bad feeling. Both he and Garrot had said that they could buy a saloon in California and be set for life with the money from this heist. California promised an appetizing environment with mild weather and wild women. All they wanted were the ladies of the night, and a few men gathered around a table of cards. But what if they weren't successful? He rejected the thought of dying alone in the wilderness. He refused to allow fear to invade his very being.

"Maybe it's the Indians," Howey said under his breath.

They rode for two hours toward the position where they expected the Tornado Express wagons to be. They dropped down to a trot and then walked as they tilted their heads, listening for the sound of wagons.

Howey forgot his worry and couldn't hold back a snicker. "I can hear their horses from here. How about we sneak up on 'em now, take the cargo, and shoot whoever survives."

"That's a good way to get most of us killed," Sneed retorted. "I ain't sayin' that we couldn't do it, but we'd have to pay a mighty big price if we did. If we do it my way, we all might live to tell the story in our saloon in California. If we get shot all to hell, we won't be going anywhere. We'll be staying here for eternity.

"Wait here while I have a look around. I want to figure out where to make our final attack. We don't want any Indians snoopin' around when we're just about to get down to business."

"You should let me go and look for a place, Garrott," Howey said. "It's too risky for the leader to ride out there into the night. I'm more afraid of Indians than most of us, but I know what we need to do to get the job done. If something happens to you, the whole deal will go up in smoke. Nobody will get paid, especially you and me. I'm sneakier than you are, anyway, and I know exactly what you're lookin' for. You've been lecturin' me on it for weeks."

"No, that's not how it works around here," Sneed said. "Everybody's gotta carry their load, no matter who it is. I ain't plannin' to be gone long. So, keep quiet and don't make a fire. We don't want to be noticed."

The gang leader hadn't ridden five miles before he saw a shadow flash in the moonlight. He pulled up and waited. The rider was heading his way. He sidled his horse next to a boulder to hide. The Shoshone messenger ran at a trot and seemed determined to get wherever he was going. Sneed had other plans for him.

WHEN THE GANG leader returned to where the others waited, they were surprised he wasn't alone.

"I caught another one of these shit-birds snoopin' around out there in the dark," Sneed sneered as he pushed his captive and jammed his pistol barrel in the back. When he cocked the hammer, the click seemed loud in the night.

The Shoshone male wore life-like, painted, white, wooden false teeth. He must have made them himself. The rest of his face was painted yellow, white, and red. It all made him look fearsome.

"I might keep them teeth," Howey said. "Half of mine have already fallen out. They won't do him much good where he's going. Did you try to see if he speaks any English?"

"From what I can tell, not a word. Go ahead and give it a whirl," Sneed suggested.

Howey began questioning the warrior, but he just looked puzzled. It was obvious that he didn't understand a single word said.

"Nothin' I could understand, boss," Howey replied. "All that comes out of his mouth is that Indian gibberish."

Sneed surprised everyone by raising his pistol and shooting he warrior in the head. He dropped to the ground like a sack of potatoes. His lights went out before he hit dirt.

Gunfire repeatedly exploded as Sneed kept shooting until his revolver was empty. He continued to pull the trigger, but the hammer fell on spent rounds. It was no secret that Garrott hated Indians almost as much as Howey feared them. He hadn't even given him a fighting chance, but shot him dead where he stood.

Howy raised his open palms, trying to calm his angry boss. "Keep your cool, boss. Now, everybody around knows where we are. You shouldn't let your temper get the best of you. If we want the gold this cargo is gonna bring, we've gotta keep our wits about us." The smell of cordite hung heavily in the air as smoke rolled from the empty barrels.

"Clean up our campsite and store our gear. There's no sense in trying to make it look like we weren't here. I figure everybody from here to Hades knows we're behind the cargo wagons. I should have stabbed the damned Indian, but I lost my temper. It's time to get rich or go bust, boys. Make sure your weapons are loaded, primed, and in good working order. You don't want to go up against those shotgun guards and find your guns don't work. Mount up and let's get this show on the road. We've diddle-daddled around for long enough."

The outlaws didn't hold back. They knew exactly what part of the Oregon Trail the cargo wagon train would be on, so they set their spurs and began to close the distance. It was time to go to work and earn a living. Nobody thought about what might happen if they failed. All of them were doing the same. Counting the dollars they would earn in their heads.

When they got the wagon trains blazing campfire in sight, they veered off before they were seen to flank the wagons. If they could get far enough ahead of them, they could catch them in an ambush, and that would end the chase. Flames danced fifteen feet into the sky as cinders rose skyward only to burn out in the night.

They were close enough now to hear the snap, crackle, and pop. They listened to men's voices but couldn't make out what they were saying. The Toronto outfit never suspected they would be attacked at night. With two guns for each one of the teamsters, the outlaws were confident they could easily mow them down. The ambush was perfect, the time was right, and the outlaws were ready for action.

"Make sure you remember not to kill the horses. Without those teams, we won't be able to deliver the goods to the highest bidder. We'll send the whole lot of 'em to hell, though," Sneed ordered. "I want them dead to the last man. Maybe if we leave the Shoshone a few guns, they won't bother us anymore until we get to Fort Boise. Just enough to satisfy them, but not enough to turn on us."

"How are we gonna explain how we ended up with the cargo wagons?" Howey asked. "Everybody we run across is gonna ask."

"We'll blame it on the Indians and tell 'em we killed them to save the cargo, but we got there too late to save the teamsters. They were dead when we arrived. Whatever is left on the plains is our property. It's the finders-keepers law. The buyers won't be in a position to negotiate anyway. That's the beauty of the plan. They need the cargo too badly to make much fuss. Even if they suspect us, there will be no way to prove it. That's why it's important to make sure they're dead to the last man. All we've gotta do is shoot a few arrows into the bodies and the wagons to make it look real."

"After we get the money, where will we go, boss?" Howey whispered to the Sneed when he had a moment. "We ain't gonna stay with this hired trash, are we?"

Sneed gave his right-hand man an evil look that sent chills up Howey's spine. "Maybe none of them will survive. They might end up like the teamsters and bullwhackers. Then, you, me, and the boys from our gang can carry on across the Oregon Trail to California. I hear there's a new south pass that's shorter. The sooner we're out of Indian territory, the better. The more money we have will make life better for us. Let's wait and see who earns their living and who's shy of gunfire."

"By this time tomorrow, we'll be rich, Jessy Crow cackled and mimicked a Mexican jig while sitting in his saddle.

The adrenaline of the chase was already coursing through their bodies, making them grind their teeth and the horses chomp at their bits while stomping their hooves. The feeling was contagious, even for the animals. They all had bloodlust in their eyes and had decided it was time to strike, come hell or high water. It was far too late to change their minds and turn back now. It was a matter of do-or-die.

"You're right, boss. Those Indians wouldn't dare mess with us in the daylight," but Howey's voice didn't hold the confidence he had wanted. For a while, he was too afraid to open his mouth because his voice would give him away. His fear was so intense that he could smell it.

"Like I always say: you never know a town until you've spent time in its jail." Howey chuckled, trying to act brave when he wasn't. "Hopefully it won't be in Fort Boise."

"Only you would be so stupid as to say something like that," Sneed retorted.

"I should know." Howey laughed. "I've been locked up six times, mostly back near Folsom, where the lawmen are onery and shoot to kill. Way back then, the lawmen—what few there were—were as mean as snakes. Lucky, I'm smarter than your average outlaw. I busted out or bribed my way out all six times."

"That's enough!" Sneed said. His long face was as red as a beet, and his mouth was no more than a tight line. "You're makin' too much noise. Quiet, all of ya."

"That's right. The boss's gotta take care of little Howey, or he might get hurt. How about a round with me, big mouth? Then we see how well you talk when I knock the rest of your teeth out of your head," Parkins snapped.

Howey knew that Slim could lick him eight ways from breakfast with his bare fists, but he felt the anger rise in his throat, and he had to reply. "You might beat me in a punch-up, but you can't outdraw me with a revolver in your dreams. I'll shoot you dead before you make three steps. I'll be keeping your nasty comments in the back of my mind for the right moment. You'll never know when my bullet hits you, Slim. If I were you, I'd hold my tongue."

"I said that's enough, you two!" Sneed snapped. "We need every man we've got to capture those wagons. You lay a hand on Howey, Slim, and you'll be answering to me. You know damned well what you'll get. Now get back on your horse and let's catch those Tornado Express wagons. If you two wanna, have it out after we're done, you just let me know. One less man will make a better split for everyone."

"Have you thought about those three others we've seen about?" Jessy asked.

"I might have read about those three in one of those dime novels," said Danny Ramrod, one of Sneed's spies. "I think it was called Mountain Men of the Rockies. It said that one was an old marshal from Folsom in the Arizona territories."

"I wonder if that's the old law dog I ran into up north. How old did they say them boys were?" Howey asked.

"Two young fellas are in their twenties, and the other is middle-aged," as I recall. "The older one is a US Marshal."

"It's too late to worry about some broken-down marshal and a couple of pups. Buck up, boys, things are just about to get interesting," Howey said as Sneed walked away.

"Talk about old. Look at the way that son of bitch walks. The boss looks like he has a corncob up his ass," Slim whispered.

His words were not appreciated by Howie, who angrily countered, "You're not only stupid. You're crazy, too, Slim. You're lucky the boss didn't hear that, you stupid son-of-a-bitch."

"You loud-mouthed bastard," Slim retorted. "If you call me a sum'bitch again, I'm gonna knock all your damned teeth out, fool. While I'm at it, I might cut out your tongue."

"You might wanna be nicer, and less of a horse's ass before I stick my pistol up your ass and pull the trigger until it goes click," Howey threatened.

"Do you want some of this?" Slim asked as he dismounted and waved his fist before him. He was ready to trade fisticuffs. "You're not man enough to stand up and fight me fair and square without a weapon."

Slim Parkins was hell on wheels when it came to brawling, but he couldn't shoot his way out of a boxcar. They only had him around because he was good at blowing things up. Now he was running everybody's patience thin. He already ticked Sneed off, which wasn't a healthy move.

Suddenly, Sneed saw a flash of gunfire in the distance. "What the hell?" Sneed yelled.

As soon as he said it, a bullet zipped so close to his ear he felt the tiny disturbance it made in the air. Slim, standing directly behind Sneed, was struck and flew backward as if kicked by a mule. He landed five feet away with a hole as big as a fist in his chest. A gaping wound the size of a wash pan obliterated his back.

The bullet that struck Slim was made to shatter on impact. Each round was carefully designed and loaded by its expert owner.

The outlaws ran for cover. Sneed and Howey sought the protection of a large boulder. Garrott's second in command squinted into the dim light, shocked by the sudden attack. It was clear that he had been drinking. It was like he was looking through filmy eyes. He stood, planting his feet so he wouldn't sway with his hand wrapped around his revolver.

"Be careful where you point that pistol. If you do decide to use it, try not to hit one of us. What's wrong with you, man? Here it's time for action, and you're already too drunk to hit the broad side of a barn," Sneed chided and stared him down until Howie released his grip on the gun. "Just do as you're told and keep your head down until we figure out who's shootin' at us."

When Sneed realized a second shot was not coming, he stepped out from behind a boulder and began giving orders.

"Stay calm, boys. Two of you grab Slim's body and drag it off to be buried. I'll be along soon enough to say a few words over him before we head out."

"And what about that sharpshooter with the long-range rifle?" Howey asked. "It didn't sound like any rifle I've ever heard. I didn't even see the muzzle fire or smoke."

"I doubt you'd have noticed if the shooter was five feet away, stupid. You're supposed to set an example for the others," Sneed barked.

"Sorry, boss. Should you be standing out in the open?"

"He hasn't taken another shot, has he? I reckon he took his chance and then hightailed it back to the safety of the wagons. We can't be bothered to go looking for a lone shooter. If we don't move on those cargo wagons now, they might make it to Fort Boise before we catch them, and we'll still be broke."

Just as they began to drag the body away, another round struck a tree ten yards away. The percussion echoed through the air.

"See, it was just a lucky shot," Sneed added, dismissing the shooter and his skills.

Ambushed

"I'll bet that really pissed 'em off," Levi said with a smirk. "It looks like they were getting ready to move in for the kill, and they weren't bein' shy about it. Now, we have one less outlaw to deal with. That should have dropped them down to fourteen or fifteen. We should be able to take out another six or so when they come at the wagons."

"Hold on, I have a bead on another one," Walker said. He cuddled his cheek to the wooden stock and prepared to take the shot, slipping his finger into the trigger guard. "Wait for it."

"Hold on, Joseph," Will snapped. "We don't want them to know there's more than one shooter, or that we're expert marksmen. With one man down, the gang leader will figure it was lucky. If we kill two or three, they'll know that the boys from Tornado Express Cargo Company have hired top-notch gunmen. Take a shot at that scraggly tree beside them so they think the shooter missed with his second shot. Hopefully, they won't notice how far away we are.

"That'll help boost their confidence, and they'll be more reckless. There's nothing like a bunch of sassy outlaws when they think they smell easy prey. We don't want to play all our cards yet."

"Now that we know where they are and their proximity to the wagon train, we can ride out ahead of them and set up an ambush," Levi said. "That will be when they'll be the most reckless and we'll be our most effective. I've scouted out ahead and found a quicker path to our wagon train.

"Remember, Rooster's gotta take the best trail to drive the teams fast without mishap and busting up the wagons. I've found a trail that doesn't even have Indian signs on it, so I know it's been seldom used. It'll get us in position in half the time as the outlaws, and we won't run our horses to death doin' it."

The captain looked at Joseph. His long, thin face was taut and ready for war. He didn't like the waiting part of the game. For him, the sooner they jumped into action, the better he felt. Still, he knew, as an ex-cavalry officer, that planning was everything in battle. If somebody jumped the gun, it could cost lives. He knew precisely how the marshal felt, but in the end, they both knew better.

As the sun sat squatting on the earth's rim, they saw a thin line of brown dust as it climbed high into the sky. Levi slid off his horse again and pulled a handful of grass, letting it fall to indicate the direction of the wind. It whistled through the grass toward the riders.

"We'll have to swing around so they're upwind, or their horses will smell ours and nicker or neigh, giving us away. We need to get ahead of them without them catching sight or smell of us. Once we get their line of attack, we can place ourselves between them and the cargo wagons. I've already told Rooster to slow down through the next stretch. That's where we'll ambush these rattlesnakes. We just can't let them get too far ahead of us."

Watching Levi, the marshal realized there was much more to Indian knowledge than he imagined. He seemed to know the earth's secrets just like the Indians. He was aware of things unknown to most White men. Rusty Steel taught him well, but Levi relied heavily on instinct. It was like he was born to scout. All his senses were honed to perfection. Then again, he grew up in the forests back East, where he learned to trap and hunt at an early age. By twelve years old, he was a crack shot, putting food on the table and even designing his own traps. That was where Levi got the nickname Beaver.

"I snuck up close to those rascals last night. From what I could hear, this Garrott Sneed fella's gotta be the gang leader and the one he calls Howey is his second," Levi said in a hushed voice. "I take it half of 'em are no more than mine rats and guns for hire. That means if we deal with the professionals first, the others will run for home. We'll be able to tell by the way they handle their guns. Half the men who hire out in these parts don't know what they're getting themselves into. I was so close I could have spat and hit 'em, and they didn't even suspect I was there."

"Well, I'll be damned," Marshal Walker said. "I locked that fool Sneed up in Foolsome ten years back. This bunch must be hard-up to come thievin' this far west. Sneed is the dangerous one. Back in the day, his second man was a halfwit. At least when he was young, he was. Maybe he's learned a thing or two by now. If I remember right, Howey was his name, and that fits with what you heard, Levi."

"I reckon they're just about to move, lock, stock, and barrel," Levi said. "We'd better mount up and get our tails movin' so we're in position to take them down."

With the shortcut that Beaver discovered, they covered the distance in half the time, as promised. It was not only faster, but it also kept them out of sight of the highwaymen. They knew they would have to ride close to the gang as they swung around in a large circle to keep from being seen.

When they were close enough to see their faces, they counted nine riders. They had stopped by a slow-running stream to rest and water the animals. Healthy horses were tied to ground stakes as they grazed, whisking their tails and sliding their jaws. By the time Levi and his friends had passed, they were mounted up again and on their way.

"Come on, let's put some distance between us and them before somebody stumbles on us," the captain said.

THEY RAN on foot with their horses with leads in their hands. Once they were far enough away not to be heard, they mounted up and broke into a gallop, following Levi down hidden paths, unused for ages. He clung to the shadows and dark places where it was hard to see. The soft clopping of horses' hooves was the only sound. They moved undetected. They had made it to their first hurdle. Now, to reach the spot where they planned their first violent attack.

"This looks like as good a place as any," Levi said, pulling his gelding to a stop. "We have a place to keep the horses out of sight, with hills on either side to help block sound. The top of that rock cover is a perfect place to shoot from. This is the best position for an ambush."

All three stepped down and hobbled their horses in the deep depression between two hills, making them all but invisible. They climbed to the top of a rocky ledge and used piles of rocks and small boulders to hide behind as they waited for the assault. All three brought their collapsible spyglasses from their saddlebags, along with their long guns and plenty of ammunition. They lay their bedrolls along the ridge, providing a soft support for their fourteen-pound rifles. Each shooter laid a box of bullets beside their firing positions.

"They should be by here in about thirty minutes," Levi said as he turned his eye to the direction the outlaws would come from. "It won't be long unless the Shoshone have another go at 'em. There is no telling where they might be. I don't doubt the Indians know we're here. Hopefully, they won't have a go at us."

"I wanna see the look in Sneed's eyes when he sees me again after all these years," the marshal growled. "I ain't gonna let him by with no stretch in prison this time. I'm gonna send him straight to hell. How can a man live the life of an outlaw for so long and still be among the living?"

"Do you really think he'll remember?" the captain asked.

"He'll remember, all right," the marshal replied. "Men like Sneed don't take kindly to bein' locked up for five years. I've even had a few come after me when they served their time and got released. I'm happy to report that they are no longer with us."

"I sure as hell hope we get to the outlaws before the Shoshone do," Will said. "If not, we'll have to chase down those warriors and retrieve the outlaws' weapons. That might be a harder nut to crack than these outlaws."

"Do you think you're gonna walk right up to a war party and demand they return what they've spent three days to acquire?" the marshal asked jokingly. "They'll shoot ya with the same guns they risked their lives to get, and you'll be dead."

"Let's worry about that one when the time comes," Levi whispered. "There's no sense getting into a fuss about something that might never happen. And keep your voice down. They might have sent a scout to do reconnaissance before they strike. Right now, we've gotta focus on our target and nothing else. There'll be no room for mistakes, boys. This will be our only chance to turn the tables and ambush them while they think they are going to catch us by surprise. So, we'd better get as many as we can before they run, hide, or slip away."

Time dragged. Seconds seemed like minutes, minutes like hours. Half an hour seemed to take all day. They used their hats to bat away the flies as sweat rolled down their brows, stinging their eyes. Nobody said another word. Everything that needed to be said had been spoken. Now, they knew all there was to do was wait. When their targets showed everything would change, and chaos would ensue. They intended to take out the leaders before they could take cover. Then they planned to pin down the rest and pick them off one by one.

All three scouts were surprised when they saw a single rider running like his hair was on fire, heading straight for the mountain men. Levi smiled and stood, but the man was blinded by his focus on the wagons, which were just out of sight. They could see the dust cloud as it hovered in the sky. The wagons had slowed to a trot, as instructed by the captain. They didn't want them to put too much distance between themselves, giving them cover from the actual threat. Hopefully, Levi had timed everything correctly.

That was when the outlaw suddenly pulled up to a sliding stop and looked to his side. He dropped off his horse and had a look around. He heard the click of Levi's Colt Walker, but it was too late. It was either fight or die, and there was no time to think. Surrender never crossed the outlaw's mind as he went for his gun. Beaver pulled the trigger. The shot slammed him against a large rock.

A man had wiry red hair, a goatee, and a mustache. He was over six feet tall when standing. His face was suddenly full of surprise when he felt the round hit his shoulder and spin him like a top, nearly blowing his arm off. It hung by tendons as the outlaw blinked in wonder.

Red Hawkins gasped as his legs went limp and he slid to the ground, leaving a streak of blood on the boulder behind him. He felt his face hit the dirt, and his heart stopped pumping as he sighed his last breath. Levi continued to hold the smoking gun in his right fist.

Hawkins was drunk, but he wasn't a bit scared. When the Shoshone Indians struck, he had nearly lost his courage and bolted. Lucky for him, he didn't, because Sneed would have probably shot him. He wasn't afraid of many things, other than hostile warriors.

Now, with a gut full of whiskey, he was ready to take on the cargo train all by himself. It gave him the false courage he needed to follow the boss's orders. It wasn't a new crutch. He had been using it for years and was inebriated most of the time.

"Let me ride out front a distance to see if I can get sight of their dust cloud, Garrott. Then we'll know exactly how far we've got to go. I've got this, boss." Without another word, Red wheeled his horse and rode off.

Sneed looked up and shook his head. He knew his intentions were good, but he wasn't sure Red was sober enough to remember to be careful. Then again, half of his men drank whiskey daily, and when in town, most of them stayed drunk for days. He knew once they finished this job, there wouldn't be a sober soul in the bunch for a month.

Red rode out at a gallop, as he scoured the sky in the distance for dust. In less than thirty minutes, he saw what he was looking for. He was too far away to see the wagons, but he was close enough to spot the thin string of dusty clouds just beginning to form fifty feet in the sky behind what he knew would be racing wheels and thundering horses. The cargo wagons were nearly in sight.

As Red had intended, he easily located the wagon train, but still, he wanted to get a closer look. He had expected a larger dust cloud, which could only mean that, for some reason, they were no longer running flat out. Maybe they had gotten lucky and one of the horses had been injured. It wouldn't surprise him with the way they traveled. A small smile touched his face as Red pressed his horse harder. He knew he needed time to get back to the gang if he found anything out of order. If not, they would make their attack easily, just as Sneed had promised. Soon, they would all go home as wealthy men.

At least some of them, Red thought to himself.

Hawkins wasn't as stupid or drunk as the gang leader believed, though. He had been thinking about the gang and its current leader for some months now. To him, Sneed seemed to have become weaker, and his voice didn't hold the fire it once had. He had his own plans after they acquired the money from the stolen cargo. He and Jimmy Johnson planned to kill Sneed and Howey and take the money for themselves. They figured the teamsters and wagon guards would take care of many of the less experienced men. Those who stayed loyal to him could ride along with the new gang leaders.

When nobody was expecting it, they would kill the old man and his sidekick, take the loot to California, and do just as Sneed had planned. Red was tired of being second to a fool like Howey and believed it was time to take over the gang. If the rest of the gang didn't like it, they would get a bullet for their efforts. He knew this was his only chance and didn't plan to let it slip away.

Now that the end was near, he wanted to see the four wagons more than ever. He had been working his plan since they left the backtrail of the Tornado Cargo wagons. Jimmy was just as ambitious. Red briefly wondered whether he could trust Jimmy with his plan, or whether his new partner would try to kill him, too. With so much money at stake, an outlaw might do just about anything. Hawkins reminded himself to keep an eye on his partner just in case. When money was involved, nobody was to be trusted.

When he saw a brown outline step onto the trail he was riding, he instinctively pulled to a sudden stop, pulling back on his reins and standing in his stirrups, his horse's hooves sliding to a halt. Red jumped out of the saddle like a German jack-in-the-box. He was shocked to see a buckskin-clad White man standing before him with a cannon-sized pistol pointing at him. Red blinked, hoping it was a mirage. He moved his hand toward his gun. That was when he heard the heavy-metal click of a single-action hammer. He waited for the impact.

Red found himself spun like a top until he tumbled to the ground. He tried to reach for his gun, but when he looked, his arm wasn't attached to his shoulder. He took a deep breath, shuddered, and went into shock from the fifty-caliber blast. He bled out in minutes, never regaining consciousness.

Billy Rooster

The lead bullwhacker bounced around like a drunken sailor while sitting on the spring-loaded seat. He had the reins wrapped around one hand. In the other, he gripped his bullwhip. Everything was in constant motion. The experienced driver was in sync with the team of horses and never missed a beat. The cracking of his whip and slapping reins grew monotonous.

In comparison, the shotgun guards had to hold on for dear life with one hand while clutching their scatter guns with the other. The horses' hooves hammered the ground like constant thunder as the wheels spun over the well-traveled trail. Despite the cargo being well secured for speed, it threatened to shift and break the bindings, allowing the contents to scatter to the wind.

They all knew a broken-down wagon at this point could be disastrous. Simultaneously, they realized the need to be swift. All they could do was push their horses and wagons to the limits and hope for the best. Both money and fear were what kept them driving forward to an unknown future. Hopefully, the three scouts hired by the businesses in Fort Boise could fend off the outlaws until they all reached safety.

Billy Rooster had spent half his life as a teamster, but he had never had such a valuable cargo, nor had he been offered so much cash to make the long run from Fort Laramie to Fort Boise. He also had never taken on a job that was so risky. The added threat of a Shoshone war party increased the odds against a safe delivery. Sure, he had heard of Levi Johnson's reputation as a tracker and mountain man along with his two friends, but he still felt the odds were daunting.

They had seen their outlaws' daunting numbers during the first attempt to capture the wagons. The teamsters were outnumbered two to one, and all the outlaws rode fine horses. The outlaws didn't know about Levi, the captain, and the marshal, though. Rooster felt the mountain men, if they lived up to their reputations, would tip the odds in their favor due to the element of surprise. Everyone had read about Johnson's shooting skills in the newspapers. He won every contest he entered from his first during the last Rendezvous in 1840. He even beat Rusty Steel.

Initially, they had been assured that, at most, they would encounter road bandits. Given the amount of money they were to be paid upon arrival, none of the drivers and guards believed it would be a cakewalk. Given that they were traveling the Oregon Trail, they all knew that anything could happen. One little mistake could cost them their lives and the settlers their food supplies. A lot of people were counting on this cargo, and the loss of the wagons could start a chain reaction.

"I hope those mountain men live up to their billing

and ward off any serious attempts at robbin' us," Rooster shouted to his guard. "When they show their hand, maybe the outlaws will break off and run."

"Well, we made it through the first couple of days without mishap, and we're getting closer to the fort with every mile," Buster shouted. "Maybe they've already scared 'em off, especially with hostile Indians involved."

"I wouldn't bet my life on it, pard. That first go they had at us was too close for comfort. Had we needed to travel a few more miles, we'd never have slipped away. As it is, we just made it to Fort Hall by the skin of our teeth. You keep your eyes sharp for trouble. By my reckonin', it's comin'."

The first long day had gone without a hitch. Levi Johnson had assured them that the Sneed outlaw gang would wait for the second day of the journey, but they missed their target again. This was the outlaws' last go at the racing wagons and the valuable cargo. The fact that the teamsters hardly ever saw the three mountain men wore heavily on the minds of the Tornado outfit. Buster wondered if the outlaws hadn't already had them for lunch and they were all long dead. They were the ones wandering out in the dark, where it was the most dangerous.

"I figure in a few more miles we'll see the signs Levi told us to watch for. Then, we're supposed to slow down to a fast trot," Rooster yelled over the roar of the wagons. "He doesn't want us to get too far out in front of them so they can give us cover fire if needed."

"I hope the hell they're out there like they said or we're up a shit creek," Buster spat.

Marshal Walker had told the Tornado crew that the gang leaders were Garrott Sneed and Howey Dundurn.

They were outlaws he had locked up in Folsom years back, convincing them they weren't dealing with amateurs. All the teamsters were aware that when things got tight, it might be hit-or-miss, and one or more of the wagons could be captured or break down, not to mention that some of them could die.

Until then, they had been lucky that none of the horses had fallen or broken a leg. Despite their careful selection and training, the teamsters had never pushed their teams so close to their limits and beyond. The men in the wagons were nearly as tired.

If they had a breakdown or lost a horse, the entire operation would be jeopardized. Rooster knew, on their own, a gang with between fifteen to twenty gunhands would have them dead to rights. According to Levi, the Indians were after the outlaws' firearms. Hopefully, they would get lucky and eliminate the road bandits before they caught up with the four wagons. To allow such an arsenal of weapons to the hostiles would be a grave error.

That was when they heard a shot in the distance. The crack somehow sounded different. It wasn't the report of a typical Colt Patterson. It sounded like something much more powerful. They had all noticed the Colt Walker revolvers in cross-draw holsters and the fancy rifles the three hired scouts carried. In the heat of the chase, they hadn't asked exactly what they were. They didn't appear to be like any rifles they had ever seen or heard of.

Rooster waited for the next report, but there was none. The only sound was the hammering hooves and steel rims of wagon wheels racing as fast as they could across the last stretch of land between them and the best payday ever. That was when his heart sank. If Levi and his men had shown their cards and nothing happened, all they could expect was the worst. Silenced gunfire might mean their precious escorts had fallen into a trap. Paranoia pumped through the veins of every man in the Tornado Express wagon team. With grit, they kept focused and driving forward. They all wanted to keep their hair and get paid.

THE DAY WORE ON, and still no sight of Levi, the captain, or the marshal. They hadn't seen them since first light when they slipped out of camp, leading their horses into the morning mist. With only about four hours of daylight left, Rooster felt they could expect the attack at any moment. He knew they wouldn't want to wait until sunset, or they would lose the chance to escape after stealing the goods. For everyone, timing was paramount.

Despite all the wrong signs, Rooster did as Levi had instructed, standing and holding up his hand for the other drivers to follow his lead. He pulled back on the reins of the raging horses while using the foot brake. He brought his team to a comfortable trot and could hear the horses struggle for air. As soon as they slowed down, the amount of dust immediately diminished. The horses' coats glistened with sweat, as did the dirty faces of the guards and drivers.

Perspiration rolled down Rooster's neck and back, further drenching his shirt. He took the moment of relative silence to remove his hat and wipe his brow. He pulled his revolver, cocking it, and laid it on the seat. He knew he would soon need it. He found the lack of the thunderous noise nearly deafening. He ground his teeth as his jaws clenched tight. All the men who worked for him were jumpy, but they held the line. No one broke into a run.

All the teamsters knew that Sneed would put them all to death. Then, they could escape to California and outrun a posse from Fort Boise.

Of course, it hadn't crossed Rooster's mind where the outlaws intended to sell the stolen cargo, but the marshal said that he had already figured that out. They would sell the cargo to the very people who were waiting for it, the starving overlanders who wanted the supplies so they could continue on their way.

The brash irony shocked even Rooster, who had been working as a teamster for years. He had never even heard of something so daring and bold, but it made sense. Where else would they find a place where the cargo was so valuable? At that moment, nowhere on Earth could wagons full of supplies sell to the highest bidder.

That was when Rooster and his mates were assured that all witnesses to the theft would have to be eliminated. Then, the outlaws could sell the cargo to the fort's hardware stores and haberdashery, and nobody could prove they didn't find it abandoned along the overland trail. With Shoshone Indians on the hunt, the story sounded increasingly feasible. It would be easy to shoot a few arrows into the sides of the wagons and claim that they had buried the dead teamster's remains somewhere on the plains.

Bald and golden eagles made lazy circles in the sky, looking for their next prey with keen eyes. Occasionally, they would see one tuck into a dive only to rise again, flapping its wings with its talons clutching its catch. The paradox of what they saw wasn't lost on any of the teamsters. They knew that they were the prey, and the Sneed gang was hungry. It was just a matter of time before they dove for the kill.

Money & the Shaman

When Potak walked up to the visitors, they all turned their heads, but he wasn't looking at any of them. His eyes were glued to Money Penny. At first glance, you would think that for the medicine man, the boy was sitting alone. He completely ignored the others' presence. He locked eyes with the growing child and smiled. His eyes twinkled like stars.

"Do you want to come with me, so I can show you how to do magic?" Potak said, smiling. "Well, it's not exactly magic, but it is a sleight of hand. I will show you how to make others think they see things that aren't there. How would you like that, Money Penny?"

"Well, I'd like it fine, but I don't know if my ma would want me to go now that she's frettin' so about Pa being on such a dangerous job."

"She won't mind," Potak said knowingly. "Where could you be safer here in the Crow stronghold than in my care?" Still, Potak didn't acknowledge that Bar-chee was there, but he knew she would never deny the camp shaman his wish. She sat with her lips sealed and stared straight ahead.

Without another word, the two walked deeper into the camp, disappearing among the members of the tribe. His mother knew these were her people, her brother was chief, and her son would be safe anywhere in the village. Everyone knew who Rusty Steel and his clan were and remembered his close relationship with Chief Hachta. They honored him still, something that Chief Wanata secretly despised. Time would tell if those feelings had changed or a grudge still existed.

"Did you know that the first guides and scouts called the Rockies the Shining Mountains?" Rusty said after the shaman and boy left. "I reckon it's a fine name. Those same men were called Squaw Men, Angus, when they married Indian women." That's where the term began.

Angus glared at his friend as he chuckled. He didn't think the name was very funny.

Rusty dug into his possibles bag for his pipe and leather pouch of tobacco. In minutes, the glow reflected orange in his eyes, and smoke swirled around his head. He blew lazy smoke rings, puffing one through the middle of the other.

"Come on, folks, lighten up," he added. "Levi, Will, and the marshal can take care of themselves. Why, Beaver and the captain are my apprentices for Pete's sake."

"None of us are Psalm singers like Virgil, but he does keep us walkin' the straight and narrow." Angus chuckled. "Why all the glum faces? We've been in much tighter spots than this. Virgil is always prayin' for one thing or another and had probably said a few words for us mountain men."

"I feel useless and foolish sitting here," Bar-chee said as tears streamed down her cheeks. "Terrible things might happen, and I don't know how to deal with them. It seems that all I can do is think of myself. I should be ashamed, but I keep getting the feeling that Joseph isn't coming back." Bar-chee bit her lower lip again and looked at Angus with moon-sized eyes.

Swirls of glowing red sparks spewed from the numerous campfires across the stronghold and drifted into the night. Smoke, as dark as coal, streamed along the treetops as black as the sky. Far overhead, behind a light covering of clouds, they saw the stars twinkling millions of miles away. One, two, three comets streaked through the heavens only to vaporize when they reached the Earth's atmosphere.

The only one who noticed Wanata sulking was the mountain man mentor, who spied on them from the shadow of a nearby Indian lodge. Rusty wondered what Wanata was doing. His usual face was a fierce mask, but now sagged sorrowfully. There was no telling what was in that Crow chief's mind. For the first time, Rusty saw him as a simple man feeling the pain of everyday life. He began to look at him in a different light. Maybe he wasn't all bad after all.

Rusty studied the war chief carefully. Wanata's tired eyes showed thin, red veins. Maybe he had been wrong about the new chief. Somehow, he seemed to have changed. For the first time, the aging mountain man saw him display his feelings on his sleeve.

Potak and Virgil had done all they could for Wanata's wife and unborn child. Oddly enough, Betty remained to care for her until her fever broke or the woman died in her arms. Somehow, Davy Crockett's niece had bonded with the sick woman in a way no one understood. She only left her side to fetch food and tend to her own personal needs.

The chief saw there was nothing he could do, so he wandered around the camp, lost in worry and insufferable pain. Nobody volunteered to comfort him in his time of need. Wanata's past behavior had turned away many of his followers. He had isolated himself from the villagers by being a rude bully.

Virgil stood with his head bowed to the fire's glare. His hat was pulled low over his eyes, and his tattered Bible was in his hand. The words hissed between his lips as he muttered a near-silent prayer. He, too, had toiled over the woman for the last days. Somehow, she continued to live. If she hadn't been with child, she would have had a much better chance of survival. Lovejoy knew her life was in God's hands. Potak argued and claimed that it was all up to the Crow spirits. White man's spirits had nothing to do with it. Virgil knew better. She was a Crow and not a White woman, but Virgil believed all of God's creatures were the same.

"Don't you think it's high time you made us something to eat, Angus?" Rusty asked. "If I remember right, we haven't had a bite since breakfast, and that wasn't much. How about scrounging around camp with your wife, Pine Needle, and see if you can come up with some good cuts of meat and a few baskets of berries? I've had my fill of mush."

"That sounds like a fine idea, and I know just where to start. Members of the tribe are always bringing Potak food, beads, and blankets in return for his healing powers and spiritual guidance. In the Crow camp, he's big medicine, so they treat him like he was the chief instead of Wanata. I bet he'll have some extra food sitting around."

Angus said it just loud enough for the chief to hear as he hid in the shadows. Of course, only Rusty knew he was there. Few people, even Indians, could hide from the mountain man mentor. Of course, he didn't mean to insult Wanata. He was hurting enough. Rusty wondered if the chief would see Potak as an example of how a leader should act and how his people responded to Potak's kindness.

THE INSIDE of the medicine man's lodge was much larger than Money had expected. The walls were covered in strange, often unidentifiable objects. A glass jar of dried lizards sat on one end of the table next to the skeleton of a large rodent. Colorfully painted noisemakers, made of gourds, hung from hooks.

Rattlesnake skins hung from the rafters, fluttering in the breeze that came in the door and out the ceiling vent. The medicine lodge was adjacent to another smaller sweat lodge with a distinctive interior shaped by ritual practices and spiritual symbolism. The high ceilings made them seem more spacious, even though there was hardly a place not covered with some trinkets, hides, or bones.

The dwelling's shape was elliptical, made by bending willow branches and posts. It was covered with small animal hides, providing insulation and privacy for his secret rituals. The ground was covered in cedar boughs and sage. The fire pit sat in the center. The bottom was covered in round stones. Flat rocks were piled around the hearth's exterior, which represented the womb of Mother Earth for the medicine man. It signified rebirth and spiritual cleansing.

Money was both mystified and curious about everything around him. A sage mat sat beside the fire where Potak made his prayers, rituals, and sang songs to the Indian spirits. On his mat lay a long pipe, tobacco, a bleached white buffalo skull, and what he took to be offerings to the spirits in the form of flowers and feathers. Overhead, hung weapons and bundles of unknown contents. The boy could only imagine what was hidden inside. He saw bows, arrows, and lances of all shapes and sizes. By their markings, they appeared to come from several tribes.

Potak had breached the void between the enemy tribes with his wisdom and fame to become an important shaman. All the tribes respected and feared the Tonkawa Indian, giving him free passage across Yellowstone Valley and the surrounding mountains. Even during conflicts, all sides respected the medicine man's right to go when and where he wished without being stopped or hindered. Rather than showing their aggression, they showered him with gifts in every form imaginable.

The room's light came from a sizable fire in the center and ceremonial candles. Unlike White men's candles, these were made of a variety of natural materials for illumination, such as animal fats, pine knots, and fish oil. Unlit torches pierced the walls on four sides. They were made of birch bark and river cane, and lighted when the medicine man invited the tribe's elders to partake in spiritual ceremonies.

A small but intricately carved totem pole graced the entrance, standing guard over all who entered. It was made of a strange black wood Money had never seen before. Round pieces of colored glass were used to represent eyes that missed nothing. The growing boy found it frightening, but when he looked at Potak, he laughed.

"Think of it as a simple piece of wood. Before it was carved, that was what it was, nothing more. Why be afraid? Humans fear what they don't understand. When you realize it is no more than a tree branch, your fear will vanish."

Along the inner walls of the lodge were two-foot-tall platforms constructed of poles and covered in mats, buffalo hides, and grizzly bear blankets. Thin elk hides attached to ropes hung above the beds to provide privacy if the shaman had guests. It was used when one of the tribe's members was ill, badly wounded, or in need of more serious treatment. Potak's bed was beside an altar.

Money knew nothing about what Potak was talking about, but he was naturally curious as all young boys were. More mats in bright colors lay scattered about the floor. Beside the shaman was the ever-burning piece of eucalyptus wood, releasing a stream of smoke with its unique and potent aroma.

The boy suddenly realized that he felt light and free, like he didn't have a care in the world, but he didn't know why. There was something about the place that gave him a deep sense of peace. He breathed out a sigh he had been holding for days.

"Do you want to spend the day with me here in my lodge full of curious items? I can tell you what all those strange things are on my walls and the secrets to live life free of fear."

"How can a person live free of fear, Potak? I ain't ever heard anyone say such a silly thing. We all get scared. Heck, lately I'm scared most of the time."

"Are you scared right now?" Potak asked with raised eyebrows.

"No, sir. I feel strangely at peace. And why is that?"

"I'm not afraid, nor do I worry, ever. For me, it is all a wonder to be marveled and not to distinguish between what you perceive as good or evil. We are all one and the same thing. Deep inside, we are all equal. That makes us all brothers and sisters regardless of our skin color. Money, power, and fear are what make us believe we are enemies when we really aren't. We are all here on Mother Earth to enjoy what she has to offer us for our short stay on this side of the spirit world."

"I must admit it would be nice to be happy all the time." Money grinned. "I can't even imagine how good that must feel. I feel like laughing just thinkin' about it."

Money felt heat as he squinted in the dim light, his senses assaulted by strong aromas. He imagined Potak sitting in a trance-induced state of mind. Little did he know that the old shaman was invoking spiritual assistance for his latest guest. The medicine man knew it was useless for the boy to worry like his mother. Barchee knew better, but she couldn't help herself. So, he whisked Money away to show him another world, a place of awareness and inner peace.

For the shaman, his lodge was the center of the universe and from where he launched his spiritual journeys. It was his launching pad into the dark world of spirits and the unknown.

"Why do you have raised beds when all the other Crow teepees and lodges have ground beds, Potak?"

"Because I belong to a faraway tribe called the Tonkawa. My people are a dying race, and we have been scattered to the wind like leaves during the Harvest Moon."

"And where was that?"

"My family comes from the Edwards Plateau region of Texas. Before that, the Tonkawa lived in the northwest part of the Indian territories, better known as No Man's Land because its terrain was inhospitable and no state or territory claimed it. We were a smaller tribe and were pushed south by the Apache and others who banded together to wipe us out. They thought that our customs were evil. That was because they didn't understand. Again, men fear the unknown. Today, there are fewer than seven hundred of us left. I fear that our future will be grim, but do I worry about it? No. Do you know why? Because it makes me unhappy and serves no real purpose. I can worry for the rest of my life, and it won't make the slightest difference. All I would do is make myself unhappy."

"I don't rightly know why, but I feel like I'm beginnin' to understand. Maybe Indians are happier than White folks."

"Don't be fooled. Most Indians are unlike your mother and don't show their emotions, especially men. It is rare to find anyone who does not worry. The formula for happiness is simple and easy to achieve if you know the path."

"Why don't more people know, then?"

"Because they are not shamans like me."

Next, Potak stared at Money so intently that it made the boy quiver inside. It was like he was just about to open the door to the secrets of life.

Money kicked off another round of questions, but Potak didn't mind. It provoked another round of important information for the young boy. Potak was happy to take his father off the young boy's mind. Rather than worry, he was using his time wisely by learning important things in life and enjoying it at the same time.

Of course, Money barely understood the way of war and the euphoria associated with the killing of one's enemy. Strangely, spending a few days with Potak had answered many of the young boy's questions. Now, he wondered why men fought when all it brought was more suffering. His father always told him it was about the letter of the law, but what laws are those? It seemed the Crow Indians had completely different laws than the White men.

Money's eyes swelled at the extravagant notion of being happy and carefree all the time.

THE FINAL STRIKE

"ARE YOU READY FOR WHAT'S TO COME, HOWEY?" SNEED asked. He watched as he struggled to stay upright in the saddle. "Maybe what you need is a good lickin' to make you mend your ways."

"Nah-huh. I reckon I'm as ready as I'll ever be." He hardly heard what his boss said.

"Don't you dare drink another drop from that bottle you have in your pocket," Sneed warned, realizing he had too many drunks in his gang. It was hard to find dangerous gunhands who didn't drown their sorrows in a bottle. Most had a sad past behind so much violence, and it encouraged them to take the edge off with liquor.

"Nuh-uh!" Howey said, his words slurred and eyes blurry. "Whatever you say, boss."

"On second thought, give me that pint of whiskey. I can't have my right-hand man drunk when we attack the wagons. The whole bunch of you can't spend a single day without a drink. With what we're up against, we need to stay sharp."

"But you drink whiskey yourself, boss," Howey

whined. "I've even seen ya drink tequila when you're bored."

"Yeah, but I don't get drunk unless I'm in a safe place and this ain't it. This part of the country is about as dangerous as it gets. What you don't want to do with those Shoshone warriors around is lose your edge. Stay sharp! Whiskey makes you dull and slow. Just because those teamsters don't look like much, don't mean that they'll be a pushover."

"It calms my nerves, Garrott. I've had a bad feelin' about this one ever since we missed our chance before Fort Hall. Maybe it was a sign, and we ought to give it up. We've never been so close to a big prize like this, and it gives me pause. Maybe this is bigger than we can handle. Remember, we've lost more than fourteen men so far. They're whittling us down is what they're doin'. Maybe that Tornado Express paid the Indians to come after us."

"Now you're talkin' pure foolishness. Give me the corn liquor before I've gotta take it from ya!" Sneed snatched it out of Howey's hand and threw it into the weeds. Howey cringed when he heard the glass shatter.

"What did you have to go and do that for, boss? I told ya I wouldn't drink another drop. Now, I won't have nothin' to drink afterward."

"That'll teach you and the others a lesson. I'll have no more drinkin' until this job is complete. We've already botched one go at the cargo, and I don't want any mistakes, not with something so serious. We don't have a margin for error here, boys. We want to hit 'em hard and fast and get the wagons to that big gully we stayed in a day's ride back. When we've got the wagons far enough away from the scene of the crime, you and I can ride into Fort Boise and make our offer. Now, everybody, stick to the plan or you'll answer to me."

"Just you and me? Don't you think we ought to take half the gang, Garrott?" Howey asked.

"Then, they won't believe that we just happened across the cargo wagons, stupid. If we make a show of strength, they'll suspect us right off. If we do it right, there is no way the soldiers can challenge our word. You trust me, and we'll walk away with a small fortune."

Ignoring the gang leader's order for quiet, another drunken outlaw yelled, "Yippee-ki-yay!" Sneed's eyes bore holes in the man, but he was too drunk to notice. It appeared that the entire gang sought courage from the bottom of a whiskey bottle.

Jessy Crow, the harsh-spoken outlaw grumbled something in a low-voiced string of unintelligible Spanish. It sounded like swearing. None of the men liked to be told they couldn't drink. Most of them didn't even want to be told what to do, especially when there were hostile Indians around. The Shoshone made one and all as nervous as a long-tailed cat in a room full of rocking chairs.

Aboriginal tribes had inhabited these vast areas for over 10,000 years. The outlaw gang knew they had their teamsters in front of them, but they also suspected that the Shoshone war party was somewhere behind them. So, they had to be careful not to get wedged in a crossfire and slaughtered.

WILL PULLED AT HIS SHIRT. It stuck to his body with sweat. The overhead sun pushed more heat into the pan-like desolate plains. He passed his tongue over his dry, cracking lips, rubbed his stubble, and frowned. He hated to go without a shave, and it had been two days, pushing three. After a long, hard ride, they had finally come to the moment of truth. The waiting was almost over. Soon, the lead would fly, and the violence would rage in every direction.

The mountain men believed their plan was nearly foolproof and that they had complete control. They still held the element of surprise. Sure, they had shot a few of the outlaws, were convinced Sneed was not able to put together too many professionals who could actually launch a viable attack on the wagons. Of course, the gang believed, all they had to deal with were four bull-whackers, four shotgun guards, and some Indians juiced up on the White man's spirits.

Levi suddenly froze as his hearing became hyperacute and his sense of smell sharpened. He kneeled, put his ear to the ground, and announced, "They're coming, and they'll be in sight in a couple of minutes. We'd better get ready, boys. It's time to see what these outlaws are made of."

They sat patiently in the windless heat as the sun wavered in the distance. Not one of the sharpshooters took their eyes off the narrow pass.

When the string of bandits came into view, it was clear they weren't trying to conceal themselves. They brandished pistols as their horses hammered the ground, and they burst into a full charge.

They chose the narrow trail to launch their assault, as Levi predicted. The gang didn't want the teamsters to see them until it was too late. To their own detriment, the narrow trail forced them to ride in a single file.

Beaver foresaw the mistake and knew that it would work to his team's advantage.

"Pick your targets carefully, gentlemen," Captain Forrester said, rock steady and confident. He would fire the first round, then the other two Sharps rifles would bark, sending .50 caliber bullets into the unsuspecting gang. With their 1844 John Çhapman scopes, they could easily identify their targets, and each shot was a solid body hit. At such distances, they aimed for the torso. If things didn't go as planned, they would have to shoot the horses as a last resort. They tried to spare the animals, though. Horses in the wilderness were a valuable commodity, a bonus that would be added to their wages.

Levi sat in the shade of some boulders as he stared across at the summit hundreds of yards away. He saw a single file of outlaws show over the ridge. The lead rider raised his arm, throwing it forward to signal a charge, and they broke into a dead run. A clinking sound and squeaking leather drifted across the stretch between them and their now visible targets. Outlaws slapped their horses' rumps with their rein poppers as they gigged their flanks with sharp steel spurs.

Marshal Walker smiled wolfishly, then wrapped his hands around the gun's stock and aimed. "This is gonna be a turkey shoot. If you see Sneed, he's mine."

"How are we going to know who he is?" Will asked as the shooting began.

"He'll be about my age and looks like a jailbird. That scum ain't no more than a scalawag, but I must admit, he does have balls," Walker said as the chaos began. "Look at him just sitting there with bullets popping all around him."

Joseph peeked through his spyglass and saw that the Sneed was looking back at him. He wondered if the gang leader knew who had him in his crosshairs. He knew it was impossible. Joseph would be the last person that Sneed would expect to find in the barren plains.

Rifle fire went off like Chinese fireworks as the mountain men aimed, fired, and reloaded quickly in a rhythm they had practiced for countless hours. One outlaw after another dropped from their horse, raising puffs of dust from the ground as their mounts screamed and ran for safety, leaving the dead and wounded behind.

As soon as the gunfire started, instead of taking cover, the lead rider suddenly stopped, making the riders behind them all bunch up as they tried to figure out where the incoming bullets were coming from. Until they found the source, they couldn't defend themselves or know where to take cover. They were easy targets as they bunched up tight. The marshal was right. It was a turkey shoot.

Amid the chaos, the longer the surprised gang stayed in one place, the more men they lost. Finally, the leader called for his gang to retreat, and those still seated on horses followed.

Levi pulled his spyglass and had a final look, but could not count how many escaped because of so much dust and gun smoke. Beaver guessed that they took out seven to eight men. It didn't dampen the villains' determination, though. They regrouped and charged again. At this point, they probably didn't know where to turn. They knew the heavy, long-range rifles didn't belong to the Indians. With enemies on three fronts, their situation had gone from dire to desperate.

Once the onslaught stopped, they mounted up and ran for the wagons. Rooster had followed Levi's order to the letter. He had pulled them up into a tight circle with the horses inside. Dead bandits littered the trail, but maybe half of the original fifteen were still alive and willing to fight. Now, it wasn't only about money, but more about revenge. The outlaws located their firing position and mounted their final assault.

The outlaws had no idea the sharpshooters had already vacated their lofty ambush positions and were racing to provide extra defense for the cargo wagons.

Levi, Will, and Joseph moved in synchrony without speaking a word. They knew the plan and stuck to it. Levi was the first to jump into the saddle of his mount. The horse reared, and Levi flattened himself along its shoulders. Will and Joseph followed him to where the teamsters were circled and ready for round two.

Levi quickly peeled back the hammers on his heavy Colt Walkers. In his massive hands, they almost looked small. He emptied all twelve chambers right before he reached cover, shooting over his shoulder and around his side as Rooster and three men pulled one wagon back, giving the three scouts room to jump the tongues and arrive safely in the center of the round-up.

As the captain spoke, his eyes watered, and his throat choked as cordite hung heavily in the air. "Damn, that was as close a call as we've had for years, Levi. Maybe this deputy marshal job isn't what we were cut out to do."

"We've all but won, now," Marshal Walker shouted over the constant din of gunfire. He picked off another rider as his Colt Pattersons bucked in his hands. Another bandit slid out of his saddle, but his boot got caught in his stirrup, and the panicking horses dragged him away, banging his head on the stone-covered trail. Soon, the horse and rider disappeared in a puff of dust as the rest focused on the last of the outlaws.

Immediately, every man fired rifles, pistols, and muskets. The harsh noise of gunfire was so continuous and loud, dead men, buried long ago, covered their ears. The outlaw rode around the perimeter of the wagons, firing at anything that moved in a last-ditch effort to steal the cargo or die trying.

Finally, when the shooting stopped and silence settled over the survivors, it was time to celebrate. Forrester hadn't had that feeling since his last battle during the Indian Wars. It felt like ice was injected into his veins. A cold chill ran down his spine, spelling relief. It looked like neither he nor his friends would die today.

ALMOST AS SOON AS they started the charge, the late afternoon erupted into flashes of gunfire followed by a cacophony of bullets as the outlaws all fired at once at the invisible enemy. When Sneed pulled out his spyglass and took a closer look, he saw powder flashes in at least two locations, if not three. Still, they were too far out of range for their rifles. He didn't know what kind of rifles they were using, but they were deadly accurate. All the outlaws could do was blindly return fire.

Sneed was jolted by the realization that he finally had the cargo wagons in sight, but they were on a barren hill with no cover of any kind. He felt a bullet whiz by his ear and slam into the hired gun beside him.

Sneed kept his cool and carefully studied the horizon for muzzle flashes. He felt his riders bunch up around him.

"How in the hell can they shoot at us from so far away?" Jessy Crow asked. "I can't even see 'em without a telescope. From what I make out, there's three of 'em, and if we don't do something now, they're gonna wipe us out."

Hot lead seared across Sneed's hip, creating a line of blistering fire. It felt like a bullwhip's popper sliced through his skin.

"I'm hit!" Sneed shouted, his breath coming in ragged gasps as he fought to remain conscious and in his saddle. The powerful round nearly sent him into shock, and it wasn't a direct hit. His body and brain sought relief.

When he looked down, all he saw was blood. His eyes resembled dark chips of polished obsidian as he fought through the pain. If he was still sitting in his saddle, he knew it couldn't be too serious. He wheeled his horse again and set the spurs to his horse's bloody flanks. He made a desperate charge for the circled wagons, which were already in sight. Now, it was just a matter of who got there first. He could see three riders hightailing it for the wagons. Garrott knew that he and his men had to get there first.

Nobody considered retreating after getting their target in sight. All they could think about was the money they would make if they managed to steal all four. They became more reckless by the minute. As they neared the round-up, the shotgun guards and bull-whackers began to give the three buckskin-clad men cover as the men in brown dusters closed in.

Sneed was ready to fight for the prize the cargo wagons promised, and more than prepared to die trying to make it his. As he lay on his back in the dusty plain, he wondered what went wrong. Confused, he looked at the sky as clouds drifted by. He was surprised when he saw they looked like funny animals. Then someone familiar came into his vision, blocking everything else out. All he could see was a bearded face.

When the marshal dropped his hand to his hip, he brushed his coat aside, showing the Colt revolver in his holster. He smiled at the man before him. Garrott recognized Walker the moment his eyes regained focus. He was older but hadn't changed much.

Joseph watched his bullet catapult Sneed from his horse. He couldn't pass up the chance to confront his old enemy face-to-face when the shooting stopped.

All the color drained from Sneed's face. His eyes swelled. Suddenly, the bull boss realized there was nothing he could do to stop what was about to come.

"I ain't gonna let you take me back to jail, Marshal Walker. I ain't gonna go back to livin' like an animal in a cage."

"Who said I was takin' you in, Sneed? I ain't as easy goin' as I was when I locked you up the first time. If you have any last words, now's the time."

"Walker," he huffed through bloody lips. "And here I thought you were dead."

"I reckon you were misinformed, Sneed," Joseph replied. "I'd try to take you to jail in Fort Boise, but you'll never make it. I guess you've seen your last rodeo. Live like an outlaw, die like an outlaw, I always say. If I let you go, were you to live, you'd just turn around and rob and kill again. There's only one cure for your kind. A bullet with your name on it."

Sneed sounded like most men when they are wounded badly and afraid of dying.

Garrott gritted his teeth, his eyes on his executioner. The outlaw tried to reach for his gun. Sneed smiled, thinking he had the lawman who put him in prison all those years ago dead to rights. Time froze, and Walker had a gun in each fist and pointed at him before Garrott could clear leather. Sneed felt the impact, but the sound of the shots seemed to echo in the distance.

Sneed's horse stood frozen beside its rider's body. Its lungs were worn out, making it breathe through its mouth. It stood wavering in the heat and dust, then dropped to its knees and finally onto its side. It looked like his heart gave out. Garrott rode him to death, and the animal died at its owner's side.

WATCHING THE CONFRONTATION FROM AFAR, Levi's mouth was so dry his teeth stuck to his lips as his heart roared in his chest. Sweaty palms clutched at his rifle, and rivulets of sweat ran down his back. He was determined not to let the outlaw shoot his friend. He sighed in relief when the final shots rang out.

The captain's mouth was filled with water from his canteen, but his eyes spread as wide as his mouth. His sunburned face showed through his scraggly stubble. They all had their hats pushed back and were dirty and tired. At least the fighting was over. Now, all they had to do was escort the wagons a half day to Fort Boise.

As nightfall approached, they knew they wouldn't

make it to the fort the same day. Everyone voted to stay where they were, circled up, and surrounded the dead bodies of the outlaws.

The captain felt the anger drain away, leaving him bewildered. The cargo company owner knocked back a glassful of corn liquor in one toss. They could see his eyes were already blurry with drink. One and all were relieved that they had fought off the Sneed gang.

Of course, they knew the Shoshone Indians were still out there, so they had to continue to be on their toes. They tried to retrieve as many rifles and pistols as they could before darkness set in.

Half the men stood guard in two-hour shifts to keep everyone alert, while the other rested. For most, sleep didn't come.

That night, they heard the Indians rifling the dead bodies outside their barrier. The bullwhackers and their guards were ready to open fire. It looked like hostile Indians upset outlaws and normal people just the same.

"Don't shoot," Levi whispered. "They've come here to take what we don't want. It's a good thing for us that we collected most of the pistols and rifles those fellas had. We don't need to go lookin' for another fight."

The following day, they hitched the six-horse teams up to the heavily loaded wagons and covered the last few hours of the arduous journey.

The War Party

Chief Pocatello lay beside Sagwitch as they watched the violence unfold. The chief was the only member of the war party with a spyglass. So, he shared it with his war chief. They had been following the outlaws and the three buckskin-clad men for two days. Right when they thought they had their chance to attack the bandits, the mountain men stepped in and stole their thunder. They stole their guns and bullets, too.

They nearly attacked the three lone men from the rear, but then they watched as their long guns killed their targets from unimaginable distances. Even the chief, with his keen eyesight, couldn't see clear targets. But he could hear the screams from both horses and men. There was no question as to what was happening. He used the telescope to spot three dirt clouds in the distance. He knew the first one was the cargo wagons with colorful letters on the side.

The second belonged to the outlaw gang. Last, the

smaller, less pronounced puff of dust, stirred by the mountain men, raced to rejoin the wagon train.

The Shoshone had watched the wagons coming to and from the fort among the overlanders for months, but they knew they were too hard a target. Many of the chief's warriors only had bows, arrows, and spears. If they attacked the White men with only a few muskets and their crude weapons, he knew he would lose too many men.

White people always had the advantage because there seemed to be endless replacements. Something that the chief knew he couldn't count on. At this time and place, for the Native Americans, it was pretty much every band of warriors for themselves, and none of them could allow their numbers to be wasted needlessly.

The Shoshone war chief waited until the heat of embarrassment drained from his face. Luckily, he hadn't executed his original plan. Now, he had lost face with his warriors by proposing a disastrous idea. Had he carried out his plans, it would have cost many lives, if not the entire war party. They would have been killed just like the White robbers. The buckskin-clad scouts seemed to have magic guns that had no limit to how far they could shoot. Even the sound they made was different. With such weapons, they couldn't even consider taking them on, especially after the chiefs saw how they easily wiped out the band of thieves.

Luckily, the war party was buried in the shadows of a rock formation above them all as they watched the drama play out. So far, the mountain men scouts hadn't discovered the Shoshone warriors spying on them. Unlike the outlaws, the three warriors were too dangerous to confront. They went through half of the outlaws in minutes. Indian war parties weren't partial to having so many casualties. They couldn't return to their tribe missing so many husbands and fathers. Unlike the White men, who were only interested in money, the Shoshone put great value in their warriors.

Chief Pocatello had heard in the Indian gossip that it was Levi Johnson and the one-armed captain scouting for the wagon train. If it *was* them who shot the outlaws, they knew better than to get further involved. Johnson had a reputation that stretched beyond the Rocky Mountains, spreading across the Great Plains and all the way back East. He and Rusty Steel were known everywhere.

As their warriors lay as still as stones behind them, the chief and his war chief continued to watch the slaughter. They were in wonder and simultaneously mystified by the behavior of the thieves as they recklessly rode around the circled wagons until they were picked off one by one. They had a total disregard for life and paid the ultimate price.

"They had all been committed to their plan and never wavered," Pocatello said. "At least, in the end, they showed bravery."

"Sometimes even fools are brave," Sagwitch replied. "Still, it is strange. They must have known they would die in the end, especially after they were picked off with those magic rifles. But regardless, they charged straight forward. They didn't even try to dodge the bullets. Did you see the outlaw chief sitting still on his horse as chunks of lead fell all around him? Was he a fool or had he simply gone mad?"

"They lost their minds to greed," Pocatello whispered, as if avarice were something evil to the Indian Nations. "They don't even respect themselves."

EVEN THOUGH ALL THE outlaws were dead, the wagons stayed circled, and no one took a chance to see if anyone was alive. They knew that it could cost them their lives, so they waited patiently until they were sure there wasn't a living person among the dead. With men of such determination, there was always the chance that a wounded man might try to take one of the mountain men on a death walk.

That night, the Shoshone braves snuck through the dark outside the circled wagons to capture their rewards, albeit not what they had counted on. They crept cautiously from cover to cover when a mournful sound cut the stillness.

They all remained stone-still for a moment until Pocatello whispered, "Night Birds."

Still, they got leather goods, clothing, tobacco, coffee, and lots of whiskey, which Pocatello didn't allow his men to drink. He had seen firsthand how it affected them and immediately passed a law that forbade it. He smashed all the bottles.

The chief shook his head with a jug of liquor in his hand as he studied the debauchery. He realized that the thieves were probably drunk, and that could be part of why they were defeated so badly. His men had taken their scalps, too, to capture the White warrior's strength. Bare, red skulls glowed in the moonlight.

The chiefs finally awakened when they heard the rumbling sounds of the wagons. The first sign of light showed on the eastern horizon. The moon hovered on the other side of the world.

The Shoshone leaders got up and stretched. Their war paint contrasted with their dusty bodies. They stood there, dumbfounded, staring at each other. Each was wondering what tomorrow would bring. As long as they weren't sighted, they would wait until the wagons left to check the camp to see if they left anything valuable behind. One man's rubbish was another man's gold. The chief realized they might be luckier than they thought.

Had they succeeded in stealing the guns, the mountain men might have turned on them, tracked them down, and demanded the weapons back. That would have resulted in a tragedy, too. Pocatello knew they were no match for them.

As the wagons pulled away, an eerie silence crept over the gray gloom. At first, the only sound was the flies that came by the thousands. Then came the noisy crows. Above them, vultures made lazy circles in the sky. Soon, coyotes were yapping, informing their friends that the feast had begun.

When they reached the outer rim of the fort, the overlanders saw the riders with badges. The cargo wagons weren't far behind. As soon as they saw them, hundreds of overlanders clapped, whistled, and cheered. Relief had come in the nick of time.

Home Sweet Home

The compound clan was having supper on Rusty's porch table when they heard the soft squeak of saddle leather and the muffled sound of hooves clopping against the ground. The men had been gone for three weeks, and they didn't know when they would return. Rusty grabbed his rifle, and Angus did the same. Not many people, other than Indians, traveled the trails, especially when it was almost dark.

Lightning bugs raced around them, flashing their tails, calling their mates. Crickets sang their nightly choir as night birds cried out in the night. On a hill in the eastern mountains, a pale orb rose, casting silver light across the land and creating long shadows.

As Levi, Will, and Joseph climbed the last part of the steep trail to the compound, they finally left the mist below them. It clung thick to the meadows as they climbed higher onto Bear Tooth Mountain. They were almost home, and none of the three had as much as a scratch.

Light slanted through the open door, and a circle of

light shone from the porch lantern. The men in the dark, leading their horses, clopped past the southern gate and into the compound.

"Rusty. Angus. Don't shoot!" Levi shouted. "It's us. We're home."

"Where's Joseph?" Bar-chee asked with fear in her voice. Levi grinned, hooking his thumb over his shoulder.

As soon as Bar-chee saw Joseph, she dropped her tin pie pan with a clatter, screamed, and ran for her husband. Her heart flooded with joy. She hurdled for Joseph as fast as her legs could carry her. Money blinked like he didn't believe his eyes and wondered what all the fuss was about.

Joseph leaned in close and whispered in Bar-chee's ear, making her laugh loudly and heartily. "Those tickles, honey." Goose bumps instantly sprouted on her arms, but she was no longer afraid. How those two ever fell for each other, no one knew. Potak said that life was strange like that. Seeing them together confirmed that they were made for each other, and little Money made them both whole.

"Come on, let's sit down to eat," Joseph said.

Bar-chee smiled excitedly and said, "All right, Joseph." She stared at him, glistening with emotion.

"Music to my ears, Angus. As usual, I could eat a bear," Levi said and laughed heartily.

The compound members all offered their hands as the women hugged their husbands. Everyone, those who had just arrived back home and those who had been impatiently waiting for them, sighed in a deep breath of relief.

A buckskin-clad woman with long black hair in

trances rode up and slid easily from the bareback pony and ran for her husband's arms. Levi waited until the heat of embarrassment drained from his face. That was when everybody laughed as he grabbed Dahteste's hand. She was a war chief and shied from showing her emotions, unlike the marshal's wife. Still, Beaver was shocked when she hugged him like she did.

"I missed you so much," Dahteste said, showing more affection than usual. Maybe Bar-chee's fretting got to her after all.

Potak stood with his arm around little Money's shoulder and smiled. "Even I am surprised by life's little changes. This one has been for the best."

"Potak taught me how to do magic," Money told his adopted father. "But it's not really magic. It is just a trick. What do you call it, Potak? Oh, yeah, a sleight of hand."

"That's the only Indian I've ever met who speaks better English than me." Virgil Lovejoy smiled, a mouth full of white teeth. "And I'm well read."

Rusty slapped his knee and said, "Good for you, Money. Spoken like an honest man. Be honorable above all else. You've got grit, I'll give you that. The truth is, if you don't have a wagonload of grit, you'll never make it in this country. Not with rain, snow, lightning storms, and flash floods, not to mention forest fires, wild animals, outlaws, and Indians."

"That's enough, darlin'," Rusty's wife, Silvia, said. "Everybody's been worked up enough as it is."

The mountain mentor went to retort, but then he looked into his wife's eyes and smiled. "You're right, and I'm man enough to admit it."

"So, did you learn a lot on your visit with Potak the

medicine man? He didn't scare ya, did he?" the marshal asked his son.

"Potak, scare me? But why on earth would he do that? He's one of my best friends. Yes, sir, and he's teaching me his ways too," Money said. His father couldn't manage to hide his smile.

The aging medicine man beamed. He had become so attached to the young boy that he had returned to the compound with them so he could continue teaching him what was important in life before he got too old to learn, as some of the others in the compound had. But it looked like even Rusty Steel was learning to be a mellower person from his recent marriage.

"That coffee is thick enough to float a rock," Joseph grumbled, pushing the cup aside. He grabbed the jug and took a belt of corn liquor, making his mouth pucker as he shook his head. "You'd better get back to practicin', Angus. Your old age is makin' you lose your touch." The sour taste of whiskey filled Joseph's mouth and nose.

Rusty slapped the dinner table and laughed until tears wet his cheeks. "Some things never change."

Rusty thought about what had happened during the last week with Chief Wanata. His wife and the child survived with the help of Betty, Virgil, and Potak. Before, nobody liked Chief Wanata, even those who had just met him. Now, old conflicts seemed to vanish, and the last he saw of him, the Crow tribe's leader's eyes softened, and his face relaxed. Maybe they were heading into a new era that held a better future.

Soon, the smell of more freshly cooked food floated from inside the cabin and Angus's kitchen at the back. Stakes piled high on the table, surrounded by fruits and vegetables, and a large pan of cornbread. The perpetual gallon pot of coffee stood in the middle, the spout popping brown bubbles.

"What about that trick that Potak promised to show you back at the Crow camp?" Angus asked. "You never did show it to us, or was it a fib to get you to go with him?"

"I can show ya right now if ya want." Money smiled. "Anyway, Potak don't fib."

The nine-year-old unrolled a soft mat about two feet square. Then he pulled out his three hollowed out walnut shells and a single dried pea, and turned them over, one at a time. Then he held up the little green vegetable in his little fingers.

"Now, you can see all the shells are empty," he said after turning them over until they were all sitting on the table upside-down. Now keep your eye on the pea. "If you can guess which one it's under, you win the game."

"And what's the prize?" Virgil asked.

"The prize is winnin'. Potak said that gambling is a fool's game, as we gamble with our lives daily. He said that we only have so much luck in life and not to waste it on silly notions."

He flipped them over again, slipped the pea under the center shell, and then began to shuffle them around at fantastic speed. They could see that he had practiced. Rusty and Angus looked on with hawk-like eyes and were sure they knew exactly where the hidden pea was.

"Now, which shell is it under? How about you, Angus?"

"I ain't no fool. It's still under the center shell. Your little hands are fast, but they're not as quick as my eyesight."

"And Rusty, what do you think?"

"I'd have to agree with Angus. There's no way your hand can move fast enough to trick me."

Money lifted the center shell, but the pea was gone. It wasn't there. He raised the one on the right, and nothing was there either. Finally, he turned over the one on the left, and there the supposed pea lay.

"How did you do that?" Angus asked, shocked. "I would have sworn it was under the center shell."

"The hand is faster than the eye." Money laughed. He was having the time of his life tricking his friends.

Of course, Penny knew it wasn't magic. The trick was the sticky mat Potak gave him and the fake pea that was actually made of rubber. When he moved the shell backward, it popped out of the back, and before anyone saw it, Money palmed it in his hand. It looked like magic, but, like Potak said, it was just a sleight of hand, that's all. Still, he loved it that he could trick them all. All except Potak, that is.

A Look At Book Thirty-Three:
Blood Moon

A rabid wolf is spreading death, and the wilderness is no longer the greatest danger.

When Levi Johnson and Rusty Steel discover the aftermath of a brutal wolf attack, they race the survivors back to the Bear Tooth Mountain compound. As fear of rabies spreads through their friends, every passing day becomes a desperate fight for survival with no known cure.

Meanwhile, Captain Will Forrester rescues a mysterious Blackfoot woman and takes possession of a wagon loaded with valuable Scottish whiskey. But British spies, ruthless killers, and hostile warriors are all hunting the stolen cargo, forcing Levi, Will, Rusty, and U.S. Marshal Joseph Walker onto a perilous journey toward Fort Boise.

Winter closes in. Wolves stalk the mountains. The infected grow weaker. And every mile brings the mountain men closer to enemies determined to stop them.

And if Levi and his friends cannot survive the trail ahead, more than one life will be lost beneath the blood moon.

AVAILABLE AUGUST 2026

Thank You

Thank you for taking the time to read *Tornado Express*. If you enjoyed it, please consider telling your friends or posting a short review. Word of mouth is an author's best friend and much appreciated.

Thank you.
Ash Lingam

About the Author

Ash Lingam was born and raised in Southern Ohio, not far from the mighty Ohio River. He had somewhat of an isolated upbringing on a family farm with his sisters. His best friends were his horse, Sugar, and his grandfather.

Born in 1886, the family patriarch grew crops, raised cattle, and doted on the young boy. At his grandfather's side, Ash learned about livestock and firearms at an early age. His grandad carried an old Colt with him at all times. It helped spawn a young boy's dreams of yesteryear.

Ash was only eight years old when his grandad taught him how to trap muskrats to prevent them from draining the farm's ponds. He gave him a double-barreled shotgun at twelve and taught him how to hunt to put food on the table.

It wasn't long before Ash was breaking horses. His spirited Tennessee Walker never allowed any other rider on her back. Together, they searched through the plowed fields in the spring, looking for Miami Indian arrowheads to add to his grandfather's ample collection.

Ash's family was among the early settlers in pre-

Revolutionary America. He has traced his lineage back to around 1746 when his ancestors immigrated from Europe to the aspiring American Colonies.

A retired marketing executive, Ash devotes his spare time to training police dogs and writing novels. He has found his niche in the Western, historical fiction, and adventure genres. With his vast vault of experience, he never runs out of sources for new stories. He has lived in eleven different countries and worked in a total of forty-six to date, Ash has written approximately 130 novels, short stories, and poems. More than one hundred of his eclectic titles help the American frontier come alive for his readers.

https://www.ashlingam.com/

Join the Lawless Waters Western Readers & Writers Facebook Group

www.ingramcontent.com/pod-product-compliance
Lightning Source LLC
LaVergne TN
LVHW040217110826
845146LV00005B/1316

* 9 7 9 8 8 9 5 6 7 3 7 2 0 *